CHANGED *hart*

HART'S BAY

E. DAVIES

Changed Hart / E. Davies. – 1st ed.
ISBN: xxx

To those who caught my hand, healed my heart, and pulled me to my feet when I was down.

1

RAIN

Rain's ass nearly took out a lamp, a pile of porn DVDs, and a still-warm pizza box on the way to the living room wall.

He slammed into the wall with a thud. Rain barely had time to gasp before lips pressed against his neck and hands slid under his clothes, wandering up his chest.

"Fuck," Rain hissed, his heart thudding at the impact. He hitched one leg up and tried to wrap it around Clay's waist.

Rain was long and lean, but this guy was all muscle. He easily pressed Rain into the wall with no more than a tilt of his hips. The line between adrenaline and arousal was thin and addictive.

He'd met Clay barely an hour before, and most of that time had been spent feeling each other up, eating pizza, and watching old-school gay porn while laughing at their mustaches. The best kind of hookup, really.

No wasted time getting to judge each other, or "know each other," as most people called it.

Rain was so hard it hurt, but at the same time, something

inside him was clawing back and fighting the moment. And he knew just what it was.

Damn that Desmond Curtis all to hell.

Rain had ditched him three months ago to move back to his hometown of Hart's Bay. He'd wised up to Des's tactics—finding guys with no other options and leeching them for all they had—but he hadn't stopped craving the sex.

Rough, fast, and unforgiving.

"Please," Rain panted, rolling his head back against the wall to bare his throat to the stranger. It was an incredibly vulnerable move, and Clay didn't miss a chance.

His teeth nipped along Rain's windpipe, his breath hot against Rain's skin. "Please what?"

"Make me lose control," Rain whispered.

In the background of the shabby living room, men's grunts filled the air. It was some flick about a sauna full of supposedly straight men, and if Rain ignored the cheesy transitions and faded colors, it helped turn him on.

Except Clay's teeth landed on the side of his neck, and he'd just bitten—hard.

"Ow!" Rain whimpered. He tried to ignore the hard line of his dick throbbing in response to the possessive move. As good as it felt, it was also too much for him tonight.

He wanted to be fucked senseless, but not tonight, and not by Clay.

Damn it, this had seemed like such a good idea. It was safe to screw strangers an hour's drive away from his tiny hometown, where he never had to see them again. No explaining his history when he walked out, like he was about to do.

Okay, maybe not *quite* yet. Clay's tongue slid into Rain's mouth, so he let his eyes close as he choked back a gasp of pleasure. His nerves were on fire, even if the pit of his stomach rang hollow.

Clay's hand had closed around the line of his cock in the confines of his jeans. He was stroking in small, jerky motions that sent shivers up and down Rain's spine. He could disappear into the heat wrapped around him.

"Gonna fuck you 'til you beg me for more." Clay spun Rain around with his free hand, still gripping his cock like a handlebar. Rain stumbled and went, his knees wobbling.

Then Clay nearly body-slammed Rain into the wall, his broad torso trapping him there. At least his hand shielded the important bits.

"I... I'm not sure," Rain mumbled.

Clay pulled his hand free, and Rain's sensitive length instantly complained. He ached to be touched again, so much so that his head spun. "What's that?" He didn't move away yet, still crushing Rain against the wall.

Rain sighed and thumped his forehead against the wall, one of the few free parts of him. "I'm not up for fucking."

"Well, that's what I thought you came here for." Clay's voice was abrupt now. Finally, he backed away, leaving Rain half-melted against the wall. The huff of his breath was sharp and exasperated.

"Me too." Rain's strength returned, and the cloud of arousal started to ebb from his mind. He shook his head once, hard, to clear it. "But I can't."

It was the right decision, because the relief that set in the moment he admitted this almost blotted out the disappointment radiating from his blue balls.

The last thing Rain wanted was to break down in front of a stranger. If they went through with it, his first really interesting hookup since the breakup, he had the sneaking suspicion that was going to happen.

"Well… shit." Clay didn't sound mad, at least. Just frustrated.

A smile touched Rain's lips. He knew what Clay meant. "Yeah. Same. I better go," he added, averting his gaze.

They'd still been fully clothed, at least. No scrambling for stray socks or figuring out whose shirt was whose. It didn't take long to grab his shoes from near the door and flee the apartment for his car.

He was parked outside on the street, an inconspicuous little car tucked among the others in this suburb of… wherever the fuck he was.

Rain couldn't think straight, and his brain barely supplied the state: *Oregon.* It felt too much like Colorado, like the place he'd escaped just months earlier.

He managed to keep his hands from shaking until he got to the car. Once there, he fumbled with the keys, eventually bracing one hand around the lock and splitting his fingers around it to guide the key into the hole and turn.

Finally, Rain collapsed into the car and locked the door before he closed his eyes and let the full-body shiver pass through him.

Fuck me, he thought. If only he could let anyone do just that. If only life were simple. If only, if only…

Once the shakes subsided, Rain turned the key in the ignition and popped his phone into the holder, punching in his hometown. No need for a specific address.

Just Hart's Bay would do.

The moment Rain walked into Cher's End Table, the one and only bar in town, his face gave him away.

"Cher? A beer for my buddy here." Justin was sitting at the bar, and he waved Rain over as he spoke.

Luckily, it was a quiet night, so only a few people were around. Justin was alone at the barstools except for Cher, the bartender and owner. Rain could tell them the truth. Besides, they were the only two people in town who knew about him being gay.

And that was its own sob story that he didn't want to think about.

"Coming right up."

Rain collapsed onto the stool and folded his arms on the bar top. He glanced around, a frown tugging at his lower lip, before he finally brought himself to meet his best friend's eyes.

"That bad, huh?" Justin clapped Rain's back while Cher slid him a beer.

Rain pretended not to notice Cher hanging around, scrubbing down that end of the bar. She already knew everything anyway. She'd hosted the one and only date between Rain and Justin, closing down the bar to the public so that they could safely act a little bit normal. Cher's heart was too big, even if she hid it well.

"Yeah. That bad," Rain sighed. "Just no spark at all."

It was a story that Justin would accept. After all, it was the truth between the two of them. He'd met Justin a couple of months ago. They worked on the same construction crew, and before Rain's arrival, Justin had been the newbie.

They'd hung out enough that dating hadn't seemed like a disastrous idea. But even after a full evening spending time together, the chemistry hadn't been there. Both of them being gay wasn't enough to click, apparently.

At the end of the date, the art gallery had caught fire, and their chemistry—or lack thereof—had pretty much cemented the platonic nature of their bond. They hadn't even cuddled for comfort afterward. At least Rain had gotten a friend out of it, and he needed one of those much more than getting laid.

But right now, his cock disagreed entirely with his head. Because whatever he told Justin, there *had* been a spark between him and Clay, however mild. He'd just been too chickenshit to pursue it.

"Ahh, man. That happens. Plenty of fish in the sea, huh?" Justin was trying to cheer Rain up, his tone annoyingly uplifting.

Rain pasted a smile on his face and clinked his beer bottle against Justin's. "Sure," he agreed.

His hollow tone must have caught Cher's attention. "Hey, he wasn't a dick, though, was he?" She kept her voice quiet, which was out of character. Her usual idea of quiet was a muffled bellow.

"Nah," Rain said quickly and shrugged. "Just incompatible, you know."

"Well, you know where to come if you need privacy again." It was a funny offer since usually Cher's was the least private spot in town. Eagle eyes were good at spotting budding romances—or flings. But it was sweet of her to offer. "Any night but a weekend," she added firmly. "You're on your own on Friday. Mama got bills to pay."

That made Rain grin, at least. "Yeah, no. I get it. Thanks, Cher."

As Cher wandered off, Rain's eyes landed on the picture behind the bar. Two men holding hands, overlooking the clifftops that were just a ten-minute walk away from here.

So close, and yet so far.

Plus, the artwork was a reminder of unfinished business for him. Rain had stuck his neck out to defend the artist and his friends that night of the fire, and... well, they'd reached an uneasy truce.

For the other guys, it was finished. For him, it was still day-to-day life.

"God," Rain remembered, thumping his head on the bar top. "It's Saturday."

"Yeah...?"

"Tomorrow is Sunday lunch with my *family*." Rain let the word fall from his lips quickly, as if it could get a divorce that way. Lose its meaning, and therefore the power to hurt him.

"Ah." Justin cleared his throat and patted Rain's back again. "You'll get through it. Just smile and nod. I'll come over sometime next week. We can watch a game and talk shit about them."

Rain pushed himself upright and turned to face Justin, grabbing the bottle. Justin was right. He had nothing to complain about, really. "Yeah," he agreed. "Sounds like a plan."

The door rattled and thumped closed, drawing Rain's gaze. Oh, shit.

Rain had never believed in types—at least, for hypothetical future boyfriends. Personality was more important than looks, he'd said.

He ate every word with a silver spoon right now.

The guy standing in the doorway made Rain turn slowly on the stool until his whole body faced him, like gravity itself had flipped on its side to suck Rain toward him. He was a black hole, and Rain's whole orbit had just been thrown out the window.

The stranger was tall, and his shoulders were so broad he

had to sidle carefully through the door, nearly filling the frame. His shoulders were thrown back, filling out his dark gray suit jacket.

His chin was tilted up, his lips thin—or maybe just pursed. High cheekbones and a straight nose gave him an air of arrogance, not aided by the way he glanced around and slowly lifted one foot to step forward, like he was expecting the floor to be sticky and covered in peanut shells.

Maybe he didn't want Hart's Bay dirt on his gleaming black leather shoes.

God, his hair was as perfectly manicured as his nails, streaky highlights running through gelled-up spikes of hair. He looked like he'd stepped straight out of a boardroom.

Except Hart's Bay definitely didn't have any boardrooms, except the back room of Jack's Surf Shack. Rain smirked at his own pun, but that did raise the question of what the guy was doing here. Maybe he'd broken down by the highway and didn't want to get engine grease on his pretty little hands.

Rain didn't have to wait long to see what the stranger would do. He strode straight for Rain, and the pulse that had quieted since driving back home sped to a near thunder.

For a crazy second, Rain searched his memory like he'd maybe arranged some public coming-out stunt. But he'd remember paying for that, surely. He'd remember anything to do with this man.

Oh. Rain felt stupid a second later. Where the hell had *that* thought come from?

"A beer and some information." The stranger was talking to Cher, leaning on the bar like he owned it. Then, he added, "Please," almost an afterthought.

Cher bristled but gave him a polite, fixed smile. "Sure.

Whatcha want?" She popped the cap off a bottle of beer and handed it over.

"Thanks," the guy said to Cher, to his marginal credit. He slid a ten across the bar top and waved away change, then sipped his drink. "Who owns those crappy warehouses down by the water?" The guy pointed toward the door like they were right in front of the bar. "The ones that are falling apart?"

Rain's jaw dropped. Even after a lifetime of carefully schooling his reactions to his family, the abrasive words took him aback.

Cher's brows steadily climbed. "By the docks?" To her credit, her eyes didn't even flicker to Rain. "How come?"

That gave Rain a few moments to adjust his expression into a mask of calmness and slight curiosity. Like his teeth weren't already set on edge by the guy's attitude.

"Looking to buy some cheap land."

Oh, God. The irritation flushed Rain's cheeks. He couldn't resist commenting, "Nothing worth having comes easy."

The stranger turned to look at him, and for a moment, his eyes widened as he took Rain in. One sweep of his gaze from head to toe and back up to Rain's face and his lips quirked into a smile. "We'll see about that. And you are?"

"Rain." He bit his lip. *He'd better not be implying I'm cheap*, he thought.

Even more infuriating, a tiny part of him whispered that he might *like* that. Might like being bossed around by someone so cool and confident. Giving up control, and giving his trust for just a few precious hours...

No, Rain told himself. *Don't throw yourself at every jerk who comes your way.* He managed to keep his anger sizzling in that spot in the middle of his chest where he kept it when he couldn't let it out.

For years on end sometimes.

The guy scanned Rain as he sipped his drink. "Rain, huh? Like the weather?"

"Short for Rainier."

"Like the mountain." He smirked. "All natural. The way I like it."

Rain bristled as heat crawled into his cheeks. The retort on the tip of his tongue would probably get him into more trouble than it was worth.

You wanna find out? He so badly wanted to break the tidy rules that governed his life and ask the stranger to fulfill his wildest dreams for a night.

Judging by the way their gazes had locked and never broken, the other guy would be just as into that idea. Was that a fighting or a fucking stare?

A quiet cough brought him back to reality. Fuck. Justin was right there, next to him, watching all of this. He wasn't going to let Rain pick up a stranger, was he? And he'd be right. There was no way that someone wouldn't see Rain bring this guy home. If he did, he'd be out to everyone in town by tomorrow morning.

"And you are?" Rain added, a little more brusque than he'd meant it.

"Colt."

"Like the forty-five?" Rain pressed.

"Or the horse. Can't say it doesn't fit me." Colt's eyes gleamed with a touch of self-deprecating humor. *Was* he hung like a horse? Or stubborn as one?

Oh, God. Rain should have known better than coming straight to the bar after getting turned on without satisfaction. It was like going grocery shopping while hungry. But he hadn't expected there to be a buffet at Cher's tonight.

Rain smirked. "Well, I've been told I'm explosive. Make of that what you will."

Cher snorted and left them to it. "Two peas in a pod," she muttered to herself as she walked away.

"Hey—" Colt started, looking over at her.

"If you wanna know more about the warehouses, I'm the guy you want to talk to." Rain still didn't want to arm Colt with the knowledge that *he* owned them, but he was curious about Colt's intentions.

This might be a way out of his financial mess, after all.

Or a chance to test his negotiation skills.

Or, just maybe, a lot more than that.

Colt tilted his head, his interest renewed. He looked back at Rain. "I'm glad to hear that. I wanted to talk to you. Now I have a good excuse."

Justin hummed and shook his head. "Hmm. I better get home. I'll leave you to it." He clapped Rain's shoulder as he stood up, but his glance was undeniably curious. And there was a hint of a warning.

Rain nodded slightly as he read the caution in Justin's gaze. He wasn't going to do anything in front of the whole bar that he didn't want getting back to his family instantly.

Then, he raised his hand in a wave. "See you, man." Justin jerked his chin and headed out, looking over his shoulder once more at them.

The moment he was gone, Colt's gaze landed on Rain again and fixed him to the spot.

Like he was a tree, roots spiraling down into the earth, Rain stood perfectly still under Colt's look.

"That your boyfriend?"

That uprooted him. A rush of fear and excitement hit Rain

like a tidal wave. He'd been pretty damn sure Colt was flirting, but that question confirmed it.

Which was also a big problem, given where they were right now.

Rain snorted, doing his best to walk that line between the truth and the lie. While they weren't dating, he wanted to come across to everyone who knew him as straight. But he also didn't want to exaggerate his reaction and lose the chance with this guy.

"Nah. Way off base there."

Colt looked surprised. His pretty lips wrapped around the bottle again as he swallowed a few more sips. He wiped his mouth with the back of his hand. "I rarely am. My bad. Think you could show me around those warehouses, then?"

Rain sighed, playing up the reaction as he glanced at his half-empty bottle. "In a minute." He kept his tone flat and cool, but his pulse was fluttering in his throat like it was about to take flight.

It was hard not to be too eager or too disinterested. He was walking a lot of lines tonight. One of them better lead him to a payoff.

"In your own time." Colt's tone was almost jeering, like he thought his time was worth so much more than anyone else's. Like he was doing Rain a favor by asking, not the other way around.

God, Rain couldn't deal with that attitude. Part of him wanted to just run Colt out of town. If nothing else, he could have that satisfaction. It was a better channel for his frustration than sitting here with blue balls, wishing he were being fucked into a mattress by a hunk three towns over.

Rain tipped back his head and gulped until the bottle was empty, then pushed it back.

"Come on," he said and turned for the door, not looking over his shoulder to see if Colt was following. He was keenly aware of the few people who *were* in the bar watching them leave together, so he added, "It's not even a five-minute walk from here."

"You have the keys on you?" Colt *was* following, then. Rain could tell from the prickle along his skin and the distinct feeling that someone's gaze was on his ass.

"Lucky for you, I do."

Colt's breath was hot on the back of Rain's neck as he paused behind him so Rain could open the door. "It's my lucky day," he said, but it was soft enough that Rain was the only one who could hear.

Rain's hands almost trembled with the adrenaline rush that hit him at these words. Still, he wasn't going to roll over that easy.

"We'll see." Rain pulled open the door without looking back at Colt and strode out into Hart Square and the dying light of a September evening.

Colt's response lit a stupidly bright spark under his skin, and it danced from his belly all the way down to his toes. And definitely to the tip of his dick.

"I plan to."

2

COLT

Colt Fuller had always thought the best day of his life was aging out of foster care. But he'd been wrong. That paled in comparison to today.

Finally... freedom. Well, sort of. His parents had left him a reasonable nest egg, but he had to be twenty-five to inherit it. And now he was. Seven long years of working in bookstores, coffee shops, cutting lawns, and doing odd jobs on the side had finally come to an end.

Almost. He was still working at Quaff, an independent coffee shop in downtown Portland, to pay the bills. But the shift work was flexible enough to let him embark on his own business venture, and soon he'd be able to quit.

He was ready. He'd done his homework, found out all he needed to know on Google, and he was ready to make his nest egg into a steady income. To make his parents proud from wherever afterlife they were hopefully enjoying now.

Only one obstacle stood between him and a whole new life, and it turned out he had deep blue eyes, a voice that rasped on the low notes, and lips to make an angel fall.

Rain. His name was all Colt knew of him so far—even weirder than his own.

And despite the nickname, he seemed true to his namesake. Like Rainier, he had a bit of fire to him that made Colt want to see what it would take to blow his top.

So to speak. The guy was a total bottom anyway, in need of someone to boss him around. It was written all over his smug little face.

"So, you buy up land?" Rain's tone was nowhere near as friendly as Colt might have expected, being a guest and stranger in town.

"Something like that." Colt cast sharp sideways glances, making out and cataloguing details. He'd had to rely on his instincts for years. By now, he trusted it more than any contract.

Rain had his own goals, and he wasn't afraid to go for them. Whether he'd sell him a bridge and make off with the money, Colt couldn't tell. Not yet, at least.

"What's your interest in Hart's Bay?"

If Colt told him the truth—that he wanted to develop and lease commercial units in an exciting new waterfront development—the land price would double, and Rain would pocket the difference. So he just shrugged.

"I'm half wondering that myself. The place has seen better days, that's for sure."

Colt was fishing, and Rain rose to the bait. "I don't think so. I think it's up-and-coming."

"Really?" Colt knew darn well that house prices had stopped sliding, and several large real estate transactions had recently occurred.

But the number one rule of property was never to show too

much interest. Make them think you're doing them a favor, or you'll come out worse.

"How'd you hear about the town?" Rain asked, ignoring his question.

"Art gallery," Colt said, pointing at the place as he passed. It was closed, of course, but he recognized the cute little storefront next to the harbor. "There was some grand opening."

"Like Hart's Bay is up-and-coming, not crappy?" Rain prompted. His eyes danced as he looked over at Colt. He was enjoying the give-and-take as much as him.

Colt grinned. "Just a good night out with some guy, somewhere nobody knew our names." At Rain's questioning glance, he smirked. "One of the doors wasn't locked. I snuck a guy into the warehouse and we screwed."

The guy or the sex had hardly been memorable, but the big empty building right by the docks sure was.

Rain's brows shot up, and Colt finally got a reaction. "That's trespassing."

"Only if the owner finds out." Colt watched Rain closely. Who was he, to have keys to the place? Surely not...

Rain's nostrils flared slightly, and then Colt saw it: his spine straightened and a mask slid into place.

So he had some game he was playing. What was it? Colt was dying to know.

"A bit of trespassing never hurt, did it?" Colt followed up with a grin. "We cleaned up afterward, don't worry."

"Good for you." Rain was feigning disinterest, it was easy to tell. As Colt shadowed him, the harbor came into view.

Colt could never quite get used to the ocean: the broad, dark, perfectly flat expanse stretching in front of him. He was an inland boy through and through. But something was fascinating about it, too.

"Whoo boy," Colt exclaimed as Rain took out a thick key ring that didn't look like it should have fit in those skinny pockets. "You a real estate agent?"

"Nope." Rain didn't elaborate, though. "Why do you ask?"

Every question Colt asked, Rain casually tossed back at him. He was used to haggling, then. He stood his ground, and despite himself, Colt loved it.

"'Cause you're carrying such a big key ring." Colt smirked. "Or are you compensating for something?"

Rain's eyes flickered with something Colt couldn't pin down. It was too much to hope for arousal. "Wouldn't you like to know," Rain said calmly and pushed open the door. "After you."

Colt brushed against Rain on the way past, his steps lingering for just a moment as he breathed in Rain's scent. Fresh, like the ocean, and just a bit citrusy. Not in a floor cleaner way, either.

"Mmmm," Colt sighed as he stepped inside and looked around. "Nice to be back. Place hasn't changed a bit." In the murky semi-dark, windows boarded up, he could hardly see the details of the building, but they didn't matter if the land under it was cheap enough.

The door clanged shut behind them, and Colt's heart just about stopped. Jesus fuck, he hated the dark. If there was a weakness, Rain had just found it.

The moments seemed like eternity, but after half a second of terrifying darkness and two scuffed footsteps, a single light far overhead flickered on.

Colt schooled his face into neutrality, but before he could come up with another smart-ass comment, Rain beat him to the punch. "Maybe I shouldn't be alone with you in here. What with your track record. That bar is full of prying eyes."

His eyes danced enough to make it clear he was... flirting? Oh, shit. He *did* like being toyed with. Colt's heart leapt, the traitorous thing.

"Of course, I could be bluffing. Nobody caught us, after all." Colt winked. He started strolling around the edges of the building, hoping to hide it as he started sweating.

Jesus, he'd spent weeks looking up things to search for in investment properties: good structure, a solid roof, reliable wiring. He'd rehearsed the checklist in his head. But he was suddenly swamped by the sickening possibility he might get exactly what he *thought* he wanted and find faults that would drain his money.

He had to be conservative, even if all he wanted was to be bold right now.

"How long before this falls down?"

"Never." Rain sounded indignant, which confirmed Colt's suspicion that this wasn't just a job to him. This was personal somehow.

"How can you tell?"

"How can't you tell?" Rain retorted so fast Colt's head spun. He folded his arms.

Colt tilted his head and looked at Rain from across the warehouse. He was outside the beam of the single light ahead, standing in a shaft of moonlight that slipped through a window high above. Enough light that his nerves didn't jar from the darkness.

God, Rain was beautiful. Way too distracting in a moment like this. His high cheekbones caught the light, and his dark hair gleamed like a raven's feathers.

"What's it to you?" Colt asked when he finally reached Rain, just a few moments later.

"I think you should answer questions first." Rain gestured around. "You're on my turf."

"If we're getting territorial, I'm probably the last guy who christened this place." Colt couldn't help digging further, wanting to get under Rain's skin. "But it could be suitable for development."

God, his heart was thumping and his palms were damp. Only five years of practice adapting to new families, hiding his fear under an unassailable mask as he showed up on yet another doorstep in the middle of the night, saved his face.

Rain shook his head. "I'm the owner. And I'm not gonna sell to a weaselly developer who doesn't give a shit about the town."

Colt blinked a few times. Ooh, there was some fire to his words. His reaction was less than measured. "What's wrong with developing? It helps the locals."

"Not always," Rain retorted. He folded his arms over his chest. "I wasn't born yesterday, despite appearances."

Colt flashed him a grin. "Pardon me. You'll be aware that I can just find another town, then."

"Not with an opportunity like this." Rain sounded certain of himself.

Too confident in himself. His eyes glinted with steely pride, and it made Colt's resolve and cock harden at the same time.

Fuck, he wanted to test him. To see what it would take to make him speak his real mind.

"Fine, then." Colt took another casual glance around the place and then hooked his thumbs in his pockets with a shrug. "I'll find another one." He crossed the semi-dark floor, his footsteps scuffing in the dust, the scent of old wood thick in his nose.

Just as he'd thought, halfway there, Rain spoke again. His voice was low and tight. "Wait."

Triumph flashed through Colt. He turned on his heel and raised a brow, keeping his satisfaction to himself. "Yes?"

Rain approached him, his posture still carefully restrained and guarded. His shoulders were stiff, making Colt want to drum on them with the sides of his hands and loosen the muscles.

But Colt didn't dare move or breathe as Rain walked closer, silent until he was just on the edge of a reasonable personal space bubble.

When Rain didn't say anything, Colt took a step closer—right into his bubble. There it was again; chemistry flared to life between them, raw and undeniable.

"Yes?" Colt repeated, but this time, his meaning was different and they both knew it.

What was Rain considering saying yes to? This—or them?

Oh, they could have fun for a night. If Rain lived nearby, all night long. Even right here, Colt could think of a dozen different ways he wanted to make Rain come undone.

They were almost close enough to kiss. This close, Colt could make out the green flecks in Rain's dark blue eyes, glowing ever so softly in the late-evening light that streamed through the only open windows, high above.

Rain stood directly in the path of the light, and it caught his dark strands, turning them almost cherry-red.

Still, Rain was silent. Those soft, compelling eyes gave away nothing.

"You wanted something?" Colt whispered, dropping his voice to a pitch that indicated exactly what he was thinking.

Rain's Adam's apple bobbed once. It was noisy in the

complete stillness that surrounded them. Like they were the ones trapped out of time, nobody else around to witness this.

"Yes," Rain finally said, so softly that Colt had to lean in just to make sure it wasn't a hiss of breath. "Yes," he said again, louder and firmer this time, his breath hot on Colt's cheek.

His tone was brisk and closed off. Like he thought Colt was making fun of him. A minute ago, Colt might have thought that himself.

Now, struggling with a desire even he didn't understand, and seeing Rain as if for the first time, ringed by heavenly light...

Colt had no damn idea what he was playing at anymore. It had spiraled out of control in mere minutes.

Unaware of the wrestling match going on in Colt's gut, Rain took half a step back and spoke in a businesslike tone. "I want to see if we can come to an arrangement."

Judging by that tone, he wasn't talking about whose clothes they should peel off first. Shame.

As if watching Colt's face fall, Rain smiled slightly and tilted his chin up in defiance. Colt might have something Rain wanted—his money, or the development expertise he was pretending to have—but Rain had his own leverage, and he knew it.

No, Colt instructed himself firmly. *This is too important to fuck up because you want to fuck him.* So he drew a breath and stood down, shifting backwards a pace. "Go ahead." His voice sounded steadier than his thoughts.

"I'm not selling for a lump sum. But I could lease, or split the profits... and I know a local construction company that prices fairly."

Colt couldn't quite refrain from snorting. One of his foster households had renovated over a summer. It had taken until

Christmas to get the kitchen they'd been promised would be completed in just two months.

Plus, all his Googling had told him to expect less than he was promised from any contractor. That was where he was most likely to lose money.

But if Rain was involved in the deal, he had a motivation to make sure they didn't overcharge or underdeliver.

Colt tilted his head and folded his arms, and Rain smiled, no doubt reading the signals of interest.

"I work for them, in fact," Rain went on. "So I'd have a special interest in making sure the work's done right."

Oh, wow. Colt hadn't expected that.

And sure, he'd come in here expecting to spend little up front so he had more to cover development, but if Rain could cut down the costs up front in exchange for a piece of the profits...

Colt's mind was whirling. "Why offer me a cut of the deal, then? If you own the place and work for a company like that, why not do it yourself?"

Rain snorted. "No way. Managing this kind of thing is a whole different ball game. I thought about it, but I can't. No time, no money, no expertise."

Colt smiled. Two out of three, anyway. He could make up for that last shortcoming with a mix of enthusiasm and caution.

His heart was soaring, as much as his head tried to tell him to hold out before he came to a deal.

This *felt* right. Rain might have his own game, but he wasn't lying. He did seem genuinely interested, and he spoke with a glimmer of excitement in his own voice that couldn't be faked.

This was even better than he'd hoped. Casual sex was one thing, but fulfilling his life goals was another.

Of course, both would be just fine with Colt, too. But Rain was being sensible and all business, and Colt stifled his disappointment to remind himself that one lost chance had earned a much bigger opportunity.

"Take my card," Colt finally said, digging in his wallet to pull out the slim bit of card.

Their fingertips brushed with an electric jolt as he passed it over—literally. A zap traveled from one to the other.

"Ow!" Rain hissed, jumping back. "The air in here is so dry." The moment broke the tension, though, and they both grinned.

"That's a good thing, though," Colt said, turning to head out of the place. He was cautious as he pulled open the metal door, but static didn't attack him.

"Why?"

"The building's as watertight as you said." Colt turned to take in Rain. He shielded his eyes against the faint light outside, still brighter than inside the building. Now, as long as Rain's word was just as watertight, they might just be in business.

Rain locked up and then fiddled with the card between two fingers before looking up at him. "Of course it is." There was that challenging glint in his eyes again—pride.

Colt grinned and touched two fingers to his head in a little salute. "Call me."

He didn't usually ask guys that as he headed to his car, but Rain?

Rain was something else, all right.

3

RAIN

Silverware clinked against plates, and occasionally a glass pinged against a piece of cutlery. This had been the sound-track for the majority of the late morning so far.

The Hart family's monthly Sunday lunch didn't start or finish at a leisurely pace. Drawn-out was a better description. Like an elastic band stretched until it felt as crisp and dry as a piece of string.

The mood was stilted, awkward, and lonely even with four people around the dinner table. Rain was used to it, but these days, there was nobody on his side to help deflect unwanted criticism. Both his siblings lived far away now—and he couldn't blame them. So it was just him, both of his parents, and his grandfather.

The awkwardness was not helped by the fact that a couple of months ago, he'd blackmailed one of them. Relations with his grandfather Floyd hadn't been cordial even before that.

Now, they were downright dire. What with his parents' annual vacation, this was the first Sunday lunch since the fire. Rain had considered not turning up. But that would ignite more tensions. He owed them his presence, as small and tight-knit as their family was. Easier to come here, stonewall Grandpa, and hope that the truth didn't burst out from anyone.

As far as Rain knew, his parents had no idea what had happened earlier that summer. He had no idea how they'd react if they did, but he had the sneaking suspicion they would side with Grandpa, not Rain.

There was no excuse for what Grandpa had done. He'd tried to burn down the art gallery run by a new guy in town, Jesse, just because Jesse was dating Rain's cousin, Finn.

Rain had a grudging but growing respect for Finn after having worked under him for a few months, and the reverse seemed to be true. Rain had taken his cousin's side and defended Finn and Jesse against his grandfather.

And in a family with a deep split between *these* and *those* Harts, taking the other side was unheard of.

Rain set down his water glass, wincing when it clinked his plate jarringly and his mother cast him a scolding look. Instantly, he felt like he was eight and learning formal tableware etiquette again.

"So, how's work going?" Mom asked, which was possibly the most awkward topic she would have dreamed of bringing up. Even she had to know that. It wasn't a secret that Finn was Rain's supervisor, or that Rain worked for Hart & Hart Construction—owned by his dad's two brothers, who had wound up on the other side of the Hart family division.

Rain studiously ignored Floyd's deepening glower. "Fine, thanks, Mom." His polite and distant tone came on autopilot. "How about you?"

Thankfully, Mom had interesting news from the country club where she served as secretary. The women's meetings were always full of gossip. Once, Rain and his siblings had delighted in these stories.

Over time, though, Rain had realized what a different life their family led to most other people around here. He'd grown embarrassed by hearing these stories. Now, he didn't mind, but he also tried to distance himself from it all.

A hard day's work on a rooftop was much more satisfying than gossiping about a percentage point fall in the value of a portfolio, and how the fund manager had invited the investors to a golf game to restore their confidence, and...

"Mmm. Now, that would be a good job for a Hart boy," Floyd said abruptly, interrupting Mom.

Rain nearly said, *Huh?*, but it would have earned him an even sterner glare. He cleared his throat instead and indicated his confusion with a tilt of his head. "I'm not sure what you mean," he said coolly, even if he was pretty sure where this was going.

"Hedge fund management. You have all the connections." Floyd's stare was cold. "Shame you've thrown them away to work on a building site like some unskilled laborer."

"Dad," Rain's father spoke up with a frown. "Let the boy have his fun."

That was all his career was to them—a bit of youthful rebellion. Like he'd come around and start dressing in suits and hosting lavish cocktail parties one state south.

Or get a house like this mansion. It was close to the defunct harbor, a five-minute walk from the town square. And of all Floyd's former property holdings, most of which were now Rain's, it was by far the best kept.

The interior was lavish. It had hardly changed in Rain's memory, like something stuck in the late eighties or early nineties. The thick, ceiling-to-floor curtains felt oppressive.

Dark wood side tables and dining table took up the length of the room. All the high-backed chairs were as stiff and formal as his grandfather himself.

Rain's grandma had died before he was born, and from what little his dad had told him, Floyd had become hard-edged. Now he was like a diamond, and only a few people could scratch his ego.

It had almost been a shock for Rain to discover that he was one of those people.

"It smacks of a lack of ambition," Floyd pushed. "Rain's getting to an age where our associates are wondering what he's going to do. Other than run off to Colorado on a whim." His eyes were hard, like he suspected more than he'd said.

A chill ran down Rain's spine. He'd never told his family the truth of what happened there.

He'd told them he was going away for a year of socializing. Schmoozing with the kids he knew who took ski vacations in the mountains. And he'd done that, sure. Just enough to keep them off his back. But he'd also refused to tell them where he was living, or what he was up to aside from that.

Because he'd spent that year living with Des, under his controlling thumb, caught between the rock of returning to Hart's Bay and the micromanaging of his parents and grandfather, or staying with Des and letting him dictate his life instead.

In the end, Rain had chosen family over a tainted love that made him hurt every day. He'd come home and his family had acted like the little break never happened.

Like *Des* had never happened. That relationship was a secret known only to Rain. And whatever bullshit he had to take living here, it was better than putting up with that asshole.

"He has ambition." Dad stood up for Rain, which made

him relax slightly. Rain had wondered whose side he'd take. "After all, the kid has property now."

Ah, right. They couldn't stay away from the subject, could they? In exchange for not telling their family and the whole town that Floyd was an arsonist and asshole, Floyd had transferred the long-promised properties into Rain's name.

"And what's he doing with it?" Floyd pushed back. "Nothing. He'll need to do something. Upkeep costs money. More than he'll get paid at some construction flunky job." His eyes glinted unpleasantly.

"I'll figure that out," Rain said coolly. "Thank you for your concern, Grandpa."

His mom smiled approvingly. "I'm sure you will."

Floyd continued, "He's picked up friends and associates in the upkeep business. I'm sure he wouldn't mind working nights with someone like Justin."

Sudden silence dropped over the formal dining room, an icy blanket after a gradual thaw like the last frost of spring.

The implication was clear.

Rain couldn't directly defend himself and say he wasn't seeing Justin, because that would raise the possibility that he was gay at all. And that had to stay firmly shuttered, he'd always sensed.

"I don't know. Justin's pretty busy with his love life these days," Rain said with a shrug, darting around the subject by implying he was seeing someone else. "I don't get to hang out with him that much."

The approval and relief written over everyone's faces was stark, and it just made Rain feel like shit. Because he was getting approval for a careful series of lies. *I'm not dating Justin* didn't equal *I'm not gay*, whatever they thought.

"You know, there's a youth social at the club," his mom started again, and Rain stifled his groan.

"No, Mom."

"I don't know why you're so resistant. It's good for you to meet people your own age of a certain... life experience."

No life experience, you mean, Rain thought. He bit his tongue as he fiddled with his tableware. "Thanks, Mom. I'll keep the offer in mind." He checked his watch, not really registering the time. It didn't matter for his next excuse. "I'm so sorry to run out on you like this, but I've actually got a business arrangement I need to follow up on."

Dad waved him off immediately with a pleased smile. "Have you? That's fantastic. You'll have to tell me all about it soon. Your grandpa and I would be delighted to advise you on any matters at all."

I'd sooner trust a total stranger. Rain pasted a polite smile on his face as he rose to his feet. "Thanks. I'll keep—" *Wait, I just said that.* —"working on it, and let you know."

How many times could he reuse the same polite dodges before it became obvious what he was doing?

Rain needed to take action in his life, and fast.

And there was a business card burning a hole in his wallet that would let him do just that. Maybe too fast, but that was better than playing things too slow.

Colt might drive him crazy, but he wouldn't subtly threaten his inheritance over his job, love life, or any other stupid reason. He was clearly driven by money, but that served Rain's purposes, too.

Better yet, the construction phase would be a great excuse for Rain to keep his distance from his family—especially Grandpa, who he was positive had mentally placed him into the *bad Hart* category and hated him now.

Maybe he should have let Floyd take the fall for his own stupid actions. But then... letting him retire from public life gracefully carried less risk of ugly in-fighting and rumors spilling out. For all his faults, he'd done a lot for Hart's Bay—before Rain was born, anyway.

It was time for the newer generation to take over that responsibility. Starting with one phone call to the man who had haunted Rain's thoughts and dreams for the last eighteen hours.

Damn it, this was either the biggest mistake or opportunity he'd ever had, and Rain wouldn't know which until it was too late.

"Colt speaking."

The brisk, businesslike voice that trickled down the phone line made Rain shiver. Or maybe it was just the sea breeze. He leaned on a cleat that was driven into the concrete of the dock alongside the deep berth where ships had once unloaded their fish.

When the fish stocks crashed, his family had been forced to shut down the business that had once driven the town, and it had all gone wrong.

"Hi," Rain forced himself to answer. The sudden nerves twisting his stomach were unusual. He'd been along to business meetings since before he could sign his name. But never on his own account. "This is Rain."

He'd expected Colt not to remember him. Or at least, to pretend he didn't. A sudden spike of gratitude flashed through him when he didn't play that game.

"Ahhh," Colt said instead, his voice warm. "Have you had a chance to think it over?"

"I have." Rain's mouth was dry. He scuffed his foot along the dock, his eyes on the wavelets lapping up into the air as a fine mist descended over the water.

He was growing slowly and steadily damp, but he didn't care. He'd deliberately parked his car down here by the harbor and town square and walked the five minutes or so to Grandpa's. The fresh air did him good.

"And?" Colt prompted. There was a slight tension to his voice that told Rain that he was anxious for Rain's response.

That made Rain feel much better about what he was about to say.

"I'd like to meet up today. Let's talk about how we can make this work."

Colt hissed slightly, and Rain could just imagine the triumphant smile curving those thin lips. Weirdly, Colt reacting like it was a victory didn't piss him off. It should have. Instead, a thrill ran through Rain, hot and way too deep. He curled his toes into his shoes and pressed his toes into the concrete, sitting on the flat top of the large, round post.

"Perfect," Colt said. "Are you driving here?"

"Depends where *here* is."

"Portland. Forest Park, to be precise. There's a good Starbucks close by. I'll treat you to a fancy latte."

Rain barely refrained from snorting. Sounded like a rich area. The drive itself wasn't a problem, but the attitude was. "If we're developing here, we have to meet here."

"Why? I've seen the place."

Rain shook his head. God, he was used to going toe-to-toe, but he was also used to being defensive and angry, not...

thrilled by it. "Because we're developing *here*, not *Forest Park*. This is going to be the center of your world for a few months."

There was a moment of silence, and when Colt spoke again, a grudging respect in his voice. "All right. I get you. Your place. Tonight?"

Oh, he could have said *today* since it wasn't even two o'clock yet. But he didn't, and Rain suspected that was deliberate.

Tonight evoked a different emotional reaction altogether from him. The word ignited every nerve in his downstairs brain, not the one he should have been using.

"Today would be great. No point in dragging our heels," Rain said briskly.

"Give me an address."

"The bar we met?" Rain suggested. In passing, he'd glanced over and noted that it was open. Cher opened whenever the hell she felt like it, so it was never a given. "There's a quiet corner. It's early, so we can probably get it."

"I said *your place*, not your bar. Unless you live there. There's worse life choices," Colt drawled.

Rain shivered. The idea of inviting the near stranger to his house—of Colt filling up his small living room and sprawling on his couch, all sex appeal and well-fitted shirts...

No way. He was barely able to keep his hands off the man in public, and Colt's flirtation wasn't easing up. Meeting in private would be a disaster.

"Why my place?" Rain countered with a question to keep him on the defensive.

It didn't work. Colt just chuckled. "I thought you said that bar's full of prying eyes? No need to alert the town press until the deal's done."

Rain sucked in a quick breath. Oh, he was good. And for a

few moments, Rain was just about prepared to agree. Damn it, Colt was hot when he was toying with him.

Thankfully, Rain *did* have some degree of common sense that wasn't letting his dick do the talking.

"Nah. Cher's would be a better meeting spot while we work out the details. Besides, you already know where it is."

Colt chuckled. "It would be easier not to get distracted there, if that's a concern of yours."

That attitude really shouldn't be so hot. Like he thought Rain was about ready to jump on him. Which... he was. Fuck, how had Colt laid bare the situation in so few words? He was way too good at reading people.

Rain licked his lips. "It ought to be a concern of yours, too."

"It ought to be," Colt agreed, and his tone wasn't even joking. Then, it lightened up. "So I'll see you at Cher's in... oh, an hour and a half?"

Phew. That would give him time to get home and change, at least, before Colt arrived. Then he could head to Cher's and claim the quiet corner table where they had the least chance of being overheard in negotiations.

If things dragged out, they could go to Millie's restaurant in town for a little more privacy, or take a walk along the waterfront again. Lots of options that involved staying public.

Because he needed to stay in public where he definitely, absolutely would *not* jump his potential new business partner's bones.

"Three thirty?" Rain countered. "Works for me. Cher will probably stay open until five or six, at least."

"That's enough time to find a satisfying arrangement for both of us," Colt said. "At least, I hope so."

Rain was raising his expectations by making him be the one to drive out here, but he kind of liked it.

He held the power at the same time. If he chose to give it up briefly, just for the thrill of it... well, nobody had to know what he was playing at.

Nobody except Colt, whose piercing gaze seemed to strike through Rain effortlessly.

"I hope so, too," Rain told him. "See you soon." He fumbled to hang up, his hands shaking as he pocketed his phone.

This was by far the ballsiest move of his life, including running away to Colorado without leaving a forwarding address. Now he just had to hope he wasn't about to fuck everything in his life up at the same time.

No pressure, then.

4

COLT

The scraggly pine and hemlock trees were opening up into cedars as the state forest vanished into the rearview mirror and the ocean opened in front of the car.

Colt drove on autopilot, his brain whirling at a mile a minute. Thank goodness today had been a day off. He wasn't quitting this job until he had a steady income coming in—or at least until he had to oversee construction.

It was a quick drive to Hart's Bay from Portland. That was one of the reasons he'd chosen this town and not a place farther south on the coastline. Far enough away from Cannon Beach so as not to be a direct competitor, and close enough to Tillamook so he could sell to the nearby tourist population when leasing the finished units. Close to the coastal highway so important to surfers and family vacations.

It was the perfect place. He just hadn't expected the perfect guy to be there, too.

In two conversations, Rain had thrown Colt utterly off balance. He'd never met a guy like Rain before. He'd slept his way around half the state, and he'd had a few boyfriends.

Nobody had caught his interest like this—standing up to him, yet dancing with him verbally.

It was impossible not to imagine that Rain might be like that in bed, too. And in life, and business.

But behind closed doors, people were very different than the face they presented to the world.

Colt ought to know. He was brutally practical, so he'd never fallen victim to daydreams and fantasies like this before. Growing up as he had, moving from foster home to foster home, he had been quickly disabused of the notion that family and a white picket fence meant anything.

Rain, though? He made Colt want to know more about him. So much so that he'd dress up in his trustworthy gray suit and shiny black shoes—the biggest purchase he'd made with his inheritance, aside from leasing this car—and drive all the way to the coast after one phone call.

Colt slowed down as he reached the edge of Hart's Bay, letting his gaze skim the humble houses and run-down stores around here.

He didn't stop until he reached the parking lot next to the town square, alongside the art gallery. On one side was the short road to the warehouses and dock, and on the other was the vibrant little green square in the middle of four wooden buildings. Roads snaked away at each corner of the square.

It was a quaint little place. Brightly painted houses, even if the paint was peeling, and so tiny that he'd spotted people actually walking instead of driving.

"Here we go," Colt breathed out, pulling down his visor to check his hair and pat it. Time to put the mask into place, just like his hair. He had to be Colt Fuller, property developer.

It was all about instilling confidence, just like parenting. The households he'd actually enjoyed were the ones where his foster parents had seemed to know what they were doing. Only later had he realized how many of them struggled to know what to do with a reclusive, headstrong young teen like Colt.

Colt nodded briskly, slapped up the visor, and pushed open the car door. He narrowly avoided taking out a passerby who was heading from the square to the parking lot. "Oh, hello! Sorry."

The guy laughed in surprise and raised his hands, sidestepping the door. He had long red hair that swished around his shoulders, half of it coiled up in a bun, the other half hanging free. He shook his head. "No problem." He squinted at Colt, and Colt had a vague sense of recognition.

Please don't let me have slept with him. But no, Colt figured, he'd recognize that hair anywhere.

"Oh, did you come to the gallery opening? I'm Ezra. I think I remember you."

Aha. One of the artists. The town really *was* a small place if Ezra remembered him from one event a month or more ago.

Colt remembered meeting each of the artists at the co-op, assessing who might be most useful to stay in contact with. In the end, his desire for physical contact had won out quickly. He and his date for the night had vanished to sneak into the warehouse instead.

"Yes, I did. I was impressed with everyone's work," Colt admitted. Credit where it was due. "How's the gallery going?"

"Oh, great." Ezra was out of breath, dressed in an old T-shirt and jeans, streaks of paint covering his arms. He must be a painter, then. "Stop by sometime and see what's new. We've been growing quickly."

"I will," Colt promised. If all went well, he might need

Ezra's services in the finished space sometime next year anyway. "See you."

Ezra waved, and Colt headed for the bar on the corner of the square. It was a nice, fresh day outside, and the short walk across the square was pleasant. The smell of the sea was still strong to his nose, but nobody else seemed bothered by it. Kind of like coffee for him, then. Most people walked into Quaff and breathed in deeply, but he hardly noticed.

This time, he wasn't entering Cher's End Table in search of information so much as commitment. A bar was an odd place to look for commitment, he had to reflect as he pushed open the door.

It was a small place, and not too crowded, just like the last time he was here. Tables dotted the place, and two pool tables were at the back. It looked like the place old guys would hang out and discuss the economy while smoking and swigging pints.

But there at a table in the corner was Rain, dark hair and dark blue shirt instantly drawing Colt's eye.

God, he looked handsome. The shirt brought out the deep tones of his eyes, his skin practically glowing.

Fuck. Handsome wasn't even an adequate word. Gorgeous? Stunning? Colt searched for a word and fell short. Rain must have known exactly what he was doing to choose an outfit that high-lighted his best features, and Colt was a sucker for a pretty face.

"Hi," Colt managed, striding up to the table. "Get you a drink?"

Rain gestured in front of him with a slight grin, his white teeth flashing. "I've got me a drink."

"Oh. Right." Colt cleared his throat and nodded. "Be right back." He hadn't even noticed anything about the table besides the man sitting at it. The room was suddenly hot, and he resisted the urge to tug at his collar. What the hell?

When he got up to the bar, the proprietor—Cher, he could only assume—took her time wandering over to him. "Can I help you?" Her voice was slightly disinterested, like she didn't know him. Or, more likely, she did remember him.

He'd taken a bit of a harsh tack when he came in here yesterday. Colt softened his approach this time. "Hi. A Coke, please."

"No information?" she quipped.

"I think I've got an inside source." Colt nodded over to Rain.

Her gaze followed his as she grabbed a glass bottle and flipped open the cap. "Mmhmm. You sure do." Whatever the hell she knew, she wasn't going to say. Colt could tell from one look at her that she'd be a hard nut to crack.

"Thanks," Colt made sure to say straight away, leaving a five on the bar and waving off the change again. Good tips were the way to most bartenders' hearts. Or at least to a well of gossip that never ran dry.

Colt headed back to the table and joined Rain, his brain finally ticking along. He could objectively observe that Rain was handsome without being so distracted that he couldn't form a sentence.

"So, hello," Rain greeted him. God, how his voice made Colt weak at the knees. Good thing he was sitting down.

"Hey," Colt answered, giving Rain a smile. "So, let's talk about that warehouse facing the waterfront."

"Great spot to develop," Rain agreed, leaning back in his chair and folding his arms.

Colt nodded. "But are you sure you want to be part of this

project? It's not without its risks. If I bought it outright, then regardless of how it goes... you're free and clear."

The way Rain chuckled made Colt feel like he had half the story, yet again. "No, I'm not. None of us around here are."

"So people will blame you if anything goes wrong?" Colt arched an eyebrow. That didn't sound healthy.

Rain half shrugged in a motion that wasn't quite an answer. "I'm not going to sell outright to you." He lowered his voice to the quietest tone that could still make it across the table. "No matter how much you want me."

Had he *said* the word *to* at the end of that sentence, or just mouthed it in a soft exhalation? Did that mean something? Colt couldn't tell. His head spun for a moment before he gripped his Coke bottle firmly.

A shot of dark soda and carbonation brought him to his senses. "You're not going to back down on that, are you?"

"Nope." Rain popped the *p* and tilted his head slightly, watching him. "Is that a deal breaker?"

Colt might have thought so at first, but the other assets Rain brought—his connections to the town, his knowledge of the place, and the construction experience—slowed his tongue.

Instead, he shook his head. "Not necessarily. It would just be easier if I didn't have to worry about pleasing both of us at every step."

"Isn't it always?" Rain's eyes sparkled, his tone still low. There was definitely innuendo laced into his words. "But sometimes that's what it takes."

"So you'd..." Colt struggled to think over the sudden tightness in his suit trousers. "You'd be fine with me taking over construction decisions to make sure the project gets done on time, to budget?"

"Yes." Rain leaned forward. "I'm willing to give up most of my control, in fact. As long as it pays off for me, too."

The air in here was *definitely* hot now. Colt's fingers itched with the desire to peel that shirt off Rain and find out if the carpet matched the curtains. He wanted to taste Rain, to pin him against the bed, to drag every sinful noise in the book from his lips and then some.

"I think we'd fit together well," Colt managed, not quite sure what they were talking about anymore: business, pleasure, or both.

"You know what you're doing in ways that I might not." Rain raised his bottle for a sip, then shot a look at Colt from under his lashes.

Fuck. He had Colt—hook, line, and sinker. But Colt couldn't yet trust Rain with the knowledge that this was his first big project. His only choice was to throw himself full-tilt at this project and fake it 'til he made it.

"And I," Rain continued, "can convince people nearby to trust in the project and embrace it."

Aside from being a town ambassador, working on a construction crew, and owning property? Colt blinked at him. "What don't you do?"

"Play the flute," Rain answered without missing a beat. He couldn't be ignorant of the meaning, could he? Then he hit with the clincher: "I wanted to, but I ended up learning the clarinet."

Colt's sex ed foundations had been school hallway whispers. Rain was practically taunting him with the implication that he gave fantastic blowjobs. How fucking badly he wanted to find out. Colt licked his lips. "That's a shame. You'd have nice fingers for it."

Rain eyed him as if deciding whether that was an insult,

which took Colt aback for a moment. Every now and then he seemed to get that defensive look about him, and Colt could never figure out a pattern to it.

"In a good way," Colt added quickly.

Oh, fuck. Was he trying to soothe Rain's feelings? He'd intended to wind him up, but he found himself not wanting to upset him. If he weren't so attuned to bullshit, Colt could lie to himself and say it was because they were going to be business partners.

There was a whole different reason, though.

"Well, thank God for that." Rain grinned and drummed those slender fingers on the table. "So, I figure you'll want to split the ownership so I don't run away with the money later. I'll take half the market value, and I know it's undervalued. In exchange, I'll expect a take of the rental income."

Colt had expected this. The terms weren't unreasonable. "I think we can work this out."

"It's not exactly a standard deal, is it?" Rain folded his arms. "Do you have funding access already?"

That was several steps ahead. Colt had planned to buy first, then figure out the next step one at a time. Now he had to pretend he knew what he was doing. He pulled out his phone and typed into Google.

Property development deal options.

No, those results were useless.

Contracts for business partners developing property.

Marginally more useful, at least.

"Yes, I'll take care of that. Before we sign any contracts, I'll lay out the available funding and we can get some quotes on the redevelopment. We should both know exactly what we're getting into." He didn't have to know that some of Colt's cash would probably come from credit card advances.

Rain leaned forward, his eyes flickering to Colt's screen, so Colt flipped his phone facedown and put it on the table. He wasn't risking Rain finding out that he was doing this on the fly.

"Taking notes?" Rain asked.

God, he was a persistent one. Colt scowled at him for a moment, but it didn't seem to dissuade him. "Yeah. I think we need to talk to a lawyer before we get much further."

"Before we get that formal," Rain said, "I'd like you to get a history lesson on the town. You'll need to know the demographics, traffic patterns..."

Colt itched to get moving on this. They could be talking to lawyers and construction companies, drawing up agreements right now. A history lesson was the last thing he wanted.

"Well? I'm right here," Colt told him.

Rain shook his head, the steel in his eyes surprising Colt. "Not good enough. Walk around town with me. I'm going to show you around." He leaned in, folding his hands. "If you're looking for an easy deal where you come in, gentrify the place, and leave... this isn't the deal you're looking for."

The boldness took Colt's breath away. But his respect grew several notches at the same time. Rain wasn't giving an inch on his principles, even if Colt didn't understand them.

He took a moment to mull it over. It wasn't like that was news. Rain had made it clear yesterday that he wasn't in it just for the money. That made him both easier and harder to work with—trustworthy, yet stubborn.

The perfect combination, despite the potential problems. And it only fanned Colt's desire to learn everything about Rain: what he hid behind his complicated little smiles and firm lines in the sand.

"Okay," Colt agreed. "Right now?"

"Well, I might let you finish your Coke first." Rain drained his drink and nodded down at the bottle as if he was waiting.

"Brief me in the meantime," Colt told Rain, sipping at his mostly full bottle.

"All right." Rain leaned back, suddenly confident and eloquent. What he told Colt about the town—that it had been a former fishing town, until the collapse of the fishery—was almost off Wikipedia. Like he'd been coached in what to say, or they'd both had the same source.

It was strangely fascinating, too. "How do you know so much about this? Most people don't give a shit who founded the town they were in."

Something flickered behind Rain's gaze. A complicated emotion he couldn't put his finger on, but it seemed strangely sorrowful. "Because it's pretty close to home. Are you ready to go now?"

"Now, now." Colt tutted playfully. "Patience is a virtue." Whatever Rain was trying to steer the conversation away from, he wasn't sure yet, but he wanted to know.

"And cleanliness is next to godliness, but you don't see me in my Sunday best every weekday from nine to five."

Oooh. If he was making Colt think about how dirty he was, they were going to be in trouble in the trouser department again very shortly. "I'd like to see that."

"You'll get the chance, it sounds like. Now hurry up. I think Cher wants to close the place."

Colt glanced over and spotted her glaring across the room at them—no, specifically at him.

"All right," Colt told Rain with a chuckle. He raised the neck of the bottle to his lips and drank in deep, slow gulps. When he was done, he ran his tongue around his lips, aware of Rain's gaze fixed on his mouth. "Ready to go when you are."

"Not everyone gets a guided tour," Rain told him, pushing back his chair and grabbing their bottles. He dropped them off at the bar on the way out, nodding to Cher, and then led Colt to the door.

Colt followed in his steps, a bit mystified at the weird expectation there—that they bus their own table. Small towns really were a whole different world. He'd only lived in the Portland metro area.

Now, he rented his own place that wasn't *quite* in Forest Park, whatever he'd implied to Rain. He'd wanted to fit the image of what Rain expected him to be... and to make sure they were far away from Quaff if Rain did visit. A bigwig property developer in fancy suits sure as hell didn't work at a coffee shop.

"Whew. At least the mist lifted," Colt commented as the sea air filled his nose again.

"It'll be back." The door closed behind them, and Rain led him across the road to the grassy square. "It always is. I've lived here all my life, save a couple years of college and... other stuff. I should know."

What other stuff? Colt itched to ask, but he knew better than to press yet. It felt like a test. If he passed, he might get the deal of his life. And even if not... well, he might get the deal of his life, but with very different terms.

One way or another, he was getting closer to Rain and his life goals at the same time. Despite his last decade of jaded thoughts, optimism won out. Maybe those two things—desire and stability—weren't as incompatible as Colt had first thought.

Or maybe this was a dumbass idea he was throwing himself into headfirst. Only one way to find out.

5

RAIN

It was beyond weird for Rain to stand in the middle of the town square and explain to Colt who he was. But it would come out the moment they signed a contract, and he didn't want Colt thinking he was keeping secrets.

"So, this is Hart Square."

"Is everything Hart around here? Bays, squares, buildings..."

"Well, yes. About that." Rain led Colt down the path toward the bench and flowerbeds in the middle of the square. Like an X, paths snaked inward and met in the middle in a large circle.

He didn't sit on the shiny new bench there, since he wasn't planning on sticking around. But there was no better place to talk. Everyone could see them talking, but they couldn't hear without making it obvious they were listening in.

"My last name is Hart," Rain explained to Colt.

"Fuller," Colt said unnecessarily and reached out to shake hands.

Unconsciously, Rain met the grip and took his hand. The

electricity that raced down his arm at this connection was sharp and demanding. He almost sucked his breath in, his body tingling at the firm grip.

What would it be like to have those firm, strong fingers wrapped around other parts of his body?

But Rain couldn't dwell on the moment. As Colt took Rain's hand, his gaze sharpened. "Wait, Hart?"

"Yes." Rain pushed away the distractions and let go of Colt's hand after one firm shake. The better to focus, after all. When he was touching Colt, his brain crackled in a way that made thinking impossible.

"As in... Hart's Bay." Colt was connecting the dots.

"The guy who founded the town was my great-something-grandfather. My grandfather owned most of the property around here until recently. He's retiring from public life and passed them on to me."

Rain folded his arms, prepared to get defensive if need be. He wasn't sure how this would affect Colt's view of him.

"That's why you're so passionate about this place. And you benefit from the deal more than you told me." Colt's eyes sparkled, though, with amusement and gentle chastisement.

"What?" Rain scowled. "How?"

"Having valuable property nearby. If we develop one warehouse, the other one will be worth its weight in gold to me."

It took Rain a second to understand what Colt was implying. That was the kind of shit his grandfather would pull, not him.

But even under the weighty accusation, although his blood heated up, he kept his cool. "I'm not out to screw you over. I'm just used to people... not being a fan of my family name."

"Ah." Colt looked curious, but Rain shook his head.

"Long story."

Colt paused, his dark gaze flickering across Rain's face. Whatever he found made him stop pushing and nod. "Okay. So... thanks for telling me, I guess."

But Rain's conscience was still burning up. He couldn't stand it if Colt thought he was just trying to quietly screw him over. "If you want assurance that this isn't a deal to make you buy the other one later at an inflated price, we can write it into the contract—" Rain cut himself off.

Colt had taken his hand again. This time, he squeezed it once, gently, to cut off his nervous ramble. "No," he said simply.

Shit. Rain's cheeks burned as he glanced around. They were in full view of the bar, the art gallery, the grocery store... not to mention spitting distance from Grandpa's house.

How many people might see this body language and assume there was something going on?

Was there something going on?

"Sorry," Colt said, dropping Rain's hand like it was a hot potato.

It was strangely disappointing, actually. Rain found himself wishing that he could hold Colt's hand again, which was an emotion he'd never actually experienced before.

He'd never wanted to do that with guys he fucked. Back in Colorado, holding hands with Des had meant Des wanted to remind him that he was his property.

This... this had been intended as a gesture of comfort and reassurance. And now that he'd tasted that kindness from such an unexpected source, Rain was parched for more.

Colt cleared his throat and clapped Rain's shoulder instead. "I mean... no, I don't believe that's your game." His eyes narrowed and little lines appeared in his brow. "Maybe I *should* believe that, but... I don't know. I trust your face."

Rain managed to crack a smile. "That's a new one."

"I'm innovative like that." Colt grinned. "So, is there more to this history lesson?"

Rain nodded slightly. "I mean, it depends what you want to see." He turned on the spot, gesturing to the roads that led out of the square. "That way lies most people's houses. That way is the old mansions. There's only a few, and most aren't looking that great now. My grandpa's is the only real fancy place. It used to be the stagecoach inn."

"Oh, cool." Colt sounded fascinated. "That must be a sight."

As if he'd be welcome to see the interior, if Floyd knew the truth. Rain certainly wouldn't be. He swallowed his sigh and just nodded. "Sure is."

"Then that way is the old Main Street. There's some shops there. A couple restaurants. Some more houses. Nothing that interesting. Oh, and the sand beach and surf shack, on the other side of that point. But if you go to *that* side"—he gestured —"you find the coastal path."

"That sounds pretty."

Even though he'd resisted this tour in the first place, Colt was paying attention. It was another small note that made Rain question his brash bluster. He'd come off as an asshole at first, but his behavior didn't add up to that of a jerk.

"It is," Rain agreed. "Then there's a little path down, and a rocky beach on that side. It's a quieter cove. Too sheltered for there to be much in the way of waves, so the surfers don't go there. That's where the town holds bonfires sometimes."

"Huh." Colt folded his arms. "This sounds pretty nice."

"And, of course—" Rain finished their 360-degree tour by

swiveling to point at the last road between the art gallery and grocery store. "—that way is the harbor." And, naturally, the warehouses.

"Shall we wander down there?" Colt suggested. "Seemed like a pretty spot, if... bleak."

Pretty, if bleak. Like me. Rain's thought made him wince. He nodded. "Yeah, sure. Let's go."

This time, they walked side by side. Less like he was being shadowed, and more like a friend.

They walked slowly, neither man seemingly in a rush as they passed Colt's car. It had to be his, because it was just as fancy as he dressed and he'd never seen it around town before. Rain's gaze flicked to it and then away again. He didn't particularly care what Colt drove, but the fancy Beemer was almost a mark against him.

It reminded him too much of his own family's obsession with status symbols. Like property, even if it was slowly growing worthless, or people, even if they were miserably trapped in the life you'd made for them.

"So you've lived here your whole life except a few years." Colt had to bring it up. Rain's guard immediately started to rise.

"That's right."

Colt whistled lowly, under his breath. "I can't imagine what that's like."

Desperate to drag his thoughts away from the goddamn shadow that hung over every aspect of his life, Rain instead asked, "Why not?"

This time, it was Colt's turn to hesitate. Rain had never gotten that reaction from him before, and he was sure that he wasn't misreading the reluctance on his face.

He was about to call off the question when Colt sighed. "I

never really put down roots. My work keeps me busy. I clawed my way up, you know? I have to stay on top somehow."

Rain already admired Colt more than he'd like to admit, but it deepened now. He'd made something of himself. Rain, meanwhile, was back in his hometown, floundering in familiar waters.

God, Rain was hungry for success. This project had to work out. One way or another, he was going to make it happen.

"So we're gonna make this work," Colt said, his voice steady and certain.

"Hell, yeah." Rain nodded and let his hand brush down Colt's arm. The feeling of biceps under his fingers made him almost stop dead, but he forced himself to keep going to his elbow before dropping his hand.

God, a muscled man under his touch ignited nerves that he'd desperately held in check his whole life. But this wasn't the right moment.

Colt's gaze flickered to him for a second. And, for just a moment, that mask slipped away. He looked at Rain like a friend as he smiled. "I'm glad you're by my side."

The smile that reaction brought to his lips made Rain's cheeks hurt. He didn't know why it was so satisfying to see a glimpse of the person under Colt's attitude, but it was.

Then it was back. "So, can I exploit your feelings to get a better deal?" Colt's smirk was a bit self-deprecating, but also full of himself at the same time. How the hell did he manage *that* trick?

"No. Fuck off," Rain told him plainly. His heart pounded after a moment. Jesus, just because they were getting to know each other didn't mean he should say that to a new business partner! Floyd would be horrified.

Colt just tilted his head back and laughed. "It was worth a

try," he said, shrugging. "What about if I tell you I'm gonna pour most of my life savings into this?"

Rain eyed him, playfully suspicious. A guy like that had money to burn, so he wasn't sure it was the truth. Colt was in haggling mode again. Rain liked the give-and-take, but he wasn't going to let it affect his common sense. "These buildings *are* my life savings."

"Can I talk you down a few percent on your cut of the rent?"

Rain winked. "You can try, but I'm hard as nails."

"Me too." Colt's voice was deep and growled.

It took every single ounce of willpower Rain had ever possessed not to look down at his groin and check which sense, exactly, he meant that in.

If he did, he had the feeling Colt would never let him forget it. And he might just not stop until he had his way—in business *and* in bed.

And that sent a thrill through Rain's body that made his fingertips tingle, his heart pound, his chest tighten, his mind whirl with unbidden fantasies.

They would be great in bed together. He could tell already. The chemistry between him and Colt was off the fucking charts.

But this was a major life upheaval, and getting his dick out was the exact wrong move, Rain kept reminding himself.

Instead, Rain just said, "Good. If I'm giving up control so we can push through this faster, I want to know it's someone who will fight for both of us."

That silenced Colt's flirtation for a few moments. They came to a halt at the edge of the concrete overlooking the water.

To their left stretched an old marina where some boats

were still moored, but it was hardly active. Some boats were old rust buckets, while others were still in use. The slipways were grimy and the gates chained shut.

It was then that the scale of the project hit him: if they were redeveloping this warehouse, they had to develop an attractive path down to the waterfront for tourists. That meant dealing with things like this old marina, or finding a way to capitalize on its rustic charm.

Rain was way out of his depth, and he wished more than anything that he could ask advice from his dad and Floyd.

But his dad had once given up control of his business to his grandpa, and Grandpa's choices had impacted them all. Rain didn't trust Dad to know what the right path here was, and he sure as hell didn't trust Grandpa.

All he had to go on was his own gut instinct, and that told him to trust this man.

"C'mere." He led Colt down the long, wide section of dock that still stuck out into the harbor and was open to the public.

Near the end, he dusted off a spot of damp wood and sat on it, ignoring the dampness that soaked through his trousers.

He glanced up at Colt, admiring the view. Oh, that was enough to send a shiver through his nether regions again. Colt's groin was just about at eye level—and mouth level.

But the expression on Colt's face made Rain laugh, shattering the moment. He looked like the wood might bite him. No doubt that suit he was wearing cost more than the dock itself.

"I'll just stand here, thanks."

Rain sighed and pushed himself to his feet with another little laugh. "You're gonna have to wear more practical things than that next time you visit. If you even own any," he teased. "Or you'll never get to sit down."

"Thanks," Colt snorted at him. "I'll keep that in mind."

"That's assuming there's something to oversee next time you come here." Rain surveyed the marina and the warehouse, then turned to Colt. "So, what do you think?"

Colt pushed a hand back through his spiky hair, playing with the tips like they held the answers. His eyes roved across the view—the boats, the warehouse, the trees beyond.

It was hard to tell what he was thinking, and all Rain could do was wait for an answer.

"The devil's in the details," Colt finally said. "We need to see what's involved before we commit."

"But if the price and terms are right?" Rain pushed. He needed a guarantee of some kind from Colt.

Colt's lips curved into a slow smile as he finally looked away from the view and met Rain's gaze. He looked steady and certain, and it settled Rain's nerves. "Yes."

"Yes...?" Rain prompted, hardly daring to hope. "We have a deal?"

Colt offered his hand, and it was impossible to mistake that signal. His smile widened. "Yes. We have a deal."

On the turn of a dime, the desperation in Rain's chest grew into hope. Maybe his fortunes were changing. And if they pulled this off, he'd never find himself dependent on an asshole again.

Just a guy who tried to be an asshole, but couldn't hide a kind touch and word for Rain when he needed it the most.

He could deal with that.

"A deal," Rain echoed softly, the blood rushing to his face as he took Colt's hand for the third time.

Colt's palm was smooth and firm, his fingers strong as he gripped his hand to shake. And he held on to Rain's hand for a few moments too long. At last, the tips of Colt's fingers inched from Rain's palm to his fingertips and slid free.

Rain could breathe again. The devil was indeed in the details, so he wasn't letting himself get caught up until he had it all in writing.

"I know a good lawyer," he said.

"Wanna give him a call and see when he's free?" Colt was just as eager to get started as he was, it seemed.

Rain grinned. He liked this enthusiasm. It seemed to rebound against his own, until the energy bounced back and forth, growing each time. "Yeah. Hold on."

He scrolled through his phonebook and found the contact, then hit the call button.

Mr. Sterling wouldn't be crazy enough to answer the phone on a Sunday evening to many people, but Rain was one of them.

In fact, he was the only lawyer Rain knew who wasn't connected to his family. He had helped him slip free of his abusive asshole of an ex just a few months ago.

He'd listened without judgment and helped him get out without a scratch. Figuratively speaking, of course. Mr. Sterling would keep Rain's confidence and never breathe a word to his family until Rain was ready.

Plus, his fees were reasonable—always an important consideration.

"Hey, Rain," Mr. Sterling answered after a few rings. "What's up? Everything fine?"

"That it is," Rain rushed to reassure him, not wanting him to think Des had come crawling back. "I have a contract I need drawn up for a business partner. Do you think you could do it this week, or... what time frame am I looking at?"

"Oh!" Mr. Sterling sounded thrilled for him, and that

brought a smile to Rain's face. "Well, in that case... yes, I'll squeeze you in this week. Why don't you call the office tomorrow? Let my secretaries know it's you and they'll fit you in."

"Thank you," Rain said, smiling with relief and gratitude. "We'd really appreciate that."

"Great to hear from you, kid." Mr. Sterling sounded enthusiastic. "I knew you'd make things happen once you got out of that place."

Not the conversation Rain needed Colt listening in on. "Thanks very much. Can't wait to explain, but that's probably better in person. Catch up with you this week, okay?"

"It's a plan. See you then."

After he hung up, Colt pumped his fist in the air. "We're a go?"

It made him seem like a giddy schoolboy rather than a dignified real estate developer, and it brought a grin to Rain's face.

"We're a go."

"Great." Colt nodded once to himself, sharply, and turned to look over the water at the end of the wharf. His voice was softer as he repeated, "That's great."

Yeah. Rain folded his arms and looked back toward the town to hide the mist in his own eyes. It was pretty damn great, as beginnings went.

6

COLT

"So, this is what I'd recommend." The architect tapped the computer screen with a pen and looked over at Colt.

It was hard to focus on what Wes was saying. Colt had spent the last week reading guides and books all night and meeting with contractors in his few spare hours around his work schedule. Sleep wasn't exactly a priority right now.

As far as Colt was concerned, drawing up and signing the contract had been a formality. The most important way they'd sealed the deal was the handshake on the dock.

But it had kicked Colt and his new business partner, Rain, into overdrive. They texted constantly throughout the days to discuss the next steps.

It all came down to this—the plans for the new space.

"This is all subject to change, of course," Wes added. "It's just a start."

"Right," Colt nodded. He'd read up on stuff like planning and zoning. From what he could tell, that was only an issue if people nearby objected to redevelopment, and it was unlikely anyone nearby would want there to be *less* business.

"But I was thinking an open, airy feeling in front. Separate the space for this area with railings. Windows along there."

Feature after feature blended into a litany of costs in Colt's head. All he could picture was a dwindling balance in the trust account. But it was much too late to back out now.

That was one reason he'd been keeping himself so busy this week. If he didn't think about everything on the line, he was a lot calmer. And if he exhausted himself so he slept the moment he hit the pillow, so much the better.

In quiet moments, the self-doubt crept in. If he squandered his inheritance and this didn't pay off, Colt would never forgive himself.

Mom and Dad would be proud of me, he reminded himself four or five times a day. It had been a habit for the last decade. Some days, it had been all that kept him going.

Wes's voice caught his attention again. "The fees, of course, would be higher for that package."

Oh, man. More money. Colt nodded, playing it cool. "We already have a construction firm in mind. I think we can cover that side of it."

Although Wes looked doubtful, he kept that to himself. "Do they have experience in this kind of project? Framing the units will be key. If you want to rent out to a restaurant, the fire safety laws are stringent..."

Once again, Colt swallowed his panic and reminded himself that he'd known getting into this that there would be a million considerations he hadn't even thought of.

He didn't have to know everything just yet. One step at a time, that was all. And one step ahead of Rain.

"Right," Colt agreed, scratching his head. "I can talk to them later this week and see..." Oh, hell. It was already Friday.

This week had flown by in a blur of shifts and homework. "Saturday, I mean," he amended.

Wes rolled his eyes. "Good luck talking to a contractor out of hours."

"Actually, we've got an inside line to these guys. That's why we want to go with them."

"Ahhh." Wes nodded and leaned back. "Well, make sure you aren't being pressured into it because of family or friends."

Everyone wanted to offer Colt friendly advice, and he should have appreciated it, but instead it rankled. It reminded him of the bluff he was playing and made him feel stupid for even trying it in the first place.

He'd never been an A student. He hadn't started his own business before. Hell, he'd been fired from more than one minimum-wage job.

What the hell was he thinking?

Stop, Colt told himself. What he needed was another glimpse at the town and the site that he'd placed all his trust in.

Every time he was there, his instincts told him it was a good bet. The numbers backed him, and so did Rain's knowledge of the increasing number of people visiting the art gallery near the warehouse.

Colt had sweated it out here long enough.

"Okay. Thank you for putting all that together," he told Wes. "Can I bring a copy of these plans to my partner and see what he thinks?"

Oh, boy. It hit Colt a split second later that Wes probably thought he meant *partner*. And that sent a delighted thrill through him.

Although Wes's expression didn't even flicker, Colt quickly added, "My business partner is back in Hart's Bay."

"Ah, right. Of course." Wes fired up his printer. "We'll do

more detailed plans once you approve these. If he wants to join in our discussion next time…?"

"Nah." Colt sat straight. "I'm in charge of this part. He'll be the boots on the ground."

"Sounds efficient," Wes agreed with a cheerful smile. "Must be nice to have a partner in crime to bounce ideas off."

It was strange—Colt had never expected to have one. Now that he did, it seemed wild that it was a man he barely knew. Yet, at the same time, maybe that was what made this work.

They weren't close enough friends that they'd take any disagreements personally. At the same time, they weren't so distant that they weren't on the same page.

If anything, they were too close to being under the same sheets.

"Thanks very much," Colt said when he finally had his bundle of papers. He shook hands firmly with Wes and headed for the car.

Almost without thinking, he set course for Hart's Bay with one stop along the way—to change clothes in the back seat. From a starched new suit into old, loose jeans and a comfortable T-shirt.

If Rain wanted him to dress down, that saved him money on expensive clothing and helped him fit into town better while showing that he would listen to his business partner's advice.

Whatever got the job done, nothing was off the table.

By the time Colt reached the familiar stretch of houses that marked the outskirts of Hart's Bay, the steadily growing anxiety had almost been swept away.

It was a treat to drive along the coast, the window rolled down and the waves lapping at the shore beside the road. Despite its unsettling vastness, the ocean was undeniably soothing.

Or maybe it was getting away from the traffic and the noise of the city. Out here, life was easier. Maybe it was harder to get a quart of milk at any hour of the day, but people slowed down and remembered each other.

"Home, sweet home," Colt murmured to himself, cracking a smile as he pulled into his familiar parking spot in the small lot next to the art gallery.

Wait. Was that Rain?

He shielded his eyes as he gazed down toward the dock. The dark hair and his way of standing were distinctive. Yeah, that was him.

He was bending over something large, strangely shaped, dark gray. Colt thought until it moved that it was a canvas-wrapped package. Nope—definitely an animal.

Colt sucked in his breath and watched as Rain took something out of a bag and tossed it down, and the creature waddled closer in awkward, belly-flopping movements.

Colt's jaw dropped. "That's a fucking seal," he whispered, like it would hear him and take off for the water.

Just in case it did, he climbed out of the car and approached slowly. Rain's head turned as Colt closed the car door a bit too loudly, and he winced.

But Rain raised a hand to wave, and the seal seemed too busy enjoying its fish to care.

For a weird moment, Colt wasn't sure what Rain thought of his car. The only other car here was one he'd seen before, and he was pretty sure it must be Rain's—a modest little Ford hatchback, several years old.

Did he think Colt was pretentious? Spoiled? Rich? Or just that he knew what he was doing?

God, he needed Rain to think the latter—and the need ran so deep he couldn't quite fathom it.

Rain beckoned him closer. Colt nodded and approached, though he clutched his folder tighter under his arm against the breeze that playfully tugged at them.

When he got to the end of the dock, Colt just looked at the seal and shook his head.

"You want to pet her? She's pretty lazy. She doesn't care." Rain grinned and crouched next to her, running a hand along her sleek skin.

As if proving his point, the seal yawned and rolled onto her side.

"I can't believe I'm... am I dreaming? Pinch me." Colt set down his folder at the end of the dock, nudging a rock over it. Then, he carefully walked up to Rain and his—apparently, pet seal—his treads sounding too loud and hollow on the wooden boards.

But the seal didn't budge, apparently enjoying the way Rain tickled her whiskers.

"Nope. You're just in Hart's Bay now," Rain answered with a broad grin. "She likes hanging out here. I was passing by and saw her, so I grabbed a fish for her from the grocery store." He said it like it was the most natural thing in the world.

Colt just shook his head. "Of course." He was just a few steps away now, so he crouched as he approached and gently laid a hand on her side.

Oh, she was warm but sleek. He'd expected her to bite or something, but she didn't move much at all.

Gingerly, he scratched her side like a cat and petted her, watching how Rain did it.

Rain looked affectionate, his touch gentle as he interacted with her.

"What's her name?"

"Lucy, or Loo. For Lucille Ball. Get it? Seal?"

Colt burst out laughing and shook his head. "Yeah, I get it." Something warm came over him now as he watched Rain. He kind of liked the guy, and in more than a lustful way. He was stubborn, but that wasn't a bad thing. It was going well between them so far.

And this softer side was ridiculously attractive on him. This was real fatherhood material.

Finally, Lucy shifted her bulk, ignoring them both as she wiggled to the edge of the dock and slipped back into the ocean.

"Bye for now," Rain called out, grinning and rising to his feet. "So, what brings you here?"

"Uh." Colt had almost forgotten. Like he'd driven here just to hang out with Rain and the town mascot or something. Then, he remembered the reason for their meeting. "Oh! I have the plans. Very early stage, but the initial concept. Are you ready to walk through the place and see?"

"I was born ready," Rain said and headed down the dock toward the papers.

Colt took a moment to pat his hands dry on his jeans before he followed Rain to dry land. When he got there, he scooped up the papers and handed them over. "Here."

Rain wiped off his hands, too, and took them. "Oh..." he murmured, his eyes widening.

The first printout was an architectural envisioning of the front of the space: bright and airy with six units, an all-white exterior, shrubs in pots between the units to separate the space.

Tables and chairs sat outside two of the units, which could be cafes or restaurants.

The roof was high and sloped, with a walk-up rooftop balcony connected to a parking garage behind it.

It looked gorgeous. Rain was frowning, though.

"This isn't very... Hart's Bay."

That stung. Colt folded his arms tightly and shook his head. "Of course not. It's fresh, new, and not a fire hazard."

This was the first time he'd seen Rain go dangerously still and quiet. It felt strangely like the moment before his name-sake blew.

Fuck.

Colt really should have thought that one through better. Now it sounded like he was looking down on the town, instead of pointing out that he couldn't match the aesthetic and produce an attractive, modern, new building.

"I mean—sorry," Colt stumbled over his words. His palms went damp as his mind spun out of control, envisioning the end of this new partnership on the spot. "I meant, there aren't many new buildings around here."

It was impossible to hold to his know-it-all persona when he saw that look go over Rain's face. There was too much at stake. The project, his friendship, and... well, whatever else he wanted from Rain. Right now he wasn't entirely sure what that was.

The storm cloud passed, and Rain took a breath and looked up from the plans at him. "Good," he said. "Don't insult Hart's Bay to my face again."

Oh, that was hot. It was probably completely inappropriate, but Colt's knees went a little bit weak as Rain told him off.

"Of course," Colt mumbled, his cheeks hot. "Sorry."

Rain actually offered a slight smile after a few tense

moments. "Good. If there's one thing I can't stand, it's disrespect."

They started walking toward the warehouse as if in mutual agreement that they needed to look over the place from inside and out. There was still a chill in the air, and Colt had no doubt Rain had filed away the indiscretion.

"Yeah. I get it," Colt said and then winked. "I'll only disrespect a man if it's consensual and inside the bedroom."

"Or the warehouse, apparently," Rain parried without missing a beat. "If rumor can be believed."

Colt paused, his eyes widening, and then cracked a grin. *He can give as good as he gets. God, that shouldn't be so attractive*, he thought. He pulled his keys out of his pocket and riffled through for the freshly cut metal one. "I'll send you a couple pennies in the mail as five minutes' rent. Good thing he didn't last long."

Rain's laugh was a light, beautiful sound. And Colt's heart soared for one other reason: as Rain laughed behind him, for the first time, Colt turned his key in the lock on the warehouse door.

They walked inside, and Colt looked around. "You got something to prop the door open?"

Rain nudged a brick closer with his foot until it slid around the edge of the door. "There."

Perfect. No relying on a single long strip light flickering overhead. Even with a phone at his fingertips that could double as a flashlight, nobody needed Colt getting stuck in the dark and freaking out.

"Okay. This will be the side entrance to the unit at the end..." Colt shuffled papers and handed another one to Rain, and they began their walk-through. It took time to go through the plans, even though they were rough, and Colt quickly lost track of time.

Even though this was the most business they'd ever talked, it was impossible to ignore the tension that crackled between them. Colt tried not to let it get to him, but when Rain stepped next to him to crowd close and look down at the paper in his hands, his whole body jolted.

Oh, man. Rain would fit perfectly under his arm. All he had to do was reach out and put an arm around his shoulders...

"Yoohoo. Eyes down here, mister." Rain's voice broke through Colt's momentary trance.

Colt blushed and realized he'd been staring at the side of Rain's head, and now Rain was watching him with an amused expression. "Huh?"

"That's what I thought." Rain smirked at him and snapped his fingers, then pointed at the paper he was holding.

Right. The front face of the building.

"I was saying, if I talk to my cousin about this tomorrow, I'll see if this is even the kind of project they'd be willing to do. I'm almost sure they'll say yes."

"Are they experienced in this kind of stuff?" Colt asked, trying to keep his tone casual, like he knew the formal terminology but was just chatting with a friend. All he knew about the building process was what he'd picked up when one foster family had ordered a new house extension.

"Framing and roofing type jobs, mostly... which it looks like we'll need a lot of. But Finn—my cousin—is a foreman. He can work with other subcontractors to do whatever we need." Rain tapped the page and then held out his hands for the stack. "Leave it with me."

Colt nodded and passed them over. "Guess I get to meet the family, then." He grinned.

Rain didn't smile. If anything, he looked more foreboding. "Whether you want to or not."

Oh, man. Colt couldn't do anything right today, could he?

He was just gonna stick to sex jokes from here on out. Way safer. Not something he usually said in a professional environment, but life was weird right now.

It brought back shades of meeting new families, trying to fit in with siblings who didn't really want him there or parents who'd wanted a young, impressionable kid. Every rejection stung that much more, adding up to make him feel like he couldn't do anything right.

No, Colt told himself firmly. *I'm breaking that pattern now.* Starting this project had taken every ounce of desperation and courage he'd had.

As they locked up and walked back to the parking lot together, he cast another glance at Rain. He didn't look mad or anything. In fact, he was smiling to himself as he looked through the papers.

They were going to spend a lot of time together over the coming months. Rain already respected Colt, and Colt was going to do his best not to screw that up. He wanted to stay on his good side.

"Okay," Colt finally said as they reached his car. "This is me."

Rain tucked the folder against his chest, hugging it in his arms. "Right. Are you okay driving all the way back?"

"Ah, it's only an hour and a half." Colt waved it off. It was going to be a pain in the ass when he was here every day, but he'd deal with that as it came. He sometimes commuted for longer than that just to get to downtown Portland.

Rain looked like he was about to say something, and then

he stopped himself and nodded. "Cool, cool. See you soon, then. I'll text if Finn wants to meet and talk shop."

"Perfect." That gave Colt a day to Google things like *how to hire a construction foreman to develop your property.*

God, his life had gotten wild faster than he could have predicted.

For half a second, Rain's eyes flickered down to Colt's lips, and the world seemed to stop turning.

Did he...? Was that...?

Colt's mind raced. His tongue felt too thick to form words, and his fingertips tingled.

Was he about to kiss him? And if so, what the hell would Colt do? He wouldn't kick him out of bed, that was for damn sure. Nor would he turn him down right here, right now.

And then his hopes crashed down when Rain just smiled, raised a hand, and walked off toward the bar like that moment had been nothing.

Like he hadn't even noticed it.

Jesus Christ, Colt, he told himself as he collapsed into his car seat. Ninety minutes of driving was nothing compared to an hour of analyzing every tiny action and reaction when he was around Rain. In fact, it was a piece of cake in comparison.

How he was going to make it through these next few months of unbearable sexual tension without giving away how damn into Rain he was, he didn't know. But one thing was for sure: he wasn't going to let his past define him.

Whether that be his history of no-strings hookups or his fear of finding stability only to have it yanked from under him, he had to let go of everything and lean into the wind if he wanted to go where it took him.

With Rain by his side—and *not* in his bed—Colt was going to prove himself.

7

RAIN

Was it ever going to feel normal to meet his cousin on friendly terms?

Rain had been working under Finn for almost three months, and had even volunteered on the construction crew to work extra hours fixing up Finn's boyfriend's art gallery. Even so, he felt a familiar tingle of nervousness as he walked into Cher's and looked around.

He easily spotted Finn, who had inherited the big, burly gene that had skipped Rain's side of the family. He was sitting at the bar, talking to Colt already.

Ah, crap. Was Rain running late, or had the others been early?

Rain strode up to them, trying not to dwell on how odd it was to see Colt here on his own. Like he was slowly integrating into the town. That was a good thing, wasn't it?

So why did Rain feel so jealous?

"Hey, guys. I guess I don't need to introduce you, huh?"

Colt's greeting smile was bright and brief. "Nope. We found each other pretty easily."

"Yeah," Finn laughed. "I looked for the guy I didn't know."

Colt nodded. "And I looked for the guy who looks kind of like you."

Rain and Finn traded looks of skepticism before Rain snorted with amusement. "I could lift weights all day and not look like him."

"You already do," Finn pointed out with a teasing smile. "All the lumber in the world ain't helping."

That was a new one—teasing. On the job, they still stayed formal—no banter about their love lives or hobbies. That was mostly down to Rain, though.

He'd already put his neck on the line for Finn and his boyfriend, Jesse, that night in July. The last thing he needed was his family giving him a hard time about talking to *those* Harts.

But this was a new start, and if he was going to make it work, he needed to suck it up, ask for Finn's help, and deal with the consequences later.

"I dunno." Colt shrugged. "Size isn't strength."

"You're telling me," Finn murmured, his gaze straying to the painting behind the bar.

It showed two guys from behind, one taller and broader than the other. They were in silhouette, holding hands, standing and overlooking the cliffs and the bay just a few minutes' walk from the bar. Nobody had ever said anything directly, but Rain had always gotten the impression that the models were Finn and Jesse. The adoration in Finn's gaze confirmed it to Rain.

He rolled his eyes, took the barstool on the other side of Colt, and asked Cher for a Coke. Immediately, he saw his mistake: he couldn't see around the wall of muscle that was Colt. He had to scoot the stool away from the bar to even try.

"So I hear you two have a project in need of a good builder. Talk to me about it," Finn encouraged them, turning sideways on his stool and leaning against the bar top.

Rain nodded. "Yeah. I wasn't sure if it's a conflict of interest, us being the developers and me working on the crew... but I don't want to hire anyone else," he said.

"Agreed," Finn said and chuckled. "Hit me with it."

"This stays between us for now." The last thing Rain wanted was everyone in town offering their two cents. And Finn might have been painted for him as a Goody Two-Shoes, a do-righter who thought of himself as a martyr for helping Hart's Bay when it was really more of Rain's responsibility than his own...

God knew what Finn had been told about Rain in return. But even given sufficient reason to hate Rain, so far, Finn had been nothing but fair and honest. He believed that Finn could hold his tongue.

"Agreed," Finn said.

Rain looked at Cher, who raised her hands and nodded. "All right, all right," Cher said. "My lips are sealed."

Colt jolted at her voice joining in the conversation and looked around, then laughed softly to himself. He was probably still getting used to the fact that someone was always around to see or hear.

Rain launched into the explanation: the idea of turning one of the warehouses into commercial units, and if all went well, maybe the other one.

Hell, he owned a couple other buildings now, just as he'd been promised his whole life. But nobody had ever told him what to do once they were in his name—how much upkeep it took, or what to look out for construction-wise.

He'd taken that burden on himself by learning construction, the opposite of what his family wanted him to do. Working on job sites had allowed him to free himself from Des's control and teach himself skills for the future. It had made it easier once he moved back here to integrate by picking up a job right away with Finn's crew. Rain's foresight was paying off now.

"So you're looking to start with just the one project, and if it goes well, lots more work," Finn summarized. "Do you have plans yet? A survey?"

"Already got them surveyed when Gran—er, Floyd passed the deeds to me." Rain and Finn didn't need to revisit that night at all, ever.

"We had an architect in Portland draw up some concepts," Colt interjected while Rain handed them over. "They're all subject to change, of course. If it would be out of character in the town... we could go with more of an Americana style."

Rain glanced sideways at him, momentarily speechless. Not only had Colt heard his criticism, but apparently he was still thinking about it. Another little sign that he listened to others more than he let on.

"No, I like it," Finn mused, paging through the concepts. "It's fresh, modern... but not too modern. Adding a few finishing details would help it fit the character of Hart's Bay. Shutters, siding, those kinds of choices. Six units?"

"To start, yeah. The rent should be low enough on each to attract small businesses and entrepreneurs"—Rain crossed his fingers—"but there's enough floor space for a cafe. Not a full-sized restaurant, but a startup for sure."

"Yeah, I was about to say. You're making back your money renting them out? Cool..." Finn mused, then handed back the drawings with a nod. "I like the concept. That's definitely the kind of work we can help with. I know guys who are good at finishing, or you can do some of it yourself to keep costs down."

"That was the goal," Colt said, nodding. "Rain knows more about that stuff, but I'll pitch in."

Rain bit back a grin at the thought of Colt in a painter's overalls and boots, staring at his brush and the surrounding walls. He'd pay good money to see that.

"One more thing, though." Finn looked from Colt back to Rain, his expression wary. "Aside from knowing that we do good, dependable work... why come to me?"

Rain knew what he was asking: *Why trust me?*

And it was a reasonable question. After all, when the fishery shut down, it had caused their family to break into two. Finn's father and uncle had kept their half of the business running for much too long, lulling people into a false sense of job security.

Floyd and Monty, Rain's dad, had been under no illusions that things would get better. They'd shut down at the first signs of a struggle, giving people a chance to go find new jobs while there were still some going.

That wasn't the way the town had seen it. Rain and Finn had never talked about that history, but Rain already knew that Finn's perspective, like most people's, was just the opposite. Some said that Roy and Joseph had been right to keep people employed while their own fortune dwindled, and Floyd and Monty had been selfish to shut down early and sit on their pile of money.

A bitter family divide had ensued, and that was about all Rain knew of the situation aside from anecdotes here and there.

"Because it's a new generation," Rain said slowly, watching

Finn's reactions. "We have the same goal, right? Make this a better place to be."

Finn's expression had just started to clear when Colt interjected. "And I'm here to invest time and money to get this place back on the map. It needs a helping hand or it'll just die off, and that would be a real shame."

Oh, shit. If Rain was touchy about Hart's Bay, Finn was more sensitive than a game of Operation. Rain sucked in a quiet breath, but he couldn't think of how to defuse the situation in time. All he could do was watch.

Finn's lips pressed together in a thin line. His gaze was fixed on Colt, and it narrowed as he pushed himself to his feet. "Come back when you know anything about Hart's Bay."

Then he turned and walked out without another word.

Fuck.

Rain scrambled to his feet, but there was no point in going after him. It would only make things worse, wouldn't it?

"Fuck," Rain hissed. He took Finn's stool so he could thunk his forehead onto the bar top. Now his cousin thought Colt was some bigwig investor here to lift the town from poverty for either profit or pity. Neither would win him over.

Colt seemed stunned. "Uh..." He trailed off, his mouth hanging open. Like he hadn't already had one warning.

Rain straightened up again. His temper, usually so carefully monitored, was dangerously close to fizzling over. It was all he could do to keep his words to a fierce hiss, because he could see people looking their way. "I told you that you'd better not take that attitude again. Barely two days later, what do you do?"

"I didn't think," Colt mumbled back. "All I said was it'd be a shame if this place folded."

"You could have chosen a hundred better ways!" Rain

whirled to face Colt, his stool spinning a little too far. He almost tipped off balance and grabbed the counter. "Starting with: sit the fuck down and shut the fuck up when we're seconds away from a deal."

Colt's hand flew out in front of Rain like he'd braked too suddenly in the car and was steadying him. At Rain's glare, he pulled it back quickly. "I'm sorry. Jesus." His voice was sharp, though, making it sound like he wasn't really.

"How about you mind your business and I mind mine?" Rain struggled to keep a lid on his temper as he gradually cooled. "That's why I'm involved, after all."

"This is my business, too. It's both of ours. So I figured he'd want to know why I'm in it," Colt defended himself.

"So you as good as told him you feel sorry for us as long as you can profit from our family's failings."

Colt went still for a moment, his eyes widening. "Oh. I... I didn't think of it that way."

"No, you didn't think," Rain countered, rising to his feet. His knees bumped Colt's as he stood over his lap, looking down at him. "And you're gonna have to start soon."

"I'm *trying*."

For just a second, his blood burned in a very different way. Colt's eyes were wide, his lips parted and cheeks stained pink. How fucking hot would he look with Rain riding him, his nails digging into Colt's broad shoulders, Colt's hands sliding up his sides...

"No," Rain hissed fiercely, both to his own imagination and Colt. "That's not good enough. You commit, or you leave." He stared down at Colt, breathing heavily.

It was a stupid idea to work with someone who pushed all his buttons and didn't even know how to read a conversation. Which was weird, because sometimes Colt seemed to have his shit together, yet other times he put his foot in his mouth.

Come to think of it, it was always the same thing—ego. When Colt wanted to show off that he had money or knew his shit, he talked smack about the town. And Rain had already warned him once about it.

Colt's voice was quiet, but he bristled under Rain's stare. "I've already committed, Rain. I'm doing my best. I thought that conversation called for a different approach. I thought he'd want to see that I'm serious about paying him—we're not gonna flake and ask him to work for free."

"Of course not." Rain nearly added, *We're family*, and then he realized that would be a point in Colt's favor, not his own.

Shit, maybe Colt was a little bit right. If it hadn't been Finn, Colt's confident, even brash, demeanor might have worked. And it had been for a reason, not just to satisfy his own ego.

But Rain wasn't done bristling, and neither was Colt. They hadn't broken eye contact yet, both breathing heavily as they watched each other's every action.

With not even a full step forward, Rain could straddle Colt's lap. Kiss some sense into him—or out of him.

Fuck. It was a really stupid idea to work with someone who pushed *those* buttons.

He'd never wanted to be financially dependent on someone who had control over him, and he'd walked right into this situation because it had looked different on the surface.

This time, it wasn't Des controlling both their income and spending, or Des demanding check-ins by text every time he went somewhere.

And it wasn't his grandfather pushing him into the career

of his choice, or his parents urging him to socialize with the right people.

But it was still a relationship—whether or not they ever acted on the raw and visceral sexual chemistry that burned between them at this very second, red-hot and tantalizing. And it was still a dependency, in that they needed each other.

Colt's voice was low. "I can think of better uses for this energy. If you want everyone's attention, there's much better scenes for that."

His cheeks burning, Rain backed away and sat on his own stool again, trying not to look around and see how many people were watching. But Colt did just that—and aimed a glare around the room in one sweeping move of his head.

The conversation at the bar had been quiet for the last minute, and Rain hadn't even noticed. He heard it suddenly start up again now. Shit, they *had* been the center of attention just then.

He couldn't risk doing that again. He had to get his act together.

"Lord Almighty," Cher muttered from behind the bar, and glasses clinked. "Men. All fire and bristling testosterone. It's bad for your health, you know."

That, at least, made Rain crack his first smile in minutes, and so did Colt.

Rain drew a deep breath and let it out, then grabbed his Coke from the bar top. "Okay. I know you were trying to help," he said, searching for better words than the ones he'd just used. "But that wasn't the best way of going about it."

Colt's lips quirked into an even broader smile. "Yeah, so I'm learning."

"So next time, let me do the dealing with my family, okay?

There's decades of family history here that you don't know about."

Colt nodded slowly. "Starting to think I might need a history lesson on that, too."

No way. Talking about that shit to anyone would just open wounds that Rain kept firmly stitched up. He snorted and waved off the suggestion. "My least favorite subject. Just leave it to me to mend this one."

"We need a safe word, you know." Colt's eyes sparkled, like he knew exactly what the mention of that word would do to Rain.

The wink Colt gave Rain was too damn attractive for his own good, and Rain did his best to ignore Cher's pointed eyebrow raise from behind Colt and the bar.

Is he...? Rain gulped, his cheeks flushing as he glanced over at Colt. "What?"

"When I blunder in and take control but I'm not supposed to, we need a way for you to shut me up. Without telling me to sit the fuck down and shut the fuck up, anyway. That might be a little too obvious." Colt tapped his chin with a finger and then lit up. "How about *avocado*? It's what we supposedly spend all our money on, isn't it?"

A sheepish laugh came from deep in Rain's belly before he could stop himself, and Colt joined in a moment later.

Oh, God. This man was going to be the death of him—or remake him. He wasn't sure which. That fine line between adrenaline and arousal was snaking around his heart and pulling him closer. Like it or not, Colt was reeling him in, and every time Rain struggled against him, they only wound up closer.

He wasn't sure anymore: Who had whom hook, line, and sinker?

8

COLT

Except for his most casual and expensive clothes, everything "normal" that Colt owned smelled like coffee.

What most people didn't know was that being a barista was more than a part-time college-kid job. People studied, trained, practiced for their lives to become better at it. They just made it look easy. Perhaps most unfair of all, if they were good at their jobs, customers assumed that machines did all the work.

Compared to most of his coworkers, Colt was the rookie. He could do a decent latte in a pinch, but he couldn't draw designs on top. He could steam soy milk without burning it, but he couldn't talk about the origins of the varietals.

In fact, he rarely got to make much coffee. He'd only been working there for a couple years, mostly running the cash register and bussing tables. Washing dishes and running was more his forte, and he left making the coffee to his better-trained coworkers.

He'd bluffed his way into the job in the first place, but Lindon, his boss, had needed a lackey. He didn't mind working hard for a paycheck and didn't expect to make coffee on day one. But all the washing dishes, dealing with spills, and cleaning still meant he smelled like Quaff when he drove home.

Colt had worked there for long enough that he forgot right until he climbed into his car on Monday evening for the drive to Hart's Bay.

"Shit."

He'd scheduled himself a meeting without enough time to shower after work. He barely had enough time to drive there. He'd have to floor it through the park that lay between Portland and Hart's Bay, after stopping to change clothes in the back seat.

Well, he *had* had enough time, but he'd spent it picking up a fruit basket before taking the Metro back home to pick up his car. No good deed went unpunished.

"Ugh," Colt groaned as he started up his car, bundled the fruit basket into the passenger seat, and peeled out of the driveway.

He couldn't afford to be late for the meeting. If anyone commented, he'd just make a joke about how he lived on the stuff. Everyone could relate to that.

It was surprisingly stressful to keep secrets. He hadn't really planned on any of this being secret, but one decision snowballed into another. He'd needed to make Rain confident that he wouldn't screw up the construction project. And people trusted rich kids with money to burn.

He couldn't get the confidence of a construction firm without having money and experience, of which he only had a limited amount of one and none of the other...

"Oh, what tangled webs we weave," Colt mumbled under his breath, turning up the radio for the drive. Along the way, he pulled over at a rest stop and scrambled into the back seat to quickly change into casual jeans and a T-shirt with a collared shirt on top.

He could buy new clothes now that he had money, but it seemed like such a waste when that money could be going to building costs. If Colt ran out of money later, he'd never forgive himself for the indulgence.

Only when the ocean spread out in front of Colt did he glance at his speedometer and do a double take.

Jesus, he hadn't realized how fast he'd taken that drive. Stress, caffeine, and guilt had given him a lead foot.

Good. All the more time to make amends.

Colt had headed home last night after the disastrous end to their meeting. He might have stuck around to try to make things better, but work had called. The coworker who had swapped shifts so he could meet the lawyer last week had called in her favor, meaning he'd had to work today.

At least he wouldn't have to juggle for much longer. Rain was able and willing to supervise the actual hands-on construction, so Colt's work would be more remote—documents and town planning hassles. He could fit that around shifts.

All the more reason to keep on Rain's good side—and stop being such a jerk to him. Hence the fruit basket. It was the best way he could think of to say sorry, besides proving that he meant it by following Rain's lead a little closer in the future.

Thank God Rain had talked Finn into another company meeting after that. Colt hadn't blown it with his rashness. Still, he planned to eat crow and make amends with Finn right away, too. Whatever it took to get it done.

Colt double-checked the address Rain had texted as he pulled up in the driveway ten minutes early. When he was sure he was at the right place, he climbed out and tucked the basket under his arm, then walked up three steps to the front porch.

It took him a second of gaping before he rang the doorbell. From here, he could actually see the ocean.

What a view.

But the stretch of ocean visible between houses paled in comparison to the view when the door opened.

Rain... was dripping wet, mostly naked, and wrapped in a towel.

Any smart-ass remark Colt might have made went straight out the window at the sight of him.

He wasn't sure whether to burst out laughing or bust a nut on the spot. Rain had shampoo bubbles on his forehead and a pissed-off look; with his hair in his eyes and flattened, he looked like a cat caught under a sprinkler.

On the other hand, Colt had never been thirstier than he was at the sight of the water droplets trickling down Rain's lean chest.

His boner sprang into action. If this were a cartoon, it would have made a *boing!* sound and smacked Rain in the chin.

Jesus fucking Christ, Colt wanted him.

The towel was tucked in firmly around his waist, which was a real shame, because Colt couldn't see whether he had a treasure trail or what the treasure was at the end of it.

"You're early." If he looked like a pissed-off cat, Rain *definitely* sounded like one.

Colt tried to summon speech. He held up the basket in one hand, his eyes still glued to Rain's glistening chest and smooth stomach. "I... brought fruit to say sorry?"

"Hold on." Rain snatched the basket from him, turned on his heel, and closed the door.

Colt let a whimper escape only when the door was shut and grabbed the porch rail to lean back against it. Oh, Jesus, he needed a fainting couch right now.

Cool it, Colt, he told himself.

But his brain would not be stopped. All he wanted was to barge in and order Rain to his knees, and they were about to walk into a business meeting. His jeans actually dug into the hard line of his cock, and he glanced around to make sure no nosy neighbors saw him adjust himself.

Nope, that position didn't work, either. He tried again, grimacing and shifting from foot to foot. This didn't look weird *at all*, right? Him standing on Rain's porch, one hand in his jeans, playing with himself? *Oh, God. Come on, Junior. Work with me here*, he begged himself.

He barely had himself tucked upright, relying on his waistband to save him, when the door opened again.

Rain wore a more amused expression this time and a T-shirt that clung to his still-damp body. "That's a nice thing you did."

"I'll try not to do it again," Colt promised, smirking as Rain bent over to slip on his shoes. It was impossible to keep his eyes off the way his ass stuck out as he did so.

"Fucking up or a nice thing?"

"Both," Colt said and winked when Rain glanced over and caught him staring. "Can't let you think I'm going soft."

Rain snorted and straightened up, then patted down his pockets before stepping out onto the porch. "No way."

But this time, he wasn't sidling closer to Colt and smiling up at him with those wide, innocent eyes that seemed tailor-made to lure him in.

Colt's stomach jolted with an unpleasant shock. *Maybe he's not single. Maybe that's why he closed the door on you.*

No, that didn't make sense. Colt hardly knew the man, but he knew he wasn't dishonest. So he was either less interested or he was trying to pretend to be.

Oh, man, he hated overthinking things.

Colt gestured toward his car. "May I escort you to the restaurant, sir?"

That earned him a small smile. "As long as your driving isn't as reckless as your tongue," Rain told him and headed to the passenger side.

Colt's feet felt frozen to the last porch step for a few moments. Was *that* it? Had he pissed him off so much that he didn't want him anymore?

Oh, man. Colt bit his lip hard. Rain had given him one warning, and he'd blown straight through it. Was that it? Was he just a business partner now?

"Coming? We have a meeting," Rain called as he pulled at the handle.

Colt raised his key fob to press the unlock button, then numbly walked to the car.

Rain squinted over the car at him. "You look like you've seen a ghost. I promise they won't bite."

"Hm," Colt hummed and focused on buckling up until the wave of unpleasant thoughts had passed.

No, he reminded himself. Jumping to conclusions would only hurt them both. Rain might be keeping his distance because they were about to meet his cousin and uncle, and from the sounds of it, he was thoroughly closeted.

That was much more likely than some epic fuckup that Colt could never recover from.

Feeling a little better now, Colt pulled out of the driveway and drove to the restaurant with Rain's directions.

Just as he pulled up in front of the restaurant, Rain looked over at him. "The fruit basket *was* nice, though." His tone was different than it had been a few minutes ago. "Thank you."

Colt shut off the car and glanced over at Rain, nervously tapping his hand on the parking brake. "Yeah? I wasn't sure if it was too..."

No, wait. Don't say "too fancy," he thought.

Fruit baskets were really kind of ridiculous. He doubted there was an ornamental fruit basket place within ten miles of here. He'd half expected Rain to laugh in his face and tell him a grocery store gift card would have gone further.

But that made it sound like he thought Rain was a country redneck. Or, worse, that country rednecks couldn't appreciate fruit baskets.

Oh, God. He'd never been one to second-guess himself like this. Usually, if he dug himself a hole, he tended to stick his shovel next to it proudly and wave his arms to point it out.

With Rain, though? He was already on thin ice, and Colt desperately wanted Rain not to think less of him. It was like he couldn't quite do anything right, and he'd never actually *needed* to do it all perfectly until he'd met him, and now...

Rain's lips twitched into a grin as he scanned Colt's face. He reached out and laid a hand over Colt's on the parking brake. "No," Rain assured him simply.

The rush of warmth, the tingle in his fingertips... it was weirdly soothing. All the air rushed out of Colt's lungs in a moment as his shoulders slumped. All it took was one touch from Rain before he felt like the world stopped keeling off balance.

"No?" Colt echoed, his voice softer than Rain's. He searched those gorgeous, deep blue eyes for reassurance.

And he found it there, in spades. Rain's gaze was soft and

understanding. In his face, Colt found acceptance and... *Oh, thank God.*

He found trust.

Colt burst into a smile. He tried to turn his hand over to take Rain's, but Rain had already pulled back his hand and was turning toward the car door, unbuckling, sliding out.

By now, Colt was growing familiar with the pang of loss that ran through him every time Rain pulled away from his touch. He still treasured those moments when Rain let him get close enough to practically taste.

"C'mon, I see Finn's truck already. We'll be late."

Colt had to rouse himself to action—though maybe arousal wasn't a good word to use, given the sparks that ran through his veins with every thought of tasting Rain.

Buildings. Renovations, he reminded himself, climbing out of the car and slamming the door. Rain was already striding for the front door, so he followed in his steps and tried not to enjoy the view too much. *Erecting a new unit... oh, God. I'm hopeless.*

It was a damn good thing Rain had no way of reading his mind. Colt was starting to see where the myth came from that men thought about sex every seven seconds.

"Oh, this is cute." The interior of Millie's was kitschy as fuck, but no way was Colt going to open his big mouth and say that. There were fake vines trailed around white pillars, and booths tucked against two walls.

"It is," Rain agreed as he headed up to the waitress who was beaming at him. He gave her a friendly wave and grin. "Sally, how's it going?"

She beamed back at them both. "Oh, I can't complain. Your cousin and uncle are here, you know." There was something in her tone that Colt couldn't quite make out. "They said they were waiting for you?"

Rain's back stiffened. Colt itched to dig his thumbs into those taut neck muscles and get him to relax. "Yep," Rain told her, peering around the place. "Oh, there they are."

"Great. I'll be right over with menus." Sally cast Colt a curious glance, so Colt gave her what he hoped was a neutral smile.

It was interesting to watch Rain's body language shift. From the confident, certain man he'd been outside, he was suddenly a little bit... shifty? Maybe that wasn't a fair assessment, but his face was guarded and his movements jerky as they reached the table.

"Hey. Thanks for meeting us here," Rain greeted as both men at the table stood up to greet them.

"You know Finn already. Uncle Roy, this is Colt."

"Pleasure to meet you," Colt said, hoping the slide of his palm against his jeans before he gripped Roy's hand was subtle. Then he looked at Finn, and his cheeks flushed. "And thank you for meeting with me again. I'm sorry for what I said."

Finn hesitated for a moment, his eyes flicking between Rain and Colt before he reached out a hand. His expression cleared up just a little bit. "Thanks for that," he answered. Was that grudging respect? Colt could work with that.

They all sat and made small talk while menus and extra water glasses were dropped off. Even as they went through the ritual of choosing meals and ordering, the tension hung in the air.

Colt itched to jump straight into business, but he sensed that he was supposed to wait. Rain was busy asking about the current construction project, and Roy was describing difficulty sourcing lumber or something.

That didn't leave much space for Colt to join the conversation without putting a foot in his mouth, so he didn't.

"But I guess you know how frustrating that is," Roy abruptly said, looking over at Colt.

Colt blinked a few times. "Hm? Sorry. I was miles away there," he said with a sheepish chuckle.

"Overrunning deadlines, subcontractors disappearing off the face of the earth..." Roy trailed off with a sigh.

"Oh. Yes," Colt quickly answered, his cheeks flushing. It sounded like a test. "It's frustrating on all sides. Hopefully not a problem with... well, what we're here to discuss, though." He said it as politely as possible.

Finn smiled. "Yeah. Let's get down to business. I had a good look at those plans, and I have to say, I like them more now."

"Nothing's set in stone," Colt rushed to assure them. "I can see they'll need tweaking to fit in around here."

"That's important," Finn said, his gaze rising to Colt's. Again, a little test. Colt hoped to hell he passed it, because it didn't take a genius to work out how important that was to Rain.

"Yeah," Colt said. Even though his cheeks burned at the subtle reminder of what had transpired on Sunday, he held Finn's look with his own. "It's important to me to fit in around here. I didn't take the right tack at first. But there's no point in putting up a high-rise in a neighborhood of bungalows, or a corner store in Beverly Hills."

"Right you are," Roy agreed. His gaze flicked between the two of them. "I hear you're renting out the units when they're done?"

"Yes, sir," Colt responded, straightening up. "That's the plan. I'd be happy to let them go to locals first. I thought it'd be nice to give people that opportunity first, since it's their back-yard. Would that be all right?"

That earned him smiles from all three of the Harts at the table, and Colt finally let himself relax just a little.

Okay, he might not be totally screwed. He could do this. He really could.

It took them surprisingly little time to agree on the details: they'd share revised plans and the survey, and then Rain would walk them through and get an estimate of time and material costs.

"What about planning permission? What's that situation out here?" Colt asked, sipping his lemonade before digging into his burger.

"Mmm." Roy grunted significantly and swapped looks with Finn. "Annoying, depending on who you're up against."

"Think it'll be hard?"

"Well, town hall can be picky." Roy wiped his fingers as he worked on a delicious-looking greasy, cheesy pizza. "Depends who's at the helm. They tend to like it when we're involved, because they know we don't cut corners."

"Now that Floyd's retired..." Finn cast Rain a look.

Rain grimaced. "I know. But he'll still hear about it. The clerk is a golf buddy."

"Ah, shit," Finn sighed. "That explains a lot."

Colt was missing half the context here, and finally, Rain took pity on him. He popped a fry into his mouth and turned to Colt. "My—our grandfather," he said, indicating himself and Finn, "Roy's dad? He had fingers in a lot of pies until recently."

Finn cleared his throat. "Yeah. But I think since it's Rain's property..."

"He might go easy on me?" Rain raised a brow, then made a small sound. "Who knows."

With a sudden jolt, Colt wondered if *this* was why Rain was so reticent to show affection in public. He'd had a mix of supportive and unsupportive families in the system, so he wouldn't be surprised.

"Well, you've got one or two big advantages," Finn muttered, flattening his burger bun with one big hand. He sounded a little bit resentful.

Colt held his breath. No way was he getting in the middle of that family division.

"Sure," Rain agreed. Then he lifted his shoulders in a shrug. "So, we have a plan."

And with that, the conversation moved on—almost too deliberately.

It took another forty minutes to finish their food and conversation about the weather, the local news, and more.

By the end of the conversation, Colt felt like the other guys were starting to accept him. They looked at him about as often as Rain, and when Colt tried to make comments, they listened.

Which made it all the more jarring when Rain suddenly checked his watch and swore. "Sorry. I forgot... I've got a friend over."

"I'll drive you back," Colt said quickly and stood up. "I'll leave you with the paperwork," he added to the other guys and shook hands. This time, he got smiles from them both.

"Thanks. See you guys," Rain bade the others and strode for the door like a bat out of hell while Colt, chuckling, followed.

All in all, he reflected, a pretty damn successful meeting. Kind of deserving of a celebration. And once the agreement was formalized, they'd be in business.

"Sorry to take off in a hurry like this," Rain said.

"No problem," Colt said, trying to ignore the jolt of jealousy that shot straight through him. What kind of friend would make Rain take off from a business meeting as important as this? A hookup? A boyfriend? "I can drop you off and see you next week, huh?"

"Thanks." Rain slid out of the car as they pulled up to the curb in front of his house. He leaned down and smiled. "That went great. Thanks for coming all this way."

It was hard not to notice there was another car in Rain's driveway and a guy pacing back and forth inside, near the living room window.

And he was *not* going to jump to conclusions, but... they were leaping to mind.

"Bye." Rain waved and strode for the porch.

Colt swallowed back the disappointment and jealousy that threatened to choke him and sour their last couple of hours. Just when things were getting better... Rain drifted away from him again.

Maybe Colt had screwed up so badly that Rain was investigating his other options. Or maybe Colt was paranoid as fuck, which meant he was jealous, but he had no damn right to be.

Colt blew out a sigh through his lips as he watched Rain walk inside. He should just head home. No point in hanging around Hart's Bay without Rain's company, and Rain was busy.

Better to get home and catch up on sleep while Rain caught up on... something or other that was totally his business and not at all Colt's concern. Even if it ate at him like a seal gnawing through a fish.

Even when the front door had closed, he couldn't tear his eyes away from the shapes moving behind the lacy living room curtain. He was aware of how much of a creeper that made him, and he couldn't stop it.

Damn it, he needed to know more, but he wasn't entitled to know anything. This was a mess he wasn't sure he could escape unbruised.

9

RAIN

"You're late, asshole."

"Sorry, sorry," Rain groaned as he slammed the door behind himself and ran a hand through his hair. Thankfully, his best friend had a key. Justin had obviously let himself in while he waited. "The meeting ran on."

They'd planned to meet up and share the news about their weeks as usual. Typically, Rain just vented about his family, Justin complained that his team was losing, and they ate a lot of chips and dip and drank a six-pack between them. Nothing wild.

Justin was in the living room, nudging the blind aside before flopping on the couch. He muted the game on TV for a minute. "Who's *that* in the BMW?"

"You know damn well who it is," Rain grumbled. "My business partner."

"The guy who stormed into Cher's when I was with you?" Justin raised an eyebrow. "Seriously? He's smoking hot. You think I believe he's a business partner?"

A trickle of fear crept down Rain's spine. If Justin had

93

noticed, who else had? "What else would he be? No, don't answer that. I'm gonna wash up. Back in a minute."

Justin was uncomfortably close to the truth. Rain had been prickling with pent-up desire since the moment his smoking-hot partner had knocked on the door, fruit basket in hand. He didn't want to talk about it yet, until he figured out what the hell "it" was.

"And that basket on the kitchen counter?" Justin continued, unmuting the game and raising his voice to yell over it as Rain headed down the hall toward his bathroom. "Looks like courtship, dude. Watch out if he gives you a handkerchief."

"Oh, fuck off," Rain groaned. He got only a laugh in response.

The TV would keep his friend happy enough for fifteen minutes. And he could use that time to beat the tension out of himself.

Rain shut the bathroom door and locked it, then breathed out a sigh as he leaned against it with his shoulder, thunking the side of his head against the door.

What the hell had he been thinking when he agreed to go into business with a man whose every smile made his knees melt?

And worse yet—or better, he hadn't decided which—Justin was right. A fruit basket was way over-the-top for a business partner's apology after one careless comment.

Then there was the way Colt's eyes had skimmed every inch of his body when he'd opened the door to him in just a towel. Rain had been so close to inviting him in. It could have gone either way, but it was probably good he'd slammed the door and gotten dressed instead.

But it was a flood climbing steadily up the banks of the river. It might be swollen—much like his dick right now—but the banks were holding, if barely. The moment he gave in to one moment over the line, he'd be wrecked.

Rain rolled slowly until he leaned back onto the door, skimming a hand down to his belt. He bypassed it, pressing the heel of his palm into his throbbing cock.

All it took was one clear memory of Colt's eyes tracing droplets of water down Rain's body and he wanted to whimper and drop to his knees.

Fuck, he'd better get this over with quickly, then.

He bit back his gasp when he slid a hand into his underwear. He was already hard and sensitive, his whole body tense at the fantasies slipping through his mind.

Rain had the feeling you weren't supposed to know this much about your business partner's domineering sexual interests. But Colt kept flirting, almost nonstop, and Rain was powerless to resist. Which was just the way they both wanted it.

His movements were quick, jerky, and fumbling as he undid his belt and pants, sliding them down to his thighs. He leaned back against the door and closed his eyes, just imagining a weight pressing him up against this surface.

The fantasy sprung to mind all too easily, just like his dick sprang free as soon as he gave it a little free rein.

Instead of his own fingers closing around the velvety warm skin, he imagined Colt's. What he wouldn't give right now to be jerking Colt off in return, Rain's face pressed into Colt's shoulder as he fumbled in the narrow space between their bodies.

Rain stifled all sounds, substituting silent gasps for the throaty groans that Colt could wring from him.

Colt was so damn strong he could heft Rain off the ground, let Rain wrap his legs around his waist, and pin him here.

Meanwhile Rain would grind against Colt, taking both shafts in one hand so the hard lengths bumped and slid against one another. Their own precum was the only lube they needed for this. Already, Rain was more than wet enough.

He swiped his thumb around the tip of his shaft and gripped himself harder, his eyes squeezing shut to better picture the fantasy.

Colt's teeth nipping at his neck and ear, intense and demanding.

Colt's cock throbbing in his hand, thick and heavy with arousal.

Colt's voice in his ear, soft and panting.

I need you, Rain, he'd groan, his voice catching with arousal. And Rain would stroke them harder and faster until their gasps mingled as one.

His body would go taut, his legs gripping harder around Colt's waist as he shuddered against the door. Every wave of arousal now would only tense his muscles until he was gritting his teeth just to try to hold back.

I'm gonna come all over you, my sexy little slut. Colt's eyes would harden along with his voice. *You want that? You like that? Feeling me ready to bust a nut all over your pretty little body?*

"Yes," Rain hissed, his thighs shaking so hard he expected to slide down the door any moment now.

But he couldn't be concerned about that. He was quivering on the edge, every fiber of his body desperate for Colt's hungry gaze on his. He needed the low, demanding growl of his voice.

You want me to make you come that way? All over yourself? Right there?

"Colt!" Rain whimpered, his toes curling into the ground and nails digging into the bathroom door. He wanted to give up control—give in and stop resisting his every advance. Let Colt use him until they were both satiated and sticky.

Let Colt invade his body, heart, and soul, and mold it to the shape he desired.

Wait. The voices weren't just in his head, and they weren't coming from the TV.

"Right there?" It was Colt, outside the bathroom door.

Rain almost choked on his gasp, and he hated—yet loved—the extra jolt of pleasure that shot through him at the realization. He was spiraling into a place he'd never been before, and he barely knew how to hold back.

He was coming, and Colt was standing on the other side of the door. Maybe—just maybe—Colt was able to hear every gasp through the thin wood.

"Ah..." Rain choked off the noise after just a heartbeat and bit his lip so hard his world spun instead, and everything faded into senseless pleasure.

Distantly, he registered what was happening. A muffled response from Justin, and then the distinctive rasping laugh from the other side of the door.

Two footsteps, like Colt was moving away from the door for a moment, and then his voice. "He is? Okay."

Fuck. *Fuck*, he couldn't let Colt leave. It was completely irrational, but the imaginary crush of Rain's body against the door was nothing compared to the real crush in his chest right now.

Like he needed to touch Colt as he came down, curl into him and feel Colt playing with his hair, and hear how beautiful he was... Rain grabbed the counter and rolled his head back as he caught his breath at the sheer intensity of his need.

The footsteps hadn't yet resumed, and Rain could *feel* Colt's gaze like it was burning holes through the wood.

And he was tired of resisting this pull between them. Like holding Newton's apple aloft for days, his arm was tiring, gravity pulling it down—down—into the realm of bad fucking ideas.

Rain was a heartbeat away from opening the door when he remembered that he had his dick still in his hand, and Justin was right there in the living room.

Fuck, think for half a second! Rain thought to himself with a hard shake of his head. Instead, he stuffed himself back in his pants and washed his hands.

Which brought his gaze down to his T-shirt—and the wet streaks that painted the gray fabric white, all across his stomach and chest.

Oh, Jesus. He'd shot his load so hard he nearly blinded himself.

Which explained why Rain was so wobbly right now that he kept bracing himself on the counter, his head spinning. He hadn't had a drop to drink, but he felt on the verge of blacking out.

But Rain had been in the bathroom for... how long now? Minutes? He didn't want Justin to think he was in here doing exactly what he was doing.

So he thought fast and whipped off his shirt and tossed it into the laundry basket. He splashed cold water on his face and hair before yanking open the bathroom door. "Jesus, what is it now?" He deliberately made his tone cranky, pinching the bridge of his nose.

But nothing could keep him from the spreading flush of heat when Colt, halfway down the hall now, turned on his heel. "Oh. Sorry to bother you again." His gaze flickered up and down Rain once again.

Like he knew exactly what he'd been doing.

"I'll wait in the living room for a minute. Take your time."

"No, what's it about?" Rain casually scrubbed at his face with the back of his hand and tried to act like his eyes weren't glassy with a post-orgasm glow. Like his palm didn't still burn with the heat of his own load. Caught red-handed indeed.

Colt walked toward him. Just like that first day in the bar, Rain's whole world seemed to slow and stop. This time, Colt *was* coming for him. And the potential double entendre wasn't lost on Rain in the moment, either.

Colt was so close that he could smell that delectable mix of coffee and aftershave before he spoke. "I wasn't sure what you were up to," he murmured. "And I'm not sure if you want to say as much in front of your... friend?"

There was a question in the word.

"Uh." Rain tried to get his thoughts back on track. Any kind of track would do. "Yeah. Gimme a minute to get dressed."

Colt's gaze flickered down his bare chest in a manner wholly inappropriate for a work colleague. "Sure you don't need more?"

"Positive," Rain said, trying to raise his chin in defiance. It barely worked. All it did was make Colt's gaze grow predatory, like he'd caught sight of the tastiest morsel.

Which just made Rain burn with pleasure again. He was pretty sure he'd discover multiple orgasms today if Colt came any closer.

Colt winked and sidestepped Rain as if waiting for the bathroom.

All too aware of the evidence just feet away, Rain sidled out of the bathroom. He knew the moment he'd made the mistake—his eyes flickering toward the laundry basket.

Colt's grin just grew until he looked like a fucking

Cheshire cat. "Gonna take a leak. Go change." He shut the door, leaving Rain staring at it.

Ordering him around, in his own house! He huffed and stormed into his bedroom, trying to pretend to be annoyed, but he wasn't even fooling himself.

Rain couldn't say he didn't like Colt's attitude. Love it, even. Crave it, in moments like now.

Oh, God. What the hell was he going to do?

Even when he heard the door open, footsteps, and voices again, Rain delayed. He struggled to choose a casual T-shirt and then meticulously finger-combed his hair, but he was only putting off the inevitable.

Whatever the hell Colt wanted to talk about, he could do it on the front porch.

But Rain's steps slowed when he reached his living room entrance and found Colt leaning on the end of the couch, long legs stretched out ahead of him as he pointed at the TV and laughed.

Justin was grinning, too. "Yeah, like they have *half* a chance of getting into the playoffs."

"You never know." Colt shrugged. "Miracles happen."

The wave of jealousy that swept through Rain caught him off guard. Justin could talk sports all day long, and Colt was a big, sporty kind of guy.

But before he could even decide what to feel about seeing his best friend and... undefined romantic and/or sexual interest plus business partner...

Colt turned and looked at him, and that expression returned. The one that said he was looking at Rain, and only Rain.

And there go my knees again. Rain leaned on the frame and jerked his chin toward the porch. "Come on, let's talk."

He wasn't entirely sure he was about to make a rational decision, but none of the decisions he'd made over these past few weeks counted as rational.

But one thing was for sure: Colt *wasn't* allowed to stay in here yet, until he'd figured out what the hell this was. So they were going to march straight onto the porch, thank you very much, and figure that out.

Because if they kept on going the way they were, he was going to explode from the tension. Something had to give, and the business deal had to go on. Which meant he had to face up to this undefined *thing* that simmered between them. Tackle it head-on.

He'd had some pretty bad ideas in his life, but this was probably the worst. And yet... he couldn't wait.

10

———

COLT

Colt's heart hammered as he stepped onto the front porch and held the screen door open for Rain. Rain had to step toward Colt—right into his personal space—to let it close.

Which underscored every reason Colt was here. He drew in a quick, sharp breath as he scanned Rain's face for any sign that this was a monumentally stupid idea.

But however much Colt had caught him by surprise, Rain didn't look pissed off. And he sure as hell hadn't looked displeased earlier in the bathroom doorway, giving Colt the very bedroom eyes that Colt had imagined for days.

I'm not imagining it, Colt reassured himself. This energy between them had a life of its own. Sometimes it throbbed, building into a crescendo that was nearly impossible to ignore. Other times it ebbed away, especially when they had business to focus on.

But, like the waves and the moon, the pull between them was never absent. Even at low tide, it lapped at Colt's fingers and toes rather than carrying him off to drown in a current he didn't know how to fight.

"What did you want to talk about?" Rain's voice was low and steady. He didn't look away, though. He knew exactly why Colt was here.

Good. No chickening out this time, then.

"It would sure be dumb for us to do anything else, wouldn't it?" Colt murmured, keeping his voice as soft as Rain's.

No need for Rain's friend to overhear. Justin hadn't seemed surprised to see him there, and he hadn't acted at all jealous, confirming Rain's story that they were just friends.

But that moment of unpleasant shock had been... illuminating.

Colt had realized he couldn't drag his feet for so long that Rain found someone else. Watching him steered by someone else's hand would kill Colt inside.

Which brought him here, to the conversation he should have had that very first day.

"What do you mean?" Rain murmured. His gaze flicked between Colt's eyes.

Fine. He was right. They should be perfectly clear. "Act on *this*." Colt gestured between the two of them, his hand moving like molasses in the space that practically crackled with tension.

"Don't know what you mean." Rain licked his lips, though, and bit the lower one. When he looked up through his lashes, a lump rose in Cole's throat.

He'd never forget that expression.

Rain looked desperate, like he wanted to talk but his tongue was tied—wanted someone to take the painful wrestling of that choice from him.

He needed help, and he was afraid.

Colt's brain had done enough. It was time for his heart to take charge.

He stepped forward, cupping Rain's cheeks to hold him steady. His warm cheeks rasped against Colt's grip.

Without giving either of them a chance to second-guess it, Colt leaned down and pulled him in for a kiss.

This was no lukewarm end-of-the-first-date kiss with bated breath and ginger touches. It was an eruption between them— a shift in the tectonic plates that had barely kept their passion from bubbling forth.

Rain's hands gripped Colt's wrists as their lips slid against one another's in a hot, dirty, openmouthed explosion.

Then Rain pulled back hard, staring at Colt like he was interrogating him. He was breathing hard, his cheeks bright red and eyes glassy just as they had been a few moments ago.

His hands raised between them, and Colt thought for a few seconds that he might slap him. But he didn't. Instead, he grabbed Colt's shirt and yanked him closer, swallowing Colt's gasp in another aggressive kiss.

It took only seconds before Colt was in charge again, and he could barely tell up from down. Their tongues danced as Rain tipped his head back and yielded to Colt's explorations.

Teeth and tongue and lips all got great reactions. All it took was a nibble on Rain's lower lip and Rain let a divine whimper escape. And when he sucked that lip gently, Rain outright wobbled against him.

How much he ached to lay Rain down and kiss him head to toe. Colt ran his hands from Rain's cheeks to his shoulders while Rain's palms pressed against his chest. The touch itself lit up Colt's body, especially when Rain's palms grazed his nipples.

At last, every damn desire that had flooded Colt's brain in

the last few weeks was back—all at once, running together in an inferno of *need* that he barely understood.

For a long minute, they were lost together. All they were doing was gasping for breath or diving in again, kissing like the world was ending and there was no second chance.

Until a car engine hummed in the distance and Rain pushed himself back from Colt so hard he practically threw himself across the porch. Colt reached out to grab him, but Rain got his own footing.

Rain's wide-eyed gaze turned to scour the front porches of the houses across the street, and Colt followed his look.

Nobody there.

It was easy to make out the sigh of relief as Rain's rising shoulders slumped and the stress lines melted from his face.

Colt hardly dared to speak, but someone had to break the silence. It didn't feel like Rain was ready to leap back on him and make out some more.

They'd had their fun—brief and intense as it was. Now they had to deal with the consequences.

"You're closeted, aren't you?" Colt said quietly. "To your family and friends."

Rain's expression was wary, but he nodded slightly. The conflict written across his face was telling.

Colt's heart twisted with sympathy. He'd been there before, too. Admittedly years ago, but still... there was no easy time to face it. "I'm sorry." If he'd just fucked things up between them, Colt was going to kick himself for days. Again.

"Don't be," Rain said firmly. "I wanted that as much as you." Even now, he stepped closer, but not as close as they had been. He was just hovering there, hands clenching into fists by his sides.

Colt let him decide where he wanted to stand—he just

stood still, bracing himself on the side of the house as the adrenaline and arousal that had flooded him ebbed away.

Rain shifted from foot to foot, sidling around Colt like there was an invisible personal space bubble whose edge he followed. Colt turned to keep facing him the whole time.

"I don't know—I mean, that was good. Really good. But we're here in public, but I don't really want to take this anywhere else. I was going to ask about business stuff. How this affects that."

At last, Colt smiled and reached a hand out to stop Rain on the spot—both from talking and from sidling like he was standing on hot coals.

"You don't have to explain anything," Colt assured him.

Rain really was beside himself, in stark contrast to the self-assured man he'd started to get to know. Colt didn't know where this was coming from, but the last thing he wanted was to make him uncomfortable.

"Okay," Rain whispered and let out a breath, shoving his hands into his pockets. Colt waited until he seemed like he meant it, and at last, Rain looked up and met his gaze. "Okay," he repeated, his voice a little stronger.

"Okay," Colt said and smiled again. "Guide me in what you want here."

But Rain just stared up at him with those wide, helpless dark eyes and raised his hands in an expressive shrug. "Fuck knows. I just know I'm in over my head."

"Me too." Colt rubbed his chin and turned away from Rain at last so he wasn't pulled back into his orbit.

They'd gotten lucky that nobody had seen them yet. If Rain wasn't ready for that step, he wasn't going to push him. People were funny, and he was the best judge of the people in his life.

"But we don't want to screw up what we've got." Rain folded his arms across his chest and chewed his lip, and Colt did his best to forget how soft and full those lips were when pressed against his own.

"Right," Colt agreed breathlessly. He scrubbed at his own, but the taste of Rain wasn't going to leave him that easily. "We need this development to work out. So let's stick with what we have. What we know works."

If he didn't look at Rain, touch him, or hear him laugh, maybe that was a doable promise. As it was, Colt wasn't sure he could keep it.

"Yeah." Rain's tone wasn't light and relieved, though. It was just as stormy and troubled as his own. "Yeah, that's a good idea. Um. Was that... why you brought the fruit basket?"

Colt blinked at him a few times. What? Did he think he'd shown up to ask him out on bended knee? "No, no. That really was because I was an idiot yesterday."

Rain gave him a breathy little laugh. "Oh. Okay."

"But I've been thinking about this for days—"

"Me too," Rain whispered.

"—and yeah."

"Yep." Rain shifted from foot to foot, his gaze straying up toward Colt's.

"Yeah."

There had never been such awkwardness between them, but it wasn't the unpleasant kind where he knew he'd made a mistake in kissing Rain. It was worse than that. The tension between them was rising because they both knew exactly how fucking good they'd be together now.

Oh, God, if Rain gave him one more puppy-eyed look, he'd be sweeping him off his feet and inside.

Where his best friend was waiting, no doubt ready to hear

the scoop. Colt had gotten the impression that Justin was aware of Rain's sexuality from the moment he'd met Rain at the bar. Justin had left them alone together, very deliberately.

Colt, meanwhile, had nobody like that to talk to. Not even his coworkers knew much about his personal life, much less his distantly-related family. He'd stayed a loner since graduating high school, and he usually liked it that way.

Not right now, when he was bursting with emotions too numerous to count.

Pride for having been brave enough to finally address this honey-sweet allure between them.

Ecstasy at the warm glow that still tingled through him at the memory of the taste and feeling of Rain under his hands and lips.

Arousal at the very slim chance he might get to do it again someday—and so much more.

Confusion at what the fuck they were going to do in the meantime.

"Yeah," Colt murmured, stepping off the porch with a little wave. "So, I'll leave you to it. See ya."

He couldn't stick around and sit awkwardly around the others, even if Rain invited him inside. And he sure as hell didn't want to make Rain's life any more complicated with his presence.

That was what Colt had always done, after all. Shown up to strangers, and however hard he tried to be helpful and understanding, he'd eventually complicated their lives too much.

This time, when he hopped in his car, Colt barely waited to buckle up before he got going—and he didn't dare look at the porch to see if Rain was waiting and watching him drive off.

Because leaving the dark-haired beauty who had invaded his dreams on the porch felt like leaving behind a little piece of his heart.

The wavelets beyond the mouth of the harbor shimmered with silver sparkles. Inside the breakwater, only the wind stirred the water's surface like a crinkled velvet sheet.

At the end of the dock, Colt sat cross-legged and looking out over the flat expanse ahead of him.

He'd never spent much time just staring into nothingness. Not when there was rent to pay and coffee to be served. But now, the brine scent tickling his nose and the soft lapping of waves on wooden and concrete pillars made him relax.

It hadn't felt right to head home after that moment. Too much like he was running away, when all he wanted was to run *toward*.

Problem was, every time he had Rain in his sights, Rain found a way to sidestep.

Colt bit his lip as he leaned back on his hands before finally letting himself flop against the wooden dock. Staring up at the early evening sky offered no new insights.

Maybe he had to look inside for those.

It was impossible to ignore the difference in his mental state when he was here. At first, he'd thought it was just being around Rain that made him calmer, more eager to experience life. But there was more, too.

He liked it here in Hart's Bay, however critically he'd treated it at first. And maybe that was exactly why he'd been so harsh. Because he was jealous.

There were disadvantages to growing up in a place where

everyone knew you. Rain was struggling with one of the biggest and hardest choices in his life, which would no doubt be easier in a different city.

But then, Rain also had people who clearly cared about him: Cher, Finn, Roy, and no doubt more.

Colt didn't really have that. Didn't have a place that felt like home, or people to welcome him to it. That was what he'd been craving for years: stability, both financial—like he was chasing now—and emotional. That was the bit he'd accidentally found.

Before he'd thrown a great big monkey wrench in the works.

Colt had just sighed and pushed himself upright again when he heard splashing nearby. He glanced around and did a double take. It wasn't a seagull toying with jetsam like he'd expected.

It was the harbor seal he'd met the other day, hefting her bulk up onto the dock. With a surprisingly dignified series of flops and contortions, she rolled up onto the dock and onto her back.

"Hey there," Colt said with a quiet laugh, and she didn't budge. Great, he was talking to a seal. He might be going crazy. But it seemed rude not to talk to her.

Lucy just looked upside down at him, her whiskers wiggling.

"I don't have fish for you." He held up his empty hands as he turned to face her and slowly approached. "No fish here. Sorry, girl."

Lucy huffed, an undignified spluttering *Pffft*. Then, never breaking eye contact, she slowly rolled off the dock sideways until she slid into the water. After one last side-eye of disapproval, she darted away, a dark shape quickly disappearing into the darker water.

Colt burst out laughing at the expression. Okay, next time he came and sat here, he'd bring a fish from the grocery store to pay the dock toll.

Still smiling and shaking his head, he walked up to the concrete stretch of waterfront and picked his way through the parking lot toward the square.

His car was parked here, next to the gallery, but he wasn't quite ready to go home yet.

Not when he was just going to sit at home kicking himself for having complicated things with Rain. Kissing him might lead to the best relationship ever... or he might have just tanked his chances. Right now, he wasn't sure which. He should have left before he could get hurt, but then they wouldn't have talked things through—even a little—and he'd be hurt anyway.

"Man, I need a drink." The shutters of Cher's bar had been closed when he walked down to the dock, but they were open now. His spirits lifted and he made a beeline for the door.

The place was quiet, just a small handful of people scattered around some of the tables. And as usual, Cher was behind the bar.

"Hey there," Cher greeted him, and she even offered him a slight smile. "I saw you down by the water."

"Yep. I was making friends with the locals at the dock," Colt told her with a smile. It wasn't until the words left his mouth that the implications really hit him, and his cheeks flushed.

Cher cackled. "I'm not judging, kid. But the only sailors you'll find down there these days are ghosts."

There was no beating her, so he had to join her. "I thought

they looked a little pale," Colt retorted and scratched his chin. "Plus there's Lucy."

"Oh, you met our mascot." Cher grabbed a beer and gave him a questioning look.

Colt smiled at her. "Please." He nodded and went for his wallet.

"Oh, stop it. You keep overpaying. It's screwing up my till," Cher told him, wagging a finger.

He'd never been told off for *that* before. Colt opened his mouth, then shut it and shrugged as he took the beer. "Thanks."

"Thank the guy who's putting his neck on the line for you."

With that, Colt stared at her. "What?" How did she know about the deal already? Or did she mean someone besides Rain?

"Oh, pfft." Cher waved. "I have sources. People aren't that bad around here if you treat them right. So, you'd better do that. No friendlier place as long as you do."

The warning was clear: if he screwed Rain over, the town would close ranks around him.

Colt gulped and nodded. "Yes, ma'am."

She dismissed him with a nod. Trying not to feel like he was back in school and had just been lectured by the teacher, he collected his beer and took it to a table in the corner.

He was going to have to get used to other people knowing his business, and fast. The only problem was keeping everything straight. So far, it wasn't too much of a problem. He had his life in the city—including the work at Quaff—and his life out here.

Once the renovation was underway and he knew if there was anything leftover in the inheritance for day-to-day living, he could quit the job and everything would grow easier. And once the project was complete, it wouldn't matter that it was his first.

But something still crawled inside his stomach and made him avoid eye contact with anyone else today—something besides uncertainty about the predicament with Rain.

And that something was guilt.

Maybe he hadn't outright *claimed* to have experience, but he'd never corrected Rain's assumptions. Encouraged them, even. And now that he was in this far, he wasn't sure how to get out.

Not without screwing up this relationship, and he'd do anything—*anything*—to avoid that.

The only way out might just be to close his eyes, run at top speed, and hope he made it into the clear.

11

RAIN

Never in Rain's life had his heart told him so clearly what he wanted. No—*who* he wanted.

And that man was driving down the street in his gleaming black car, taking his kissable lips and soft, understanding eyes with him.

It wasn't like this was forever. They hadn't even broken up. They hadn't even been together in the first place. But Rain's indecisiveness had driven Colt away. He had the sinking feeling that he couldn't do that to Colt again.

He had to make up his mind on what he wanted to do, and fast.

Nobody in the world could talk him out of what he wanted, except himself. And he was pretty damn good at doing that. Right here and now, Rain realized that Colt had power over him.

Having tasted him once, Rain wasn't sure he could stay away again if Colt kept flirting like he had these past few weeks. Just one kiss—well, maybe one make-out session, to be more accurate—had been enough to get him hooked.

He craved Colt's palm on his cheek, and the smoky, sweet smell of him, and the hardness of his body pressed against him.

If he'd been horny fifteen minutes ago, this hit a different note altogether. Just after a good pipe clean, he ought to have been more self-controlled. But he'd thrown himself at Colt without a second thought.

Because it was something deeper that craved Colt's touch, his words, his soft laughs and intense gazes.

Rain smacked his forehead with his palm and then ran his hand down to cover his face. Why couldn't his heart come with an instruction manual?

The front door opened gently, and then Justin poked his head out of the screen door, holding it open. "Hey, dude. Your beer's getting warm in here." It was his way of expressing concern, and it made Rain smile a little.

"Thanks." Rain followed Justin inside and closed the door, his mind racing.

"What's the deal?" Justin didn't have to ask for any more clarification than that. He just crashed on the couch, muted the TV, and picked up his beer bottle.

Under his expectant gaze, Rain sighed and sat next to him. "He's... I don't know. We've been dancing around it a lot. So far, it's just been business, but... we also get along really well."

That was an understatement. No way could he explain the way it felt like Colt fit with him.

"Both times I've seen you together, your chemistry has been off the charts. It's like you don't even notice me in the room," Justin commented.

Rain winced. "Sorry," he mumbled. That was a dick move when his friend had stood by him these past few months.

Justin laughed and waved it off. "I don't mind. It's kind of cute, in a dorky way, to see you like that. So what do you want from him?"

He posed the question like it was that simple to answer.

"I... I just need him. It's like the moment he walked through the door at Cher's, I looked at him and I saw my future. Is that crazy?" Rain started to breathe faster as his brain caught up with his mouth. "That's totally crazy."

"Whoa." Justin pressed a beer into Rain's hands. "Not at all. That's how my parents met. Some people know right away. Some take their time to figure it out."

"It's not like I'm *planning* to marry him or anything, but it's like every time I learn something about him, I've always known it all along."

"Soul mates from a different lifetime?" Justin was smirking at him.

Rain rolled his eyes and smacked Justin's knee. "Shut up. This is serious."

"Sorry, sorry," Justin chuckled. He tapped Rain's beer bottle. "Drink up. It'll help."

Rain wasn't sure about that, but he did so anyway. After a few gulps of beer, his mouth was less dry, at least. "I... I could get used so badly."

"Mmm. That's the risk of relationships."

"But I need him, too. Like I said. This is crazy strong. Even that asshole I dated out in Colorado? It was more of a *hey, he likes me and I need to get out of here* situation. This? Pffffth." Rain sounded like a horse when he sighed like this. "Fuck knows. I'm way out of my depth. I didn't expect it, either. I was all *no boyfriends* and he went and snuck in the back door while I wasn't looking—oh, shut up!" He saw the expression on Justin's face, but too late.

Justin burst out laughing. "You said it, man, not me."

"Very mature." Still, Rain smiled. It was nice not to be so hung up on appearances that he couldn't make a dirty joke. Hanging out around Justin had been great for him that way.

Justin swigged his beer and set it aside so he could gesture with his hands. "Well, hell, man. If this is gonna get you free from all those dicks... cut the ties and fly free, little songbird."

The thought wasn't one Rain had let himself indulge before. Him disowning his family? It had always been the other way around, in his imagination—slipping up, doing something too *wrong*, and being tossed out.

But he could walk away first. Set a boundary and invite them to join *him* in his new life if they loved him. If not, he could find other people who did.

The perspective change made him reel, and he stared at the coffee table as the full meaning of those words sank in.

"I don't know," Rain finally murmured. It seemed like a huge risk to take on a guy he barely knew. "Plus, we're so different. He's some bigwig from the city. He doesn't know half the story of all the Hart family drama. He lives all the way out in Portland. How can we resolve those kinds of differences?"

Justin laughed at him, and Rain would have been mad if he'd detected an unkind note. But he didn't. Justin leaned forward and punched his knee gently. "I'm not talking resolving differences, Rain." He finished his beer and stood up, turning off the TV.

"Then what do you mean?" Rain rose to his feet, shoving his hands in his pockets.

"I mean..." Justin turned to him for a moment, his smile growing. "You're not planning the rest of your lives together... not yet, anyway. Maybe it's about being a normal twenty-five-year-old guy for once in your life. *That's* where life starts. Not with contracts and detailed ten-year plans that other people make for you."

Rain opened and closed his mouth for a moment. He wanted to protest: he'd tried to escape before like a normal twentysomething.

All he'd wound up doing was following some pretty surfer boy back to Colorado. And Desmond had turned ugly fast. Controlling his bank account, controlling his social life.

The socialite mixers Rain had dreaded at first became an escape, a chance to see vaguely familiar faces and keep the money tap flowing from his family while he figured out how to divert it away from Desmond without his noticing.

The breaking point had been when Desmond raised a hand to him in the bedroom—without asking first—and Rain was out of there, carrying a few more emotional scars.

Mr. Sterling had been his guardian angel, helping him wrest control of his finances and life again on his way back to Hart's Bay.

Justin knew most of the story, but he was the only person Rain had told. Cher had overheard key pieces before Rain glared at her to shoo her away.

Rain had never thought he'd find a guy he'd trust to take him hard and rough again, but Colt? There was no question. When—*if*, Rain hastily reminded himself—they fucked, it wasn't going to be some boring, vanilla missionary crap.

No, it would be the kind of sex that left Rain's head woozy and a grin on his face.

"I... I've never been a normal twenty-five year old," Rain mumbled.

"Do you want to be?"

Rain nodded. He'd spent years wanting to be a normal kid,

then teen, and now adult. He'd just never been allowed the chance.

Fuck that. It was time to stop waiting for chances and seize one for himself.

"Then you goddamn deserve to be," Justin told him seriously. He grabbed his jacket and shrugged it on. "And if you didn't hook up with that ten when I gave you the chance last time, you'd better fucking hurry up and do it now, dude."

Rain burst out laughing, even though he was blushing. He was so not used to people talking about hooking up with guys so casually. Like it was empowering, even. Like he had the right to be, do, fuck, or love whoever the hell he wanted.

Before Justin could go, Rain grabbed his arm and moved in for a hug.

Justin held him tightly for a few seconds, almost crushing him, before slapping his back once and giving him a nod. "Go get him, tiger."

Rain just laughed, the sound nervous even to his own ears as Justin let himself out of the house and closed the door.

Seconds ticked by as Rain sat on the couch to finish his beer.

But of course, now that he was alone, the self-doubt crept in.

Maybe Colt hadn't liked the kiss as much as Rain had.

Or maybe Rain was about to screw up a good working relationship.

But the whole time on the porch, Colt had focused on Rain's needs.

Wait. Was that what was tripping him up?

When he'd met Desmond, Rain had been drawn to his attitude—smug and certain, like a guiding beacon. Only he'd been a lamp and Rain a moth, circling it over and over in desperate search of the light of freedom while slowly roasting.

Rain shivered. "Fuck him," he muttered, tipping back the bottle and finishing it before setting it down with a solid thunk. It was time to give someone else a chance. Time to open up his heart and try letting someone else in.

And he was pretty sure he could trust Colt not to ever act like Desmond had. Because Desmond's intensity, his knowledge, and his unquestioned dominance had made Rain come harder than he'd ever done on his own. But...

Guide me in what you want here? Hell, no. Desmond had never stopped to ask what Rain daydreamed about or asked him to show him. He'd just taken what he wanted and assumed Rain liked it, too.

Rain swallowed hard and slid his phone out of his pocket, his pulse aflutter.

He opened their text messages and tapped the corner of his phone against his lips before he dared to take a peek at it.

One little text, that was all it took. They sent plenty of texts every day about timelines, revised plans, all the details they wanted to keep straight.

Another text wasn't the end of the world. Like Justin said, it wasn't like they were getting married.

But oh, that thought sent a strangely excited thrill through him. Like the ending to a fairy tale he'd never allowed himself —or been allowed by people around him.

He was making his own chance, and it started now. One tiny action, and then another.

Rain: *Hey—are you still in town or driving back home?*

And, to his enormous relief, the phone pinged almost right away.

Colt: *At Cher's. I can save you a chair. Or two?*

He knew what Colt was asking—whether Justin was coming with him, too. In essence, whether they were being chaperoned.

Rain: *On my way. Alone.*

Before he could change his mind, Rain grabbed his keys and wallet and strode for the door.

Rather than walk along the road, he took the path that snaked between houses toward the coastal path, and then looped around—all the way down to the square.

The scenic views were surprisingly soothing, actually. The sun was only two finger widths from the ocean, which meant he probably had half an hour before it set.

He headed along the dirt track down to the field behind the art gallery and emerged next to Cher's. Without lingering, Rain walked straight inside and up to the bar.

It was easy to spot Colt in the table in the corner—the same one he'd shown him was the most private.

Rain didn't glance over yet, just nodded at Cher to attract her attention.

She didn't seem surprised to find him there. "What can I do for you?"

"Shot of Jack."

"Straight?" She raised an eyebrow and took out a shot glass. "Or not?"

Rain gulped. In three words, she'd cut to the heart of it. "No mixers," he answered instead.

Cher glanced up at him and then grabbed the bottle, pouring him a shot as he took out a few bills. "That's more than one costs."

"I know." Rain picked up the glass and flung the liquid in it into the back of his throat. It burned, but he swallowed fast and bypassed the cough as he set it back down and nodded at it.

She refilled and he repeated the move.

When he set it down again, Cher raised an eyebrow.

"Come on," Rain murmured. "One more for the road."

But instead, Cher reached over the bar top to pat his hand. She took some of the bills and left the rest behind. "You don't need more yet. Go talk to him."

Rain's hand shook as he collected the other notes and stuffed them back in his wallet. "Okay. Thanks, Cher."

"Welcome, honey."

He felt her watching as he crossed the floor and walked up two steps to the table where they'd met Finn just yesterday. It felt like a lifetime ago.

"You came," Colt greeted, rising to his feet for a moment. Then, like he wasn't quite sure whether to hug him, shake his hand, or pull him in for a kiss, he awkwardly bobbed back down again like a pigeon.

Rain cracked a smile and pulled out the chair opposite, then dropped into it. "I did. And you noticed."

Colt's eyes widened. He looked around as if checking for people listening in and then met Rain's gaze. His hands were tightly folded as he leaned in over the table. "I wanted to give you time and space to figure things out."

"I have," Rain said simply. He offered Colt a smile. Maybe it was only halfway to the truth, but he'd at least come a long way in a short conversation with Justin.

Because his best friend was right. He was sick of managing everyone else's reactions and trying to be a different person for their sake. Or at least trying to wear a mask and pretend he was.

"And?" Colt asked. His voice was thick with a kind of nervousness Rain hadn't seen in him before.

More than anything else, that cemented Rain's certainty that Colt was serious about all this.

Rain smiled. "And I think we should talk about it, but not necessarily here. There's a lot to explain."

The breath rushed out of Colt's lungs. "And I've been waiting to hear."

"Have you?"

"I wanted you to share at your own pace." Colt nibbled his lips and then leaned back in his chair, his gaze still fixed on Rain. "But I think we're at that stage."

That was an understatement. They'd blown past the stage of surprising honesty and right into the complications that came with it.

"Should we... go somewhere?" Colt hesitated. "I know your house is your castle and all..."

Rain still wasn't sure how he felt about bringing Colt home. It made it way too easy to fuck first and talk second. "How about I show you a little more of the place?"

"Lead on," Colt said, rising to his feet. "Beauty before wisdom."

Rain gaped at Colt for a moment, and then he laughed. "Oh, screw you." His cheeks were flushing at the compliment hidden in his witty rejoinder.

"What?" Colt winked. "You can't complain."

"Can and I will." Rain strutted past Colt, nose in the air. "Before wisdom indeed. Hmph."

Colt kept pace with him and even reached the door first, holding it open for him once he walked through. "One of us is wise enough to know that shots of Jack are never a good life choice."

Rain gasped. "And one of us is nosy, apparently. Spying on all the new neighbors?" He led Colt up the coastal path, his steps slow.

"Only when it comes to you." Colt's voice was mild, even if his words weren't. "I don't care what you do, but I want to know all about it. What makes you tick. What makes you smile. What makes you get that stormy little thundercloud over your head. Why you never seem to get mad for more than half a second before you do that thing where you're a brick wall. How I can get past it."

Rain's heart might just leap right out of his chest. "I... do?"

"Yeah," Colt murmured. His fingertips grazed Rain's arm, but he looked around and didn't move to hold hands. No doubt he'd noticed that they were still within sight of town.

All the little ways he respected him made Rain want to ask him to disrespect him—filthily, and all night long.

"That's a lot of psychoanalysis."

"I don't make a habit of it, trust me." They were over the little grassy hilltop and into the trees, and now Colt brushed his arm again, this time sliding his fingers into Rain's hand.

And Rain let him do it. And his silly heart grew, and grew, and suddenly he was on top of the world with a smile like the crescent moon burning above a deep purple sky.

I never planned to find my dream guy in this kind of situation.

But now that he had, what the hell were they going to do about it?

12

COLT

As they picked their way up the steep path and through the trees, Colt's heart was full to bursting.

Rain's hand was tucked into his. It was smaller than his own, so Colt made sure his grip was gentle. Even though Rain worked in construction and no doubt could handle himself, Colt never wanted to hurt him.

Not unless Rain begged him to, anyway.

Pushing aside the shiver of arousal, Colt focused on enjoying the warmth shared between their skin as their fingers locked together.

"This is pretty," he commented with a look around at the mix of shrubs, grasses, and trees around them. There were a dozen shades of green, and the smell of pine and other kinds of wood mingled with the faint salty mist that seemed to be laced with the air anywhere near the coast.

The outskirts of Hart's Bay were wild in a way that the Portland suburbs never were. And they probably didn't have nutria lurking near the playgrounds here.

"It gets better. Give it about ten seconds."

"Huh?" Colt followed Rain's gaze as they crested the top of the hill, and then he sucked a breath in.

Oh. He wasn't kidding about that.

A cove stretched out before them, and for a moment, the romantic in him imagined that they were the first to stumble on some secret, sheltered little place. Which was silly, of course, given the well-marked path. But with nobody else around, it did feel that private.

"How cool," he murmured, his eyes roaming over the point and the rocky beach.

"Let's walk the other way. You can head along the coast, or down to the cove, or..." Rain pulled on his hand, and Colt followed his lead along the path to the right.

"It's crazy how you've got these gorgeous views right up here, and around the corner is the harbor..."

"Wait 'til you see what's up ahead," Rain said, smiling up at him. "We've really got it all."

"Is it a petting zoo?"

Rain laughed, the sound sharp and unexpected. "No, silly. A sand beach."

"Oh! Is that one gravel?" He squinted through the trees at the cove they were leaving behind. Now that it was pointed out, it was definitely gray and not sandy brown.

"Yeah. Try sunbathing on that if you want bruises," Rain snickered.

"Oh, I can think of more fun ways to get bruises." Colt kept his gaze firmly fixed ahead as he tried not to grin. He could feel Rain's gaze boring into him.

"Do you always talk about sex this much?"

That took him off guard. "Huh?" Colt looked around at Rain, momentarily afraid he'd offended him. But Rain's expression was just curious. "I... I didn't think it was that much more than normal."

"I guess I'm not used to normal people." Rain gave a self-deprecating little chuckle. "Or people who are cool with gay sex. Like, my parents and my grandpa—pretty much my only relatives... they're barely even cool with gay guys who go live as monks."

"Mmm." Colt knew where Rain was coming from. "Well, it's nothing to be ashamed of. I've had shallow hookups, but some people don't. Just like straight people."

"I haven't been exposed to a lot of gay culture." Rain glanced over at him. "I dated a guy once, when I lived in Colorado for a year. It was a pretty bad experience. Otherwise, it's just been... a covert hookup where I can get them, as far from here as possible. And barely even that lately."

"Oh," Colt murmured, squeezing Rain's hand. "Yeah. I've been out for a while now. Since I was a teen, pretty much."

"Is that a problem? Me not being... well..." Rain gestured with his other hand in a vague rainbow shape and then made half of a pair of jazz hands.

Colt laughed. "No, it's not," he assured Rain.

"Sometimes I feel like I'm not gay enough." Rain sighed. "And I need to get better at that before I come out, but as soon as I do..." He trailed off.

"As soon as you do?" Colt prompted softly.

He wished Rain could see himself as Colt saw him. The way he gestured and spoke, the way he flirted when he wasn't overthinking it... he was such a twink. Colt was certain that the rest of gay Hart's Bay—however big that community—was just waiting for Rain to tell them.

"Then my family will start a whole lot of shit." Rain grimaced. "My grandpa especially. They all suspect, I think.

And he loves dangling my inheritance and my place in the family over me."

"Fuck that, then," Colt burst out. Nobody should accept that kind of treatment, whatever the rewards at the end. "If you're cutting away a piece of yourself to make them love you, they don't love *you*."

Rain's eyes were suddenly glassy, and he stumbled to a halt on the path.

"Shit." Colt reached out gently with his thumb to swipe the tear on his cheek away. "Shit, sorry. I didn't mean to..." His words had been harsh, now that he thought about it.

But Rain wasn't mad. He just shook his head slightly, his gaze rising to meet Colt's. "I know," he whispered. He took a deep breath and let it out. "I've just been waiting until I was ready. I needed people around me to show me another path."

"You've found them." Colt squeezed Rain's hand hard, and he rested his other hand on his shoulder. He wished he could sweep Rain off his feet, take him straight to the Harts' front door, and tell them to go fuck themselves.

But all he could do was stand by Rain's side until he was ready to say it for himself.

Rain gave him a shaky laugh. "Yeah?"

"Yeah," Colt nodded firmly. "Besides, what about Finn and Roy? Aren't they family?"

Rain groaned quietly, and then he tugged on Colt's hand to lead him down a trail away from the coastline. "Not quite. They're starting to become family, I think. It's complicated. I didn't want the news to get to them, and then everyone else finding out. What about you?"

Little alarm bells went off in Colt's head. He stiffened slightly and glanced over at Rain.

"I... I won't tell anyone until you're ready."

He deliberately misinterpreted the question and prayed Rain wouldn't push it. Because as soon as he started talking, he risked something slipping. And more than that, he didn't want to see the pity in Rain's eyes when he talked about his teenage years.

Pity was for losers, and he wasn't a loser.

"It's between us as business partners," Colt continued when Rain looked up at him with a confused expression. "And more than that, as friends."

Rain was smiling now, the confusion clearing away. "As friends," he repeated and squeezed Colt's hand.

That much was the truth. Behind all their teasing, and even behind the bristly arguments, the moments when Rain dug in his heels and Colt found a compromise... there was a surprisingly strong friendship.

"I've gone a long time feeling like I don't belong," Colt murmured. It looked like they were heading down into a residential neighborhood, but he followed Rain without question. "It's nice to have someone to take on the world with me."

"Tell me about it." Rain's laugh was quick, yet harsh. "Sorry. I didn't mean to take over that moment."

"No, go on. I want to know," Colt murmured. He'd gotten way too close to spilling his own heart and admitting everything to Rain. But then he risked losing Rain's confidence, if he said too much. Better to let him think he had a distant but rich family, like Rain did.

"Growing up here was rough. The family got split in two by the fishery dying, I told you that much. But a lot of people didn't like my side for one reason or another. Mostly because they didn't like Grandpa's business decisions. Well, it was his own damn business."

The defensiveness that crept into his voice was odd given

that his grandpa sounded like he was a dick to Rain, but people were complicated. Feelings even more so.

Colt just nodded and squeezed his hand, his heart going out to him. "So they took it out on you?"

"Even though we were just kids, me and my siblings—and Finn and his siblings... it kept the feud going. A lot of people thought that I had it out for them." Rain bit his lip and looked away. "Or that I was going to inherit some empire."

Fuck. That had to be hard. Colt had had enough trouble with people's assumptions about him—even those who'd signed up to take him into their homes. People could be cruel.

"Well, at least you got something of an empire after all that, right?" Colt tried for an encouraging smile.

Rain glanced up at him and smiled. The stress written across his face was obvious. "You said it yourself: they're falling to shit."

God, Colt had waded into a lot more than he'd expected. All he wanted was to make Rain feel better, and now Rain was talking about his feelings and possibly feeling worse.

He felt compassion for Rain, but also something much more tender—yet rougher, too. Like he wanted to stand between Rain and the world, shield him from every little look and comment that anyone could ever make.

He cared about Rain. A lot.

"Sorry," Colt muttered, wincing again at his first choice of phrasing. Really, he'd invited the most trouble when he waded in trying to be something he wasn't. "That sounds really shitty."

"Ah, you know..." Rain was clearly trying to push it off and pretend it wasn't too big a deal. "I can't complain. It led me to this. To you."

Colt's cheeks flushed as Rain looked up at him, and he

abruptly realized where they were—back at Rain's house. And they were walking down the street, still holding hands.

What that meant, he didn't know. But he did know that he fucking loved it.

"Yeah?" Colt smiled, tentative hope blossoming in his chest. He could drop Rain off at home, give him a good-night kiss…

"Sorry for the rant," Rain said casually. Before Colt could assure him it was okay, he added, "I didn't mean to make this all a baggage call. More like a booty call."

Colt stumbled to a halt. "A—Ah?" He stuttered for a second.

"If you'd rather keep it a working relationship, you know… that's cool by me." Rain's gaze was steady, and he didn't look away from Colt.

Which made it fucking impossible to pretend there wasn't chemistry sizzling between them like a beaker about to blow up.

"But I think there's more. And for a night, I just wanna be a normal twentysomething."

"We both know there's more," Colt agreed quietly. He started to walk again. They reached Rain's front gate, and he let go of his hand at last but accompanied him up the path.

Colt was stuck in Rain's orbit, not quite sure how he'd gotten here but completely unable to tear himself away. And he didn't want to, either.

Maybe they barely knew each other past the surface, but he'd gotten a good glimpse tonight. Everything he'd suspected so far seemed to be true: Rain was a sweetheart, and a lot more sensitive than he let on. He was honest and loyal. He wanted to fight for a better life, but he needed help, too.

And every bone in Colt's body wanted to stand by his side while he figured it out.

Late summer had almost passed, but the chorus of frogs nearby apparently hadn't quieted yet. It was still a warm evening, making it seem strangely like an earlier hour than it really was. The kind of hour where he didn't feel like he was sneaking into the house discreetly.

But as their eyes met here, standing on the porch again, they both knew the truth of it.

"Coming in?" Rain's invitation was so casual it seemed almost absentminded, but his gaze was sharp and focused.

Colt let a slow, dirty smirk cross his face as he watched Rain's cheeks flush. "I'd love to."

And as he followed Rain inside, he felt his life shift. Toward what, exactly, he had no idea. He just knew—like he had when he'd walked into Cher's bar—that everything was about to change again.

13

RAIN

"Want something to drink? Water? Coffee?"

It was the second time Colt had been inside today, but this time felt different.

Instead of Colt taking Rain by surprise while showing up while he was... er, busy... it was the other way around. Colt clearly hadn't expected an invitation inside.

And the prospect of what was to come made Rain feel far more nervous than signing any contract.

"Coffee would be great, thanks."

Rain kicked off his shoes in record time and headed for the kitchen, leaving Colt to follow when he chose. But when he glanced through the pass-through between the living room and kitchen, he found Colt waiting in there instead, wandering around the house.

It was beyond odd to see him in here.

His home had become his sanctuary in the past few months, because he rarely had anyone over except Justin. Especially not hookups—the town had too many watchful eyes for that, and if things grew too intense, it was easier to leave than kick someone out.

As if reading his train of thought, Colt glanced from a photo of Rain and his siblings over to him. He had to lean down to see him through the window. "How long have you been living here?"

Rain fumbled to press the button on the machine, then leaned next to it with folded arms. "About three months. My grandfather sold it to me cheap when he got wind I was trying to move back here."

"And where were you before?"

Rain licked his lips. There was a conversation he'd hoped to avoid. "Close to Colorado Springs. I was there for eight or nine months after college."

"Did you like it?"

Rain laughed. "Hated it."

Colt sucked air through his teeth. "Jeez. Tell me how you really feel."

Rain shrugged. "I chased a guy back there, and he was a dick. Untangling myself from him and coming back here was pretty shitty."

"Oh. Sorry." Colt sank onto the couch and folded his hands, leaning forward to maintain eye contact.

The expression of sympathy just made Rain uncomfortable, so he grabbed two mugs. "Don't be. I learned a lot from living on my own."

"Like what?" Colt was asking a lot of questions, but unlike their first meetings, it was a gentle, curious exploration. This wasn't a challenge or a way of sizing him up. Colt seemed to genuinely want to know how he ticked.

Rain sighed as he poured mugs. "About life, and myself. Some good, some bad. Milk? Cream?"

"Milk and sugar, please."

Once he'd stirred in the additions, Rain carried both mugs to the living room and settled himself on the couch next to Colt. It was overwhelming to be so close to him. "Just some more coffee to top up your coffee tank. You must drink a lot of it."

Colt stiffened and looked over at him like he was offended. "I what?"

"I mean... you smell like it. It's good. Is it your shampoo or something?"

Colt's laugh was quick, forced. "Nah. I guess I do drink too much. Cheers." He raised his mug to clink against Rain's with a smile.

Rain took a good long sip, then set the mug aside and took Colt's hand. "I learned that I like it when a guy takes charge. But you've gotta find someone who deserves your trust."

Colt frowned and set aside his mug, resting his other hand on top of Rain's. He didn't say anything, but from his expression, Rain could tell that he understood what he was trying to say.

Rain let out a quiet sigh and closed his eyes to just enjoy the warmth they shared, and the sound of their breathing mingling, and the thud of his heart. Oh, how he loved the way his body reacted to Colt's very presence.

"You like being bossed around in the bedroom?" Colt murmured, and Rain cracked his eyes to have a peek at him.

Rain nodded. It felt almost shameful, admitting this. Like he shouldn't like it. But Colt already knew that much from their incessant flirting—it was no surprise.

And Colt wasn't judging him, because whatever he was offering, Colt wanted it.

"You like it rough?" Colt's nails scraped their way up Rain's arm toward his shoulder.

Oh, fuck. Rain's whole body shivered and arched toward Colt. "Please."

Colt wasn't just holding him physically. He was holding emotional space for Rain, letting him step into it at his own pace, and Rain was eager to do so.

No more fighting this attraction. Rain wanted so badly to ride it—in every possible way.

Colt shifted his grip on Rain. One hand slid into the small of Rain's back, the other to the back of Rain's neck. In this supportive hold, he turned him around and eased him down to lie on his back on the couch.

Rain lifted one knee against the back of the couch, his other foot hooking around Colt's waist. He felt decadent, like a flower in bloom, while Colt crawled over him—into him—and drank his nectar.

And Colt was swift to do just that. He draped his weight along Rain's, propping himself up on his forearms. Then he pressed his mouth to Rain's, and all rational thought escaped for a few seconds as heat burst between their lips.

All Rain had to do was let Colt have his way—and the thought alone had his dick hardening in his jeans.

The moan escaping Rain's throat turned into a gasp when Colt started pulling his shirt up. Colt broke the kiss just long enough to yank his shirt over his head and up his arms, tossed it across the room, and dove down to kiss him again.

Rain gasped into Colt's mouth and tried to catch his lip, but Colt pulled back too quickly to allow it. He was moving fast now, his touch rough yet focused. His fingertips skimmed Rain's chest, found his nipple, and pinched firmly.

"Ah!" Rain gasped, bucking off the couch and into Colt. It

just made his hardness grind into Colt's hip, which felt so good he did it again.

He expected those hands to go to his belt, but no. Colt took his sweet time pinching and rolling both nubs between his fingers while white-hot, borderline painful sparks shivered along the surface of Rain's skin.

No matter how much Rain moaned and gasped, Colt ignored his hints to go further. He had a little smirk on his face that really shouldn't have been so fucking hot.

Like Colt was enjoying tormenting him, inflicting upon him the agony of unfulfilled arousal. All Rain could do was beg, and his noises hadn't gotten him far. Colt was working at exactly his own speed.

The realization only made Rain hotter.

"Please," he whimpered.

Colt's cocky little smile widened. His eyes gleamed with satisfaction as he gazed down at Rain. Each flick of his fingertips across Rain's nipples grew even more agonizingly light. "Please what?"

Rain choked and gasped for breath, trying to press up into Colt's hands. He needed a firm touch—a hand pressing against him, nails digging into his skin.

But more than that, he needed satisfaction. Colt had shifted his hips so that he pinned Rain down, but Rain couldn't grind against him. All he could do was squirm around under him, twitching and damp and so hard Colt would be able to make out every vein through his jeans soon.

"Please get my cock out," Rain whispered. His voice was harsh already, hoarse from his whimpers, gasps, and moans. But he had no hope of catching his breath yet. Not while Colt was looking him over like he was deciding what to do with him.

Colt hummed thoughtfully, his gaze raking from head to toe before he nodded once, firmly. He shifted back on his heels, unbuttoning Rain's jeans. He carefully slid them down, along with his underwear, and worked everything off.

Rain was instantly aware that he was naked and vulnerable while his partner was fully dressed. He caught his breath, working his hands beside himself while Colt straddled him again.

"Better?"

"Much," Rain whispered. He closed his hand around himself, his eyes fluttering shut at the pleasant, tight heat. Hoping he'd be told off, he stroked himself a few languorous times.

He wasn't disappointed.

Colt gripped his wrist and yanked his hand away. "No," Colt whispered.

Rain's eyes flew open. Colt seemed to be waiting for him to say something, so he licked his lips and gulped, then nodded. "Okay. I'll wait."

"Until?" Colt took one of Rain's hands and then the other, laying them above his head.

Rain quivered. His cheeks burned as he held this pose, but it only turned him on more. Moisture dripped from the tip of his cock onto his own stomach, a sticky string that caught the light. "Until... you tell me?" He guessed.

"That's right." Colt gave a self-satisfied grin again and let go of Rain's wrists.

Fuck, this pose made him feel like an art object on display, a thrashing wild thing under the gaze of a predator. Rain's thighs started shaking, so he let one knee rest against the back of the couch, and the other foot slid to the floor.

Colt's face was the picture of calmness and control, and

Rain's quivering knotted mess of emotions slowly untangled at the sight of him.

Still, anticipation made his breaths sharp. What was going through his head? Whatever the hell he was thinking, Rain wanted him to do it.

Colt's motion was swift. He reached down to his own zipper and yanked it down, the quick rasp loud in its suddenness. He locked eyes with Rain, and then one corner of his lips hitched up in a sexy little smirk.

Colt gripped the couch behind Rain's head and shifted one knee at a time until he was kneeling over his head.

The whimper that escaped Rain was inhuman. He licked his lips, eagerly squirming from side to side as Colt worked his dick out of his pants.

The first glimpse didn't disappoint him. Colt was hard, thick, and long. The swollen pink skin looked so delicate up close, but so needy, too.

Rain gulped and parted his lips, his gaze flickering up Colt's body to meet his gaze.

"It's okay, babe," Colt whispered, still crookedly grinning down at him. "I won't fuck your mouth too hard—this time."

"You can," Rain offered, his hands shaking above his head. This adrenaline wasn't laced with the same fearful danger that it had been when he went to bed with Desmond.

Not even close.

He trusted Colt to make it good for them both—to watch him, as he was doing now, for his reactions.

"You like that?" Colt's teeth flashed in a grin. One big hand wrapped around his cock, guiding the tip toward Rain's mouth. But rather than sliding in, he tapped the tip of his cock against Rain's chin like he'd been naughty. "You want to be used like the dirty boy I know you are?"

Rain's whimper was long and quiet. His cock strained, untended but so sensitive that the slightest breeze might set him off. Fuck, he couldn't remember ever being this turned on.

Colt grinned and slapped his dick lightly against Rain's cheeks. While rubbing the head of his cock across Rain's lips, he whispered, "I knew it. You're so thirsty, aren't you?"

"Mmhmm," Rain moaned, focusing on the throbbing erection that needed his attention so badly. He darted his tongue out, and Colt let him lick his way around the head like a Popsicle.

Curling his tongue around the tip made Colt sigh with satisfaction, one hand running up Rain's cheek and tangling in the front of his hair. He held Rain's head down against the couch cushion, his other hand still wrapped around the base of his dick.

As Rain closed his mouth tightly around the head of his cock and sucked for all he was worth, Colt thrust forward, pushing into Rain's mouth.

He filled his mouth and then some, and Rain could barely breathe. Especially when Colt set into motion, holding Rain's head still and thrusting into his mouth.

Already, Rain loved it on a visceral level he hadn't expected, even with his past experiences. Since they'd met, he'd wanted Colt to be irresistibly attracted to him. Well, he was, and now the thin barrier of resistance had snapped.

"Mmm," Colt sighed, but he was casually in control still. He just sounded like a pleasant breeze had glanced off his skin in the summer.

Rain had given blowjobs where he was in control before, and this was nothing like that. Which made it ten times hotter.

Fuck, his skin was burning up. Even naked, the couch

seemed like too much against him. He was going to faint if he didn't get some attention down south.

But Colt wasn't going to grant that, and his eagle eye was on Rain's hands.

Rain whimpered and closed his eyes, and Colt thrust a little faster. His motions were sharp now, jerky and demanding. Every now and then, Rain choked, but Colt didn't stop. The salty, musky taste filling Rain's nostrils only made it more intense.

"You're so good," Colt whispered. His hand slipped away from his cock, and Rain realized that he was taking most of it with every thrust now. Instead, Colt stroked Rain's cheek, rubbing his thumb along his cheekbone until he danced it along the rim of Rain's ear. "So hot, baby."

Rain's only option was a muffled grunt back, and even that turned him on so much it hurt. He couldn't say a word—all he could do was whimper and service Colt.

"You even know how beautiful you are?" Colt whispered. His movements slowed for a moment as he scanned Rain's face.

Rain's cheeks were already burning, but now his blush deepened. He couldn't quite shake his head, but he avoided Colt's gaze.

Had a man ever looked at him quite like this?

Colt stroked the side of Rain's head and cupped his cheek again. "Well, you are." He thrust again, slowly, taking his sweet time. "Such a good little slut for me, aren't you?"

Rain gasped and choked again around the dick nearly touching the back of his throat. He whined, managing to meet Colt's gaze with wide eyes.

"You like being called that?"

Fuck. Rain didn't want to admit how much it turned him

on, but he had no real choice. He'd just leaked a few more drops of precum all over himself, and his already harsh breathing had quickened. His heart pounded.

Colt's grin was slow and knowing. "Yeah, you do. My gorgeous little slut for the night, aren't you? Your tongue's so good. Lick it, baby," he whispered, pulling back and holding his shaft steady for Rain to lap at the head. "Oh, I'm gonna pound you into the couch right here. Would you like that?"

Rain nodded as hard as he could, staring at Colt.

Colt growled. "Did I say you could stop sucking?" He yanked Rain's hair hard as he forced his cock between Rain's lips again.

He fucked Rain's mouth in shallow thrusts despite his tight grip and harsh words.

A minute later, when Rain's whole body ached for touch so much he was about ready to invent his own sign language to beg, Colt pulled away. His touch was gentle as he shifted back to kneel between Rain's legs, lifting them over his shoulders effortlessly.

Rain's ass ground against his jeans, reminding him that Colt was still fully clothed. He just had his jeans undone and pulled down around his thighs so his balls hung free and his shaft lifted proudly in the air.

"Oh, my God," Rain mumbled, his jaw aching and taste buds still filled with him. "Fuck me like this."

"Not 'til we get tested together," Colt murmured. He reached in his pocket for his wallet, humming and tossing it aside once he'd pulled out a condom packet and a thin, flat packet of lube.

"Who the hell carries lube?" Rain murmured.

Colt pinched one nipple—hard.

"*Ah!*" Rain exclaimed, throwing his head back and baring

his teeth as the surge of pain through his system made him clench. But all he could think was how fucking great it would feel if he clenched around Colt right now.

"I like my twinks defiant, lucky for you."

"And I like my hunks..." Rain trailed off. *Like you* was all he could think. Because Colt hadn't touched his dick once yet, but he was already on the edge of orgasm, his whole body alight in a way he'd never experienced. On the surface, this was the same stuff he'd done before, but it didn't compare in the slightest.

Maybe it was because it was Colt. He'd dreamed for weeks of Colt right here on top of him. And even more than he'd dared to dream, Colt seemed to be reading his mind as he found new, hot ways of turning him on.

"Hung and ready to fill their sexy little slut's ass?" Colt finished when Rain didn't.

Rain could only manage a wordless groan. His mouth wouldn't make actual words, so he nodded hard.

Colt grinned at him, his touch gentle on his thigh. His fingers were slick and ready. "You tell me the moment anything hurts in a bad way, you hear me?"

Rain impatiently waved him off. "Fine. Yeah. Do it."

Colt arched his brow at Rain's order and paused.

Excitement prickled through Rain. He wanted to test him further, but now wasn't the moment. He needed him too much. "Please?" he added.

"That's it," Colt whispered, and Rain glowed with contentment—and then twitched.

Rain breathed and pushed against Colt's fingers as they slid inside one at a time, focusing on how much he wanted Colt to fuck him. That thought helped him let go of any tension, and before long, Colt was rolling on a condom.

"Yes, please, yes," Rain whispered, his brain so focused on Colt that he forgot every other word. Did he even need any?

Colt smiled, adjusting Rain's knees over his shoulders for a better angle and bracing himself with his elbows. He leaned forward over Rain, and Rain cried out against his mouth as he slid inside.

Time itself lost focus as Colt rested an arm across Rain's wrists, keeping him from touching himself when he started to try to free a hand.

All Rain could do was cry out loud, so he did—in spades, in every volume and note he could think of.

The heat was almost unbearable, Rain's muscles so tight that every thrust seemed to vibrate deep inside him. Colt's muscles flexed as he drove into him, his cock filling every inch of Rain while his world spun.

Oh, fuck. Rain was suddenly right there, the pleasure too much to hold on to any longer. Even with only his own stomach for his poor, sensitive dick to grind against, it was enough. Colt was pressing the spot deep inside him with every thrust.

"Come for me, sweetie," Colt whispered, his hand suddenly cupping Rain's cheek. He shifted his angle as thrusts turned into pounding, rhythmic fucking.

And Rain did, shouting Colt's name as he clenched around him. Waves of pleasure rolled through his body, and he gasped raggedly for breath, covering his chest in far-flung jets of passion.

Colt pulled out, whipped off the condom, and added his load to the mess, a practiced hand wringing himself dry. Then he wiped himself off on Rain's thigh and let him stretch out on the couch, sliding onto the floor next to him instead.

"Mmmph." Rain closed his eyes, finally moving his stiffening shoulders to rotate his arms. He covered his face with his arms. "Wow."

When he looked again, Colt was smiling at him, his arms braced on the couch as his cheek rested against one hand. "Mmm?" He shifted enough to pull one hand free and rest his hand on Rain's cheek. "You good?"

"Better than that." Rain couldn't think of a word that meant *more than good*. "Gooder. Goody. Wait..." His brain was slowly kicking in again. "Great."

Colt laughed richly and kissed his forehead as he pushed himself to his feet, grabbing tissues and dealing with the mess. "Goody. I'll take that as a compliment."

"Please do." Rain was still buzzing on a strange kind of high, a smile never leaving his lips. He watched Colt clean up, bring him water, and sit with him like he was a million miles away, still in that place where Colt was deep inside him and guiding him through anything that mattered.

"I liked that."

"Yeah?" Colt murmured. He was decent again, his shirt even tucked into his jeans.

"Mmm." Rain closed his eyes for a moment.

It wasn't just the sex he liked. It was seeing Colt authentically dominant—the man who took charge and gave them both the time of their lives. Nothing like the blustery asshole image he'd tried to present at first. This Colt was confident, sensitive, and devoted to Rain's pleasure.

Rain beamed to himself. "You could stay, if you want."

But Colt's expression brought his mood thundering down. He looked away from Rain and shook his head. "I'm sorry. I can't."

"Oh." Rain had no idea why he'd expected him to. After all, this was one night between them.

It didn't *mean* anything... yet.

Rain didn't know if he wanted it to. No, that was a lie. He did want it to mean something, but he was afraid to ask for that much so soon.

Instead, he just watched Colt checking his pockets for his keys. "You gotta get to something early tomorrow?"

"Important business meeting. With a... contact. Super early," Colt murmured, not making eye contact.

He couldn't figure out if it was an excuse or if Colt had something else on his mind. "Oh," Rain said again. But he kicked himself, too. He was *not* going to be that clingy asshole when Colt had never promised him more than one good night.

"Cool," Rain said instead, pushing himself upright to wave at Colt while he headed for the door. "So I'll see you later, right?"

"Damn right." At last, Colt found a smile for him. To his credit, it was broad and warm.

Rain relaxed. He hadn't fucked up, and Colt wasn't running away from talking about this. "Okay, cool." He ran a hand down his face "Thanks for... all of that."

"Thank *you*." Colt let go of the doorknob and strode back to Rain, his gaze fixed in that animalistic way again. This time, he leaned down and pressed his lips against Rain's. Just one kiss, but it was certain and passionate.

Then he left, and Rain fell back onto the couch, and sleep took him.

14

COLT

As steam hissed close to Colt's left ear, he scooped the box of milk out of the fridge and then reeled backward with surprise.

There was suddenly a coffee cup in his face and a bored-looking hipster pouting through his beard at Colt. "More cinnamon," he grunted, like a goddamn caveman.

Colt drew a breath and let it out, ignoring the throbbing in his temple. "Certainly. Is the shaker all out? Sorry about that." He straightened up, passed the milk to Yolanda, and grabbed the cinnamon shaker.

With a few skillful smacks, he evenly spread cinnamon across the top of the drink. That much, at least, he was capable of. He still burnt the roast half the time he tried it, but he was a good sprinkler.

"How's that?" Colt asked, brightly smiling at the customer.

But he didn't even say thanks to Colt. He just nodded once, snapped the lid back on, and huffed like it had been the greatest inconvenience of his life. Then, he walked out the door, leaving a trail of root beer e-cig scent in his wake.

"Ass," Yolanda muttered, not quite loud enough for any customers to hear. "Dunno where that guy learned his manners."

Colt grinned and shook his head. "Raised in a barn."

For all it was stressful trying to juggle his job with his other career, Colt liked his coworkers. The place was a gorgeous little shop, too, right downtown. Just around the corner were the pizzerias and microbreweries, cobblestone streets and romantic river views. On their other side, the business district and lots of office workers in need of caffeine.

This was the kind of city where independent coffee shops could still make a living, rather than being swallowed by faceless conglomerates. And Lindon, their boss, did look after them.

Hell, Colt had swapped shifts half a dozen times this month to make appointments with architects and planners, or to drive to Hart's Bay and meet Rain. No other job would let him do that so much, even though Colt suspected he was wearing out his luck.

If he'd trained to become a barista, that would be one thing. But he couldn't stand in for other people easily. Nearly all of them were more skilled than him; they hardly let him near the machines.

But at least Colt was great with a cash register, and he was good at cleaning tables. Nobody needed to know it was because he'd learned that doing chores well was a good way of winning over a new foster family.

Colt ducked out from behind the counter to clean tables and collect cups, juggling a tray with his cleaning cloth on the way back to wash. The shifts passed quickly, at least, but it meant he rarely had time to duck away and check his phone during work.

Finally, he had a second, so he stepped into the stockroom and slipped his phone out of his pocket. One voicemail.

"Hey, Mr. Fuller, this is Wes. The planning application is ready. You free to pick them up today? I'm here until three." The architect sounded cheery. "Let me know and I'll squeeze you in to chat about them. Okay, see you!"

Colt mouthed a few swear words. He could race over there on his lunch break. He'd have to leave his apron here and hope the architect didn't notice his standard retail-black trousers and shoes.

He got a lot more respect in a suit. That was the first thing he'd noticed when he'd bought it—how people looked at him differently, shook his hand instead of waving to him, addressed him as Mr. and not "Hey, dude."

Colt heard the door jangle, so he pocketed his phone, grabbed a container of cinnamon, and headed out to the bar to refill it.

After that customer left, he checked for watchful eyes and then snuck behind the bar, holding his phone below counter level.

Colt: *Final plans are ready! Should I pick them up today?*
Rain: *YES! TEASE!*

Colt grinned and cleared his throat. Rain made him smile, and teasing him made him smile even more.

Rain saw past his suit, his car, his mask of not needing anyone. All it took was a few words from Rain, or a touch, or a look, and everything fell away. Everything except the thickening bond between them.

"Hey, can I take my lunch at one?" Colt leaned on the counter, tossing a towel over his shoulder. More likely the office would be open then. He ought to have just enough time to make it there and back on foot.

It had been a risk choosing an architect with an office walking distance from his workplace, but this was Portland. He'd made sure there were a dozen coffee shops between here and there.

"Sure thing, Colt." Yolanda wiped down the steamer and eyed him with interest. "Hot date or doctor's appointment?"

Colt winked. "Why not both? More efficient." She laughed, and he added, "Neither. Just paperwork."

"Zzzz," she yawned. "Come up with a better story. You've been antsy all week. For a couple weeks, come to think of it."

Colt licked his lips and smiled. "Okay. Paperwork for a friend."

"Ooh." Her eyebrows rose. "A friend."

Heat crept from Colt's collar all the way up his neck. "Uh-huh. So anyway, thanks."

His phone buzzed, just loud enough for Yolanda to hear. Her grin spread. "Why don't you get that?"

"That's fine. We're at work. I can wait." Colt was blushing furiously, though.

Yolanda laughed at him. "Oh, I could fry an egg on your face. Go on. There's nobody in here."

Colt stuck out his tongue at her and ignored the startled laugh, pulling out his phone. Then, his eyes widened.

Rain: *Shit. SOS. Just found out the application's due TODAY. Or we wait a month for the next planning meeting.*

"You look like you've seen his dick pic and it's not all it was cracked up to be."

That, at least, surprised a smile out of Colt. "No. No, it really is. It's something else. We need—he needs—those papers today." He kicked himself for the slip of the tongue. He trusted Yolanda, but he didn't exactly want the whole shop knowing that he was trying to jump ship for another career.

She hadn't missed it, though. She raised her eyebrow. "Marriage license?"

Something inside Colt jolted, right down to his toes. Because for a split second, the question hadn't seemed as ridiculous as it was.

"No," Colt said and snorted. "A site plan. He owns a building we're fixing up." He was getting pretty tired of half-truths, though, and something in his chest gave way. "It's a project together. We want to develop it into units and rent them out to small businesses."

Yolanda's face lit up. "Oh, man! That's epic! You're like, a property flipper."

Colt hadn't thought of himself that way, but it was kind of true. "Yeah. I guess?" He straightened up, pride filling his chest. "You're right."

"Work it, Colt." She high-fived him and then shooed him to the register, where another customer was approaching.

That still left him with a predicament, though. His shift was ending at five. And most government offices like town hall closed at five—if not earlier.

He managed one more text and response.

Colt: *What time does it close?*

Rain: *5.*

Then, he had to pocket his phone, because more stupid customers walked in. It was getting kind of annoying having a job.

Colt still smiled his way through the transactions, even though he felt himself receiving another text just before one.

He barely refrained from checking it until he had his apron off. On his way out the door, he read it.

Rain: *Colt? Can you bring it or email it or something?*

Colt hissed under his breath. The last thing he wanted was to stress him out, but he couldn't guarantee anything yet.

He just about ran flat into Lindon, who was walking in.

"Colt, hey." Lindon looked him up and down and then asked, "Off for lunch?"

"Yeah, I am." Shit. This was his chance. Flustered and out of breath, Colt couldn't think of a good way of coming out with it. "I know I've been swapping a lot of shifts lately..."

Lindon raised an eyebrow and stepped aside from the door so customers could walk in. "Yes?" He wore a slightly exasperated expression.

Colt swallowed hard. If he was going to win everyone over with his confidence, he couldn't let it slip here, either. "Could I take off at three today? An emergency came up."

"What kind of emergency?" Lindon eyed him, his frown deepening.

It only solidified Colt's resolve. He had to get out of here sooner rather than later. As soon as an emergency came up in construction, he couldn't be driving back and forth and trying to swap shifts.

He had to take the plunge, and soon. Not just sit on the edge with his feet touching the water, but one hundred percent throw himself into this. Which meant telling the truth to everyone in his life.

His other option was quitting on the spot, and that was a way more dick move, leaving them short-handed while they scrambled to fill their schedule.

Colt swallowed hard. "I'm working on starting a business," he said. It took balls of steel to ignore the alarm bells blaring in his head. Nobody but an overconfident blowhard told their boss that they were trying to quit. "And we've hit a snag."

Lindon clearly hadn't expected that answer. "Right. I thought you were going to invent a dead grandma."

"I could do that if you'd rather," Colt offered, shoving his hands in his pockets. He was all too conscious that his lunch break was ticking away while they talked.

Lindon thought it over for a moment and then waved a hand. "Sure. Come in two hours early for your next shift."

The air rushed out of his lungs. "Oh, thank you," he breathed out. It was still going to be a rush to get there in time, but as long as he floored it, he'd be fine.

"But shifts are shifts," Lindon warned Colt. There was an edge to his voice he hadn't heard before. "I know it's tough starting a business, but you'll find out soon that you need to be able to rely on your staff."

"Yes, sir," Colt responded automatically. "Thank you."

Colt wasn't going to be able to escape the repercussions of this double life for much longer.

Not just the fun or meaningful stuff, like not getting to spend the night with Rain after they'd had sex for the first time ever. But now it was affecting his work life—both the career and job.

He was being squeezed from all sides, like a can of Coke at a party. Colt wasn't quite sure how and when he was going to blow, but it was inevitable.

And if he had to choose between his lives, Colt knew which one he'd choose—any day of the week.

The one he was building on the coast, with a man with tender blue eyes and a defiant grin.

God, Colt had a sudden spring in his step as he raced for the architect's offices. It wasn't just knowing what he was on his way to pick up, either. The thought of Rain was enough to lift Colt's spirits sky-high.

Last night had been fucking incredible, and incredible fucking. Colt prided himself on being no slouch in bed, but Rain had lost his mind with pleasure yesterday. Any more and his eyes would have rolled back in his head like some creepy cartoon.

The thought made Colt laugh. It satisfied a piece of his soul he'd forgotten existed to take the control Rain handed him and make the most of it. In a weird way, even though he was supposedly the one in charge, he was serving Rain.

And Rain needed someone to pay him that kind of attention. Someone to look at him like he was special, and remind him that he *was*. Colt wanted to be that guy.

He'd caught feelings, hadn't he?

Colt's steps slowed for a moment, but he shook his head. There was no point in denying it. The way his heart fluttered at every dumb little text from Rain—even a form to fill in or a link to a news article—betrayed it.

The only problem was all the things he hadn't told Rain yet, like the fact that this was his very first attempt at property development, and he wasn't as rich as he acted, and he sure as hell didn't have connections like Rain did.

He'd never in a million years expected to meet someone like Rain, much less expected things to progress to the point where it *could* be a problem.

But Rain wasn't a pump-and-dump guy. And from the cues he was giving Colt, he didn't think of Colt that way, either. Hell, he'd invited Colt to stay, and if not for the stupid job, he would have.

Okay, that made up his mind.

Colt needed to get Rain alone today, and before things got

any further between them, tell him everything he never had. Everything he was afraid of, and everything he hoped Rain wouldn't judge him for.

And all Colt could do was hope that who he *really* was would be enough for Rain.

15

RAIN

"Rezoning? Heavy to light commercial? Yeah, that's no big deal."

Rain breathed a heavy sigh of relief, matched only by Colt's. They stood side by side at the desk in the small building. The Hart's Bay town hall was so small that it shared its lobby with the police station. After town hall closed for the day, they just drew a rope across that desk.

"Really?" Colt asked. "It's hell trying to rezone anything in Multnomah." He glanced sideways at Rain. "The Portland metro area," he explained.

"Oh, you're not in the big city anymore, dude," the clerk laughed good-naturedly. Rain searched his memory unsuccessfully for the guy's name. They'd been in high school together. Just about every class, too.

Colt nodded. "Oh, I'm getting that feeling." He smiled and nudged Rain. "See? No need to stress."

Rain gave Colt a fierce glare. He'd sauntered into Rain's house reeking of coffee and complaining about his all-day business meetings at quarter to five, like they had all the time in the world to get here.

Rain had only put his scolding on ice because they needed to speed to the town hall. Being pissed off would only increase the risk of fender benders along the way. Still, Colt had picked up on his mood and wisely stayed silent. The mood in the car had been icy, for once, instead of filled with hot barbs.

Their good luck didn't mean Colt should make a habit of acting like Hart's Bay was Portland. It wasn't uncommon for clerks like this to take off work early, or lock the doors at quarter to five to shut down for the night.

They could have been screwed. But they weren't, and Colt *had* made it here in time. Rain had to give him some credit and let go of his annoyance.

"Yeah. I know which building you mean. The city's been looking for a use for those warehouses for years, haven't they?" The clerk rubber-stamped a few pages and typed in his computer. Then, he riffled through the papers in front of him and checked the clock. "Just in time, too."

Rain cleared his throat and resisted the urge to look at Colt again. Last thing they needed was to be seen fighting like an old married couple.

"Yeah," Colt said, his chin rising as he pointedly avoided looking at Rain. "Thanks for helping us out."

"Of course. It's been a while since anything happened there."

Rain knew just what he meant, and he went tense. "Yeah?"

"It's bound to get rubber-stamped through. Is Floyd helping with all this?" Then, the clerk's eyes skimmed the part of the application where they named the construction company: Hart & Hart.

Those Harts were Joseph, Finn's dad, and Roy. Neither were on Rain's side of the family divide.

"Oh." The guy cleared his throat. "Never mind. So, looks like it's all good. I'll send it to the committee."

Colt grinned, oblivious to the tension in the air. "Thanks. That's great news."

The clerk kept rattling off his spiel. "You should hear back pretty quick, by the end of this week if there's no objections. If there are, it'll take a few weeks, max. You'll have a chance to respond, and vice versa, blah blah." He shrugged. "But I doubt that'll happen. Anything else I can do for you?"

"Nope. Thanks for your time."

As they left, Rain waited until they were just by the door before glancing over his shoulder.

Maybe it was his paranoia talking, but the clerk was on the phone now, his gaze fixed on the two of them.

Okay, that's paranoia, Rain told himself. *Maybe the guy's ordering pizza.* He shook his head to clear the thoughts away as Colt held the door for him. "Thanks."

"No problem." Colt gave him an infectious grin. That boyish expression and cheeky gleam in his eyes reminded Rain of the intimacy they'd so recently shared. "How about we celebrate this?"

"If we celebrate every step with a beer, I'm gonna be burping hops by Christmas," Rain said. *Unless he means another kind of celebration*, he couldn't stop himself thinking.

Colt just laughed. "Nah, we can't turn down a beer for a big milestone. Come on. Let's go."

But they'd barely made it down the road, over the square, and into Cher's before Rain's phone rang.

Fuck. His mood sank, but he wasn't surprised. A piece of

him had been hanging on and expecting it even as he nodded, smiled, and listened to Colt joking and laughing.

"You gotta get that?" Colt asked. "I can grab you a beer."

There was a tension to his smile, though. Rain had been so distracted wondering when this call would come that Colt's forced cheeriness hadn't registered. What was that about?

"Hold off that plan, and get one for yourself," Rain countered. Colt tried to disagree, but he waved him off and stepped outside.

He'd know the number anywhere. It was Floyd.

"Hi, Grandpa," Rain greeted. Floyd sometimes liked it when he called on their family relationship—but sometimes it just made him testy. It was a fifty-fifty shot these days.

He hit the wrong fifty. "Rainier." Floyd addressed him as he only did when he was in trouble. "I believe we're overdue a chat. Why don't you stop by my place? You're in the area, right?"

Rain didn't bother to ask how he knew. No doubt that fucking clerk had phoned Floyd the moment they walked away to give him a heads-up.

"Yeah, um... okay." His gaze strayed toward the bar. "I'll be there in ten minutes."

"Make it five. I don't have all night."

Rain flinched and shook his head. He never got used to Floyd's moods. "Okay. Um. As soon as I can. See you in a bit."

Colt was still waiting by the door when he opened it, and Rain blinked with surprise. Desmond would have been two shots deep at the bar already, flirting with whoever was closest. "Oh. Hi."

"What's up?"

"I've gotta go report to my grandfather," Rain murmured, sighing. "He's heard about this, no doubt."

"What? Then don't go," Colt said with a shrug, like it was the most obvious statement ever.

Rain smiled. The optimism was nice, but Colt had no idea how tricky this tightrope was to walk. Not turning up would light fuses that Colt didn't even know existed. "No, I can't just not go. But I'll be back ASAP," he promised.

If Rain pulled away from his family and went his own way, life would get harder in a myriad of little ways. He didn't have a backup family in waiting. Rain had to make sure his ducks were in a row first. And right now, they were hatching, one at a time. The last thing he needed was to screw it all up again.

"I'll wait for you in the warehouse, okay? I wanna walk around a little more." Colt's gaze was distant, daydreaming. It was kind of adorable.

Rain chuckled. "Stand there and survey the place, more like. Like it's your castle."

"You know it." Colt winked. "See you soon, okay?"

It was like walking through cement as Rain tore himself away from Colt and walked out of Cher's. Every fiber of his being wanted to be back there with him—or have Colt here by his side, at least.

But Rain had to be the man he'd failed to be for the last twenty-five years of his life. Nobody could do that for him.

And that started by walking to Floyd's house. By not letting his grandpa intimidate him into silence this time. And maybe—just maybe—today was the day he'd finally commit to coming out.

Having Colt by his side would rub it in everyone's faces, and he wasn't sure their relationship would ever recover from that. As it was, he kind of hoped his mom and dad would come around.

Floyd, though? He was a write-off. He just had to make

sure his grandpa didn't take out too many bridges when he lit up.

"I can't believe you didn't tell any of us."

His mother looked hurt, and for a minute, Rain's heart hurt, too. She was wringing her hands as she sat next to his father on the expensive formal sofa. It was the kind with curly wooden legs and armrests, and silken fabric that wouldn't stand up to a decent house party.

And opposite them, in the dark green, high-backed armchair he always chose, sat Floyd.

Rain was on a stool in the middle of them all like a goddamn child, but the only other option was standing. If he did that, he'd start pacing nervously, and he didn't want to show weakness.

So he sat and folded his hands, sitting up as straight as he could. "I'm making some investment and renovation decisions on my own. It's about time I did."

If they were reacting like this to him starting a business on his own, coming out would send everyone thermonuclear.

"Yes, but—don't you trust us enough to let us know? Do we have to find out from the planning application?" His father leaned forward, spreading his hands. "You know we offered help. Your grandpa and I know a thing or two about this."

Floyd hadn't spoken since he'd broken the news—that the family knew about Rain's planning application. His face was a thundercloud, and his nails dug into the arm of the chair, working out a thread.

His nails were the only part of him that moved besides his lips. "Who's this business partner?"

Nobody had asked that much. Rain had hoped nobody would read the application, but of course Floyd had gotten a copy—somehow—and skimmed the highlights. There it was, printed out on the table in front of him.

"Colt? He's a property developer." Rain wasn't giving them more than they needed to know.

Floyd leaned forward, venom dripping from his voice. "A property developer *I've* never heard of."

God, did he have to be so insufferable? Floyd acted like he knew everyone in the world who was important, and if he didn't know them, they weren't worth knowing.

Thank God Rain had broken out of that way of thinking early.

"Who's this guy, then? And why don't I know him? What does he care for Hart's Bay?" Floyd asked.

Rain couldn't stifle the snort. Once, he would have withered under the look he got from all three older relatives as a result. Now, he just straightened his spine, because he didn't take back the sentiment.

Like they cared for the town at all. They didn't contribute a thing anymore, and they hadn't since the business closed. All they cared about was a status symbol—being named after it. They certainly didn't care who they hurt along the way. Even if it was their neighbors or their own damn son.

"All you need to know is that he's got the best interests of everyone at heart," Rain said, his voice harsher than he'd meant it. "If you object to the proposed use of the building, feel free to write to the committee."

Rain stood up and dusted his jeans off, like that could wipe away the sneer Floyd gave him. He wouldn't dare bring this to the public eye, and they both knew it.

"You can't let your heart make business decisions. That's

the best way to get ripped off." Floyd didn't stand up, his eyes tracking Rain across the room. "And to hurt a whole lot of other people in the process."

"Who exactly am I hurting?" Rain spun on his heel as he reached the door. "Who's living in those warehouses that I might hurt? Oh, wait. Nobody. It's an abandoned industrial building. And not even that. A crappy property—"

"That you wanted," Floyd taunted, reminding him of the bargain they struck.

"That you held on to until it was falling down before passing it to me," Rain snapped, his blood red-hot. He ignored the shock on his parents' faces. He'd never talked back to his grandpa before, but it was long overdue. "I don't think you were ever gonna give it up, were you? Like you never gave Dad his fishery all those years ago, or... or gave a damn about anyone in town, really. You just wanted to own it all so nobody else could be more successful than you."

It had been a harsh realization, learning that the other Harts were right about the man he'd once called Grandpa. Still did, sometimes, because of a lifetime of memories: Sunday breakfasts, card games, and movies. He'd never been warm and cuddly, perhaps, but at least he'd acted fond of Rain a long time ago.

Now he had other memories mixed in with the man, like finding out that just a month ago he'd tried to burn down the art gallery. Hell, Floyd hadn't even known if anyone was inside at the time.

Even before then, Rain had realized that Floyd was a selfish bastard. But he'd never done anything, because he was a goddamn coward. Endangering lives, destroying property, just out of some petty vendetta? That had crossed the line.

Rain was speaking out, and it was about damn time.

Floyd's face was pale, but his eyes were narrowed under the attack. He didn't look like he was taking in a single word, but that didn't daunt Rain.

"Colt's the best man I've ever met," Rain said, his nails digging into his palms. "And he's bringing investment to the town. Just like the art gallery did, as much as you hated that. I'm beginning to think you *want* this place to fall down around you, like the tragedy that your life is."

"Rainier Jameson Hart!" That was his mother, and she had her thundering voice on.

But Rain wasn't listening. Like his namesake, he didn't blow his top often, but when it was gone, there was no stopping him. "So if you have *any* shame, you leave him the fuck out of this. Attack me directly, if you're man enough to do it. But you better be ready for a fight. It's about time someone stood up to you."

He'd never dropped the F-bomb in this house before, either. First time for everything right now.

With that, Rain turned on his heel and stormed out of the house, flying on the wings of victory. Nobody else had even formed a response by the time he was out the door.

His heart was swelling with the words he'd just said, because they were true and straight from the heart.

Colt is *the best man I've ever met*, Rain thought as he walked back toward the town square, a mile-wide grin spreading across his face. And he wanted everyone in the town —no, the world—to know that. But most of all, he wanted Colt himself to know how he felt.

It was time to stop letting other people tell him how to live, who to be, and most of all, who to love.

16

COLT

The warehouse was quiet, and it smelled of old dust and card-board. At the same time, its history was tinged with the future. It was full of possibilities, a blank canvas.

Colt had felt a hint of this promise the first time he'd snuck in here with his hookup. Now, potential was everywhere. It practically gleamed from the walls.

He'd studied the plans at every stage of design. Now, he did his best to memorize the final design before construction began. He wanted to be able to keep up with Rain and pull his weight if he showed up to supervise or make decisions.

The numbers vanished from Colt's brain the moment he tried to commit them to memory, but he could visualize the space from the computerized drawings.

Looking at the old wooden beams overhead, Colt could see the dividing walls between the units. He made chopping motions with his hand where the windows would go in and paced the length of the storefronts.

Darkness fell as twenty, then thirty minutes, passed. The

evening set in quickly here, as soon as the ocean's flat horizon had swallowed the sun.

Now, Colt was growing nervous. Surely Floyd lived nearby from the way Rain had promised to be back soon, but he hadn't returned from his summons yet.

"Knock knock." Colt spun and saw Rain standing in the doorway of the warehouse. Rain nudged the brick that held the steel door open with a toe. "Can I come in?"

Colt beamed and nodded. "You may enter my castle. Our castle," he revised with a smile.

Rain's smile brightened. "Yeah. Ours," he echoed. But, as he studied Colt's expression, he tilted his head. "Everything okay?"

He finally approached, heading through the warehouse, hands in his pockets.

Colt snorted and tried to shrug off the question. "I should be asking *you* that."

But Rain shook his head and sank onto the floor of the warehouse. He sat cross-legged and looked up at Colt. "Come on. I don't want to talk about it yet. It's too fresh."

The prospect of a heart-to-heart was a little overwhelming to handle. Colt had a lot to tell Rain, and no idea how his partner would take it. But Rain needed distraction, so Colt would take the lead. Rain would talk when he was ready.

Colt nervously licked his lips and wiped his palms on his jeans. He mirrored Rain, sitting beside him. It seemed friendlier than sitting across from him.

"I noticed you were a little off earlier," Rain commented.

Colt nodded slowly. "Yeah. I have a lot of things that I never said. I couldn't quite bring myself to do it, you know?"

So far, so good. Rain nodded once, lacing his hands and resting them on his ankles. "Okay. Better late than never."

"I'm not some spoiled rich kid on his parents' dime." Colt stared down at the floor. "You never asked me why I'm doing this."

Rain paused, his brows furrowing as he gazed at Colt. "I just figured it was because you wanted to help the town, and..." He trailed off. "Well. Make money?" His glance was apologetic.

Colt shook his head. He didn't mind Rain's assumption. He'd worked hard to cultivate it, after all. "It's more than that. I don't have a family. My parents died, and after that I grew up in the foster system, bouncing around a lot. Not a lot of people wanted to hang on to a moody teen for six years."

Rain sucked in a quick breath, and Colt glanced sideways at him. He looked like he'd just jumped into the harbor for the Polar Bear Dip at New Year's. "Shit. Sorry. My family might be shitty, but at least I had a roof over my head."

Colt was used to the reaction—surprise, regret, pity. He saw it all dance across Rain's face.

Before Rain could apologize for something he had no role in, Colt held up a hand. "It's fine. Long time ago, and all that. But I always felt like I didn't really come from anywhere. I don't have roots like you." He blushed. "I was a little jealous at first, actually. So this project started out with me wanting to make money, because I don't have... well... parents who could save my ass in an emergency."

Rain nodded slightly. "A safety blanket."

"Yes." Colt half-smiled. "But it turned into a safety blanket around my whole life. Now I feel like I might have... a home. I hope I do someday."

Rain nodded slowly, his gaze far too soft and kind. It made Colt nearly choke up. He said nothing yet, just let Colt talk.

"But I also wanted to prove myself, because..." He couldn't

meet Rain's gaze and talk at the same time, so Colt looked down and fidgeted with his shoelaces. "Because I feel like my parents would approve."

"How old were you?" Rain's voice was soft. His hand slid onto Colt's knee, steady and reassuring.

"Thirteen." Colt's lip wobbled as he smiled tightly. "My distant relatives didn't know us well, and didn't feel equipped to raise a stubborn teen. They already had enough kids."

Rain hissed softly, sympathetically, but said nothing.

It was harder than Colt had expected to dredge all this up. "But I've always been insecure about who I am. I thought you'd respect me more if I put on this front."

At last, with great effort, he dragged his gaze up and turned his head to the side again to read Rain's expression.

It was too understanding. Why wasn't he mad yet?

Oh, right, Colt thought. *You haven't gotten to the big stuff yet.* But so far, so good. Rain wasn't treating him like dirt. Colt trusted that he wouldn't run a mile if he found out that Colt wasn't quite the man whose image he'd constructed.

The overhead light snapped off in a single, jolting moment. It sounded loud, too. Wait, it *was* loud. Why?

Colt's entire body went stiff. The darkness was blinding, even compared to the single, buzzing, dim overhead light they'd enjoyed until a second ago.

Now, a wave of panic choked him and he scrambled to his feet.

"Shit. Shit, shit, shit!" Rain was doing the same, because out of the blue, with a resounding crack, they knocked heads. "Ow!"

"Fuck." Colt grabbed his head and squeezed his eyes shut, but the sudden burst of pain interrupted the spiral of panic that had been building in his chest.

He hated the dark. Hated it.

He froze for long moments, listening to Rain's receding footsteps. Then, from far away—too far away—Rain spoke.

"The door—someone's bolted us in." His voice was suddenly thin, reedy—afraid.

"Who the hell? What?" Colt exclaimed. He followed the sound of Rain's voice. "Push it harder."

"I have." A metallic thump echoed through the place. "Nope," Rain declared.

Fuck. Colt was about ready to stride over there and body-slam it open, then punch whatever punk kid thought that was funny.

"It's my grandpa." Rain's voice came out as almost a whimper. The only reason Colt could hear his soft voice was the vast emptiness here and the silence apart from them.

Colt's anger subsided into abrupt protectiveness. He might be irrationally scared of what was in the huge, dark space surrounding them, but Rain had a reason to be scared.

Rain's footsteps slowly scuffed closer. "Which way are you? God, it's dark."

Colt didn't need reminding. "I can't see a thing." Logically, he knew it was stupid. There was absolutely nothing in the darkness that could get him. "Come here. Please. I need you."

Except maybe there was. And that played on Colt's mind, making his hands shake. He was thirteen again, pulling the blankets over his head and shivering.

"Colt?" Rain's voice was closer, and a shiver of fear shot through Colt again. He couldn't let Rain down. "Are you okay?"

"I don't know," Colt admitted with a too-raw laugh. "What do we do?" He couldn't think straight and take charge like usual.

Rain was close now, his steps still shuffling. "I don't know what to do," Rain said, breathy and afraid.

Colt forced himself to think. Light—that would help. A flashlight? No, his phone! He had a phone these days.

Not like back then, afraid and alone in the attic bedroom of his first foster home. The very first night, there had been a thunderstorm rolling down from the mountains, making the roof shake. After that night, he hadn't been allowed to turn the light on after ten at night. It had been full of creaking boards and drafts.

Night after night, Colt had stuck his head under the covers and shivered himself to sleep, even if it was perfectly warm up there.

"He..." Rain's words interrupted the memory as Colt fumbled for his phone.

There. Colt flicked the flashlight on, illuminating Rain. He stood a pace away, his hand still resting on his forehead. His eyes were glassy and wet.

"Shh," Colt whispered, stepping closer and sweeping an arm around Rain. He pulled him into his chest, holding him as tight as he dared with one arm while shining his flashlight around. "Here. Hug it out."

Nothing else in the warehouse with them. Good. They could think their way out of here.

"Yeah." Rain's voice squeaked on the syllable. He cleared his throat, pressing his nose into Colt's neck. His body still shivered like a leaf, though, and Colt smoothed his back gently. "Right. Okay. That helps."

"That's it, deep breaths," Colt whispered. He mirrored them himself. "It's hard to think straight. I'm not good in the dark."

"I thought you sounded panicky." Rain took a breath and squeezed Colt. "We'll make it through, okay?"

Colt drew strength from his certainty and chuckled sheepishly. "It's dumb, I know."

"No," Rain said fiercely. "Nothing like that is dumb. You can't help it. Oh! But we have light." Rain fumbled, squirming against Colt until he had his phone light on. "There. That's double the light. Okay? I don't know what the hell's going on with the overhead light. Maybe he shut off the power from outside."

In the faint light, Colt smiled back at Rain. "I'll be okay," he murmured. He tried to choke back his own fear as the blackness around them only deepened. With their eyes not adjusted to the dark, it felt like they were in a bubble of safety together.

"Right." Rain's hand shook despite his confident voice, so Colt squeezed it gently.

"Let's focus on getting out of here first. Let's see if my weight is enough to get the door open. I assume it's not locked, or you'd be able to get out with your keys," Colt said.

Rain nodded. He threaded his slender fingers through Colt's and moved with him toward the door, their steps almost in sync. Neither of them wanted to leave the other alone for a moment, it seemed.

"Fuck," Colt whispered as he leaned on the bar with his hip and it didn't open. He tried again, harder, and then nearly threw his full weight against the door. "Okay."

"Let me check the lock." Rain fumbled, but the key wouldn't open it any more.

"It's jammed from the outside," Colt concluded. It made him almost dizzy with nerves to say it out loud. The only light from the outside was the faint glimmer of stars through the dirty windows near the peak of the roof on each end.

"It has to be Floyd. He tried to burn down the art gallery a month ago and we caught him and I yelled at him tonight and he might be doing the same thing!" Rain's last words were choked out, like he didn't have enough breath for them.

"Okay," Colt whispered. That was enough to grab his attention. He doubted Floyd was dumb enough to try that again if he'd been caught last time, but Rain's fear was valid. He wasn't going to dismiss it. "Let's think. We have phone signal. We can call for help."

Rain pulled back from Colt and took his free hand. "Yes. We're safe, and we've got these phone lights. They'll last for ages. Are you okay?"

God, he was sweet. Even scared that his grandfather was trying to sabotage and scare them both out of town, he was checking in on Colt.

If Colt could ever be lucky enough to deserve this man, he would count it the greatest triumph of his life.

"Fine," Colt told Rain, even though his heart still pounded. Having Rain by his side in this bubble of light helped. "If we can get out, I'll be better."

"We can... climb out the window?" Rain's giggle was halfway to frantic. He craned his neck to look up at the dark window, the stars visible through it.

Colt shook his head. "Wait. There's bay doors." He'd just studied the floor plan, after all.

Two, in fact, at the other end of the building closest to the water. The plan was to convert them with newer hardware and rolling doors so a coffee shop or restaurant at the end could open the place up to become a patio on gorgeous days.

"Yes!" Rain turned. "That end, right?"

Colt nodded and followed Rain's lead through the huge, echoing, pitch-black space. It was irrationally terrifying, but there was nothing they could do except go for it.

Step by step, they walked, and Colt focused on their destination rather than the dark space behind and around him. It was only darkness. It couldn't hurt him. Anyone who meant them harm was outside the warehouse. They were safer here, really.

And Rain was here, by his side, murmuring about how close they were. "A hundred feet. Fifty. Look, here we are, I see the wall. Okay, and the doors."

Colt nodded, gulping hard. With that, he pushed back the thoughts racing through his brain. This had to work. If not, he was going to be seriously panicky. "Are they locked?"

"Yeah, but I have my key ring. I think. But they haven't been opened in God knows how long." Rain paused and looked at him.

"If this doesn't work..." Colt trailed off, his heart seizing again.

"Hey, wait, wait." Rain sounded breathless. "If we're blocked in, I'll call Cher and get someone to let us out. Or the cops. Let's just try this first, okay?"

Colt nodded and drew strength from him. He crouched by the chain and held it up, turning the phone light toward it. "Here we go."

Rain found the right key, to both of their relief. He fit the key in and turned it, and then tossed his keys down. They worked together, unthreading the chain from the lock.

The handle creaked, but it turned, and the door was unlocked. "Right. Here we go. Three, two, one," Colt counted them in, and they each took a handle, pulling up at the same moment.

The door creaked and lurched up half an inch before bouncing back down again.

"Fuck. Is there another lock?" Colt rose and inspected the door, shining the light across the surface. There it was—another lock in the middle. He picked up the keys and held them up, matching them up by sight.

There. That one looked like it would fit.

"Give it one more try with me." Colt was all too aware that time and their phone batteries were ticking away.

Rain nodded. He shifted his phone into his other hand and crouched to grab the handle.

This time, Rain counted them in, and on three, Colt threw his whole weight upward.

And the door rose, slowly grinding its way up.

The salty air of the harbor met his nose, and the breeze on his cheeks had never been more welcome.

"Let me see if I can find Floyd before he runs away," Rain whispered. He ducked out of the door and nearly sprinted around the side of the building.

"Nothing!" Rain's exclamation was followed by some curses and creative insults.

The darkness at Colt's back was way more than he wanted to confront. Instead, he threw his weight into sliding that door right back down again. Fuck, no, he wasn't going to think about the monsters in the dark now.

With them safely on the other side of the door, Colt followed Rain.

A steel bar was jammed across the door, keeping it closed. No sign of whoever had done it, either.

"That motherfucker!" Rain hissed, and Colt rubbed his back.

"Look, let's sit and cool off for a second," Colt murmured.

He could use a moment to stretch after that brief, intense workout. He hadn't stretched before opening a rusty industrial bay door and then closing it again. His shoulders were going to feel that in the morning.

Rain sounded shaky, just as Colt felt. "We should check for… I don't know, fire."

But despite two laps of the building, there wasn't a single hint of anything out of place. Rain's fears had filled in the blanks, and Colt couldn't blame him. His own fears had kicked in, irrational though they were.

"Feel better?" Colt asked Rain once they reached the door again.

Rain slipped his hand into Colt's and shook his head, rolling it back to stare up at the sky. "Define better."

That drew a raw chuckle from Colt. "I know," he murmured. "Come on. Let's get out of here and breathe."

Colt shook his head. It had just been a dumb prank, after all. Whatever the hell Floyd's problem was, he couldn't be more childish.

Rain relaxed by Colt's side as they walked down toward the dock, their footsteps clomping along the wooden slats before long. Even Colt was cooling off, his shoulders dropping and breath coming easier.

The darkness outside was totally different. It was only within four walls that the darkness crept up on him, tickling his spine with chilling fingers.

Outside, Colt could breathe and enjoy the darkness. The stars glimmered, and the crisp ocean breeze dried Colt's palms. Even on a cloudy night, the darkness outside was fine with Colt. It wasn't dark like being trapped in a room.

In silent agreement, they sat side by side at the end of the dock, overlooking the glassy mirror surface of the water.

"You okay?" Colt whispered, putting his arm around Rain's shoulders.

Rain leaned into him, fitting perfectly as he rested the side of his head on Colt's shoulder. "Better now. You?"

"Much." Colt let his breath out, the adrenaline finally ebbing. "Stupid, really. Being afraid of the dark. God."

Rain shook his head. "No. We can all have irrational fears."

Colt paused for a moment. But while he was on this streak of telling the truth, it just made sense to come out and say it, so he did. "It's not exactly irrational. My first foster family wouldn't let me turn on a light after dark. My room was spooky, and I was... well, I thought my parents were hanging around. As ghosts."

That was it—he was choking up. He'd never said that to anyone out loud before. It sounded nuts.

Rain drew in a quick breath and then slipped his hand into Colt's. "Jesus. I can't blame you. It must have been kind of comforting to think they were looking after you from wherever, right?"

"A little." Colt bit his lip and looked across the ocean, squeezing Rain's hand. "But also scary. I had to live up to their expectations. Be the very best, because they could see everything I said and did."

Rain's arms slipped around Colt's waist, and then he nearly squeezed the damn life out of him.

"Oof!" Colt managed breathlessly after a few moments. "Damn, you're strong."

Rain chuckled quietly. "So are you, Colt."

But he didn't mean it physically—they both knew it.

Colt swallowed hard and looked away again. Saying it out loud made him realize why he was so invested in this. He didn't believe in ghosts anymore, but he still had something to prove.

No wonder he'd backed himself into a corner doing it. Colt's conscience pricked, but they had bigger concerns to take care of first. And he needed a distraction.

"Okay. Do we know who that was?" Colt asked.

"If it wasn't Floyd, I'll eat my shoe." Rain might have made Colt laugh if it weren't so serious. "I... crossed a line tonight."

Colt bit back his fury, since he was pretty sure Floyd was the one who had crossed the line. He chose an inquiring hum but didn't ask the question. It was up to Rain to share if he wanted to do so.

"I'm about to get kicked out of the family." Rain's voice was quiet and accepting, rather than miserable like Colt might have expected. It had to be bittersweet, but Rain wasn't dissolving into a puddle.

He's a hell of a lot stronger than he knows. Colt would have been a wreck—he had been, twelve years ago.

"God," Colt muttered. "I'm sorry."

"We can't choose our family. Or... lack thereof." Rain shifted and kissed Colt's neck. "Sorry. I don't want to rub it in."

Colt shook his head slightly. "There's nothing you can say I haven't thought or been told."

"How about I don't say anything about it?" Rain asked quietly.

Colt drew a sharp breath. Yeah, that one *was* new. He took a moment to decide how he felt about it. Good, that was how he felt.

"Thank you," Colt murmured. "And you know what? I don't care if your relatives are crazy, too. I'm here for you."

The sudden sunshine that crossed Rain's face could have

lit up the whole damn ocean. He pulled back to stare at Colt, his eyes alight with hope. "Really?"

"Really," Colt promised. He leaned in and pressed their lips together.

This kiss was more than just lust or connection or desperation. It was a promise, and they both knew it.

It was soft and warm and lingering, and tender in ways that scared Colt to the soul. But he reached for it, too, like a plant's roots sought water.

"Better not make out on the dock. People might see," Colt said.

Rain pressed a finger over his lips, and Colt blinked, abruptly breaking off. "No," Rain said simply. "I'm tired of hiding. I've been hiding myself for my whole damn life. Let's not keep this a secret. It's just a weapon that other people can use against us this way. And I don't want it to be."

"What..." Colt hardly dared to ask the question, his voice wavering. "What *is* this? Are we dating?"

"I'd like us to be." Rain spoke carefully, like he was afraid to ask for too much. "If that's okay with you."

Colt burst out laughing. *Okay* with him? Couldn't Rain see that this was what Colt wanted more than anything in the world?

"Pffft," Rain grumbled. "Don't laugh at me. I can push you into the water, you know."

"No, I mean—yes. Yes, I want to date you. Obviously!" Colt explained himself, but he only laughed harder at the threat. "I'd like to see you try."

Rain snorted. "I'll throw down with you any day."

"That's why I like you."

Colt had come *dangerously* close to the other L-word, but

this was way too quick to say that much, wasn't it? He didn't have anyone to ask for advice in that department.

"Hmph." Rain elbowed him. "So, boyfriend. We should lay down some rules about laughing at me *before* you tell me what that's about."

"I like the laying down part. Not so much the rules." Colt nosed his way into Rain's neck and kissed it once, then again.

Rain shivered, inhaling in one sharp gasp. "I know that much about you already." He flicked Colt's side and when Colt backed off, put his arm around Colt's neck. "I'm glad you said yes, though."

Colt smiled to himself. "We're stronger together. I think I've found that much out already."

Rain hummed quietly and nodded. "No more hiding," he murmured. "God. It's a scary thought. I'm not sure if I'm brave enough."

"I'll be by your side to help you find a way," Colt promised. "And to help kick Floyd in the nuts."

Rain chuckled quietly. "No, Cher has him by the balls. Stupid little pranks are all he *can* do. She knows all his secrets. Stuff she's never told me, that's for sure."

Still, locking them in the warehouse had been more than a stupid little prank in the heat of the moment. Colt had heard the fear in Rain's voice. For that alone, he wanted to go knock on Floyd's door and put the fear of God into him.

But he had work tomorrow, and getting thrown in the tiny city jail wouldn't help anything.

Colt grunted and clambered to his feet. "Okay. Let me drive you home, at least. I won't accept anything except *yes* from my new boyfriend."

"Okay," Rain agreed with a smile up at him. He reached out and Colt pulled him to his feet. Then, he rose up onto tiptoe and pressed a kiss to his lips. "When you ask, the answer's always yes."

Colt's heart melted, but he couldn't help himself. "Actually, it's usually *make me*, as far as I can interpret you."

The surprise in Rain's yelped laugh made him grin. "Oh!" Rain gasped and clutched his chest. "A low blow."

Colt scooped up his hand to walk him back down the dock, grinning. "Yeah, I like a good low blow. But we can save that for Friday, hm?"

"Is that a date?"

A smile crept across Colt's face. Yeah, he could do that. "You'd better believe it."

As they reached his car, it was Rain who grabbed Colt by the shirt and hauled him in for a kiss. This one was long, dirty, and filled with promise. "Take me home, then, big boy."

Colt's head spun as he climbed into the car for the short drive to Rain's, and then a longer drive to his own apartment.

God, he was going to be hard-pressed to wait 'til the end of the week to taste Rain... but leaving Rain's bed last night had been the hardest thing he'd done in weeks. He wasn't sure he could do it again.

Which meant one thing: Colt had a resignation letter to write tonight.

No petty asshole could stop the pieces of his life from falling into place.

17

———

RAIN

It was the first time Rain had chosen a table at Millie's with a tea light candle. He'd eaten here a hundred times in his life, he was sure. But nearly all of them had been with friends or family.

Never, ever a date.

When he approached Sally and asked for a table by the window, her grin split her face. "Of course. Come on, boys."

Colt gave Rain a bemused expression, but he didn't know any better. He did seem to register the white tablecloth and candle when Sally gestured them to a two-person table, though. "Why, thank you." Colt cast Rain a searching expression now.

Rain grinned back at him. Colt probably hadn't expected the family restaurant to show two men to a romantic corner. "Thanks, Sally."

The menus were still laminated, and the tablecloth was definitely not fine linen, but the view was stunning.

Below them, the coast sparkled in the sunset light. It was just past seven, and the sky was burnt orange and gold, fading into pinks high above them. The light caught the water in a shimmer of silvery gray.

"Wow. That's a million-dollar view," Colt marveled. His dark eyes glowed a warm gold in the light.

Rain smirked. "Don't get the development bug. Millie and her girls wouldn't sell for any price."

Colt cast him a bashful look, and for a moment Rain wondered if he'd overstepped. But instead, Colt smirked. "I have my hands full with one partner. So, this is a family business?"

"Millie started it, God knows how long ago. Now her daughters run it. Sally's one of them," Rain explained, smiling at Colt's surprise.

"It's not often you get a genuine family business like this." Colt leaned back and flipped the menu over. "It's no chain restaurant."

"See why I love this place?"

Colt licked his lips. "My taste buds agree." He hummed. "Kinda tempted by the mac and cheese."

"Mmm. I've had everything on the menu," Rain said, laughing. Still, their conversation didn't quite quell his nerves.

This was a date. A real date, in his hometown, with his business partner and now boyfriend.

It was like being eighteen again, finally getting the chance to do all the things he'd desperately wished he could do years ago. Only now, the stakes were higher.

Their conversation wandered through polite topics as they ordered and handed back menus, and then sipped glasses of house red. The weather, Rain's latest construction job, the news... but not anything personal. At first, anyway.

It didn't take long. By the time they were waiting for dessert, Colt was teasing Rain about his relationship with

Lucy. His imitation of Lucy's side-eye had Rain splitting his sides.

"She came to tell me off for dating her young man, I think." Colt shook his head. "I should have brought a fish offering."

Rain laughed. "Like meeting my mom. Only less judgmental."

"Yeow!" Colt grinned at him and sipped his wine. "Eh, screw family. We can make our own, huh? And choosing family comes with more perks."

"Less trouble when we choose them ourselves," Rain agreed. His cheeks flushed at the idea of making a family, though.

It sounded too good to be true. A man to stand by his side while he raised the next generation of Harts—or maybe Fullers.

Or Fuller Harts. How appropriate. Rain nearly choked on his laugh as Sally brought over cheesecake with two spoons.

"Hm?" Colt picked up a spoon to dig in.

Nooo way could Rain tell him that he was mentally joining their last names on their first date. "I'm just thinking about... opening day," he lied. "Making Lucy the maid of honor. Guest! Guest of honor."

"When we get our opening day." Colt bit his lip, and the *if* went unspoken, but Rain heard it loud and clear.

Rain almost held his breath. Was Colt admitting to insecurity? As more and more layers were peeled off this man, he found more to marvel over. He came off so brash, but seeing him afraid of the dark earlier that week had left an imprint on Rain.

Everyone was afraid of something.

"Are you getting cold feet now?"

"No," Colt answered, a little too fast. He frowned over his dessert spoon. "Not a chance."

Rain nodded once, firmly. "Good. Because we've got this. Nothing to worry about. You want the last bit of whipped cream?"

"You're too kind." Colt smiled at him, fondness in his eyes as he licked the last bit of whipped cream off the spoon. "I wake up with stress dreams pretty much every night these days."

Rain gazed across the table, sympathy making his chest tight. "Oh, man. It'll get easier when construction starts. Just take a breath and let your track record speak for itself."

"Ah." Colt bit his lip as he gazed at Rain. "I mean, if construction starts. We have to wait on the committee..."

This seemed like the perfect time to break the secret Rain had been keeping close to his chest.

He could barely resist his grin. He bit it back with all the restraint he had and cleared his throat. "Hm. Speaking of which, I have some news. I figured you *might* be interested in it."

"What?" Colt leaned in. "Is there a response?"

"Yeah... but I can't quite remember what it said..." Rain's grin was breaking through, however hard he tried.

Colt sucked in his breath. "No."

"Yeah. We're approved. No changes or complaints." Rain jiggled in his seat, trying not to bounce out of his seat and make a scene.

Colt had no such restraint. He leaped to his feet and clapped together sharply once. "Yes!" His voice could have carried to the kitchen.

Heads turned, and Rain's cheeks flushed red. He'd spent so long trying not to attract attention that he didn't handle the spotlight too well. He stayed sitting down, but Colt grabbed his hand and pulled him out of his seat. Rain was barely on his feet before Colt swept him off his feet and spun him around in two big circles.

Then, Colt gently set him down and plopped into his own seat. "We're in business."

Rain laughed breathlessly and sank into his seat, grabbing the table to steady himself. "Well. I'm glad I saved that for the right moment."

"Shall we celebrate another way?" Colt grinned.

Rain matched his grin. It had been a long week without Colt's touch, but he had one other thing he wanted to do now that the path ahead of them was clear. "After a quick stop at Cher's? I think someone told me we should celebrate every milestone with a drink."

"Well remembered." Colt pulled out his wallet, and despite Rain's protests, he insisted on paying for the meal.

Rain blushed when Colt walked with him to the door, Colt's hand in the small of his back. It felt like he was being escorted, and he wasn't ashamed to say he loved it.

They'd walked to Millie's, so it didn't take them long to pick their way down the coastal path—minus the few necking breaks they had to take along the way—to the town square. Then they burst inside Cher's End Table, all smiles and ready for drinks.

Rain didn't miss his opportunity: he took hold of Colt's hand to pull him over to the bar.

It was a crowded Friday evening, and curious eyes couldn't miss it. People turned their way and murmured, and Rain stood tall and proud the whole way to the bar.

At one table, Rain's cousin Finn sat with Jesse and a handful of other young men: the artists from the gallery around the corner. There was someone else, too: Dash, Finn's brother. They all spotted the gesture, smacking each other and pointing as subtly as they could.

Cher's eyes widened on their approach, and then she offered them a rare wide grin. "Well, well. What can I get for the lovebirds?"

Rain's cheeks flushed as he looked over at Colt. It was hard to make a decision when he was so hyperaware of everyone's eyes on them. Finn and Jesse made it look easy to walk around holding hands, and Rain was so not used to it.

"How about two glasses of champagne?"

Cher leaned back, squinted into the fridge, and leaned forward again. "Counteroffer: generic sparkling wine?" She probably assumed he'd turn up his nose if she didn't warn him.

Rain laughed. "That's fine," he told her. He paid as she poured the glasses, and then they faced each other at the bar and clinked glasses with a delicate *tink* noise.

They each sipped. The bubbles went straight to Rain's nose, and he set it aside after just the one sip. Besides, he had something else he wanted to do.

It was time to fuel the wild speculation already being passed around the place.

Rain nodded for Colt to put down his drink. He ignored the question in Colt's eyes when he did so. Instead, he just grabbed Colt's shirt and leaned up.

Their lips met in one hot, hard press that tasted like victory and freedom.

That caused a stir.

Rain pulled back, breathlessly laughing as he heard more than one exclamation.

Most of all from the table of gay guys their own age who

had so recently moved here. Most of the artists looked surprised, except for Jesse. Finn most of all.

"Okay," Colt laughed, out of breath and grinning at Rain. "That's one way of doing it."

Rain winked at him and picked up his glass, then laced his fingers with Colt's. "Let's say hi to Finn and the guys."

He'd largely avoided hanging out with them over the last month or two despite invitations. It was too close to being outed to spend time around all those gay men, and his family would cast him out for fraternizing with the enemy. But so far, Finn had proven reliable, friendly, and fair, which was more than Rain could say about his grandfather.

"Wow. What?" Finn greeted them, his jaw hanging open. "I didn't see that coming."

The rest of them laughed, especially Jesse. "I did. I kept your secret, though," he said with a wink.

"He's so oblivious." Ezra, the redheaded artist, leaned forward to touch Rain's arm. "Good for you." He sounded sincere, and his smile was too.

They all seemed to like Rain despite his family connections, maybe because they were from out of town. And because Rain had worked overtime to help them fix up the art gallery in time for the grand opening in August.

"Good for you, yeah." Finn had taken a few more moments to process it. Rain couldn't blame him. After all, Rain had just upended years of careful half-truths.

Rain just smiled back at him. "Thanks. I wasn't sure if I'd get your support."

Finn blinked at him. "Huh? Why not?"

"Well..." Rain squeezed Colt's hand and sipped his champagne. "The family business in our past."

Finn snorted. "And because you're throwing another grenade into that rift?"

Dash cleared his throat subtly. He was slighter than Finn in height, but just as broad-shouldered now. Years of workouts while he'd been away, living and teaching in Connecticut, had helped his frame. Rain, meanwhile, had inherited the "skinny no matter how much you lift" gene.

Rain just blinked at him. He knew his side of the family took every chance to ridicule Finn, but something wasn't adding up. "What do you mean?"

"You know. The great big fight."

Rain's brain wasn't catching up to wherever Finn was. "Uh... you mean the fishery split?"

Everyone else around the table seemed to be holding their breath, letting the cousins talk.

Even Dash wasn't interjecting yet. Rain didn't know how much he'd seen. He'd taken off for Connecticut at eighteen, partly for his career, and partly to get away from the town where he was born. Unlike Rain's escape, Dash had needed the space in order to transition. He'd blossomed into himself now, though he was still quiet and unlikely to step in the middle if a fight brewed now.

"No, the fight before that."

Rain's gut sank. Instantly, it made sense now that he thought about it. Why else would they have divided the business so conveniently? "I... didn't know the fight wasn't over the business."

"Oh." Finn blanched and opened his mouth, then shut it as he glanced around at the others. "Right."

Dash pressed his lips together nervously, watching both of them. He might as well have been screaming *careful* at Finn mentally; even Rain could see that from his expression.

Rain stepped closer, his grip so tight on the glass that Colt reached out to ease it out of his hand. "What are you telling me? It wasn't?"

"Fuck," Finn muttered. He eased himself to his feet and tugged Rain aside, and Rain nodded for Colt to stay with the others for a minute. Dash stayed where he was and started a conversation—too loud and cheerful—about the best beer brands on the west coast.

It was impossible to get any real privacy, but close to the door, nobody was lingering and listening in to their actual words, at least. Once they reached that spot, Finn turned to Rain. "I'm sorry. I thought you knew."

"Just tell me." Rain had his suspicions now, but he didn't want to make any more assumptions. His life had been full of too many of them.

Finn nodded slowly. "Um, Uncle Roy came out. Monty—I mean, your dad didn't like it. And Floyd didn't, either. They said a bunch of stuff. Then they mentioned me, and my dad flipped out."

"You?" Rain echoed. "But you were... like, three."

Finn's half-smile was rueful. "Apparently they could tell early. So anyway, my dad told your dad to go to hell, and I guess... that's where it all began. They agreed to split the business rather than keep working together. And after that, the industry collapsed, and... you know the rest."

The breath rushed out of Rain's lungs. He didn't see a hint of a lie on Finn's face. He'd heard a bit about this when listening in after the fire—enough to convince him to take the guys' side instead of his grandfather's—but not the full story.

Damn it, he believed Finn.

"I was told it was *because* of the fishing ban and stock collapse. Nobody ever mentioned a word of that fight to me."

"Me neither." Finn gave a rueful sigh. "They turned us against each other for bullshit reasons."

"And I thought my side of the family didn't like yours because you guys, uh... I mean, Uncle Roy and your dad..." Rain trailed off cautiously. He didn't want to reignite this debate.

"Gave everyone false hope?" Finn filled in the blank. The tension thrummed between them as Rain nodded, and Finn ruefully smiled. "I've heard it before. And I'm sure you've heard our opinion of Monty and Floyd. We're supposed to hate you for being greedy."

Rain knew most of the town thought his dad and grandfather had shut down the business almost overnight out of selfishness. And it hurt to realize that maybe they were right, and *he* was the one who was wrong. After all, Floyd did seem to like sitting on his hoard of money these days.

His grandfather had lost half his business and family over his refusal to get with the times. No wonder Floyd had been so viciously petty toward the group of gay men coming in here, revitalizing his failing town now. The perfect storm, and Rain had been right in the middle all along without even knowing it.

Rain nodded slowly. "Yeah. I don't know what to think. But I'm pretty sure I'm not invited to family supper anymore."

Finn hissed, the noise low and sympathetic. "That's bullshit. They can't just kick out their own kid. I'm sorry, man."

"I've been defying them in every other way." Rain shrugged. "If it wasn't for this, it'd be something else."

"Still," Finn murmured. "If there's anything I can do... you know where to find me."

The tightness in Rain's chest was unexpected. So was the prickle in the corners of his eyes.

He leaned in and hugged Finn tightly, and he felt the air rush out of Finn as he hugged him back.

They pulled apart and looked around the bar for a minute, giving each other a few moments before they wandered back toward the table.

"—I was thinking of renting that place above the grocery store," Colt was telling the other guys. "Anyone know if it's the owner who rents it out?"

"Yeah!" Ezra beamed. "It'd be great to have more neighbors."

Rain's jaw dropped. *Colt living here? In my town?* God, he'd never get a moment's work done with Colt right here.

Finn rejoined Jesse, and the group politely pretended their little diversion had never happened. Dash looked at Finn first, but Finn just smiled at him.

"Anyway, we have to go soon," Colt said. Rain's heart had just started to sink when Colt looked at him and grinned. "I have a place to stay tonight, and I'm hoping there's a curfew."

It took Rain a moment for his brain to kick in: Colt was asking to stay with him.

"Yes," Rain just about yelped. "I mean, yeah. There is. In, um... ten seconds." He took back his glass of champagne and downed it in a few gulps, and then his knees wobbled as the bubbles attacked his nose and throat all the way down. "Ow! Jesus, never let me do that again!"

Colt was laughing, but he grabbed Rain's shoulders to steady him. "I'd better get you home before that kicks in."

"Oh, you don't need to make excuses to go have wild sex," Aaron smirked, leaning forward. "Just tell us all about it, now that you're all bared to the public eye." He managed to make that sound filthier than Rain had imagined possible.

"Aaron!" Jesse groaned.

Finn and Dash both covered their ears. "I don't want to know," Dash muttered, while Finn nodded in agreement.

"Bye, dude," Finn chimed in.

Rain laughed and waved to his cousins and the rest of the table. "Bye, everyone."

They left their empty glasses at the guys' table and made a beeline for the door before anyone else could stop them.

Normally, Rain might have stopped to gauge the goodwill of those in the bar. He would have wanted to make conversation and see if they were all okay with it.

But now? He didn't care. He was showing up as his whole self, and nobody else in the world could stop him.

"I could just drop you off here." Colt's words hung in the air between them, an unsubtle promise of what was to come otherwise.

Rain snorted and turned the key in the lock. "Why do you say that?" His chest was tight with anxiety. Was Colt changing his mind about dating him?

"I want to respect you and take it at your pace." Colt's voice was soft. "And if I come in... well..."

His hands slid down Rain's sides as Colt crowded behind him, and then he squeezed Rain's ass. With that hot wall of muscle behind him, it was nearly impossible to focus on his words.

"You're irresistible, Rain, and I think you know how I want you. If you're looking to take things slow, I'm the wrong guy."

How could Rain explain the need that burned inside him? The way he felt taut enough to break, like he'd been under tension for years? Did Colt know what it was like to hide himself, push back his desires, and treat his love life like a dirty secret?

Rain had always been okay with himself. Loving men—submitting to them, too—had come as naturally to him as breathing, so how could it be wrong? The stress of tiptoeing around his family had been enormous, though, and Rain was done with it. He was ready to lose his carefully maintained self-control.

When he snapped, he snapped. One day, Colt would learn that.

Rain pushed open the door, and then turned and tipped his head back to face Colt. "You'd better come in. I didn't get myself a hot-ass boyfriend to be chaste."

A grin spread over Colt's face, and he stepped forward—so close their chests pressed together as he wrapped one strong arm around Rain's waist. "Hang on."

"Huh—oh!" Rain exclaimed as Colt grabbed Rain's ass and hefted him off his feet.

Colt barged through the open doorway and kicked the front door shut, then spun Rain around to press him up against the door.

Rain whimpered and closed his eyes as Colt's lips found his neck. He pressed hot kisses along the side of his neck, behind his ear, and even along his throat.

It was vulnerable, yet liberating to cling to Colt and grind against him, hot and desperate for him.

And then Colt found Rain's weak spot. "I want you on your knees," he whispered, his nails digging into Rain's ass. "I'm going to enjoy making you suck me off. Would you like that?"

Rain's heart pounded, but he couldn't have nodded faster or harder. "Jesus, yes."

Colt's chuckle was deep, and it thrummed through them both. "You trust me to make you feel good?"

"Yes," Rain whispered. He closed his eyes and shuddered when Colt's tongue danced along his collarbone, his lips finding spots just below it that made Rain's brain switch off. His cock jumped to life as heat pulsed within him.

Especially when Colt whispered back, "Then give in to me, Rain. You're mine tonight, and I'm going to make sure you know it." Rain was pinned against the door, both physically and with his words.

Rain surrendered—to Colt's body crushing him against the door, and to the fantasies finally playing out in life instead of just his mind.

Colt's cock was pressing into him, and Rain was eager to see it—even more eager to taste it. But Colt took his time to kiss every inch of his neck and chest, growling when Rain's T-shirt got in the way.

"The bedroom's that way," Rain managed.

Colt's chuckle was low. "Maybe I want to fuck your pretty, smart little mouth right here. That way I'll make you remember the taste of me every morning you leave for work and every evening you get home. Would you like that, my gorgeous?"

Rain's cheeks burned. He tried to avoid Colt's gaze and close his eyes, but Colt had claimed his mouth. He kissed like a vampire intent on drawing pleasure from Rain, and Rain couldn't help but give in.

"Yes," Rain finally panted against Colt's mouth, his eyes flickering open as he gasped for breath.

"Yes, what?" Colt paused mid-kiss, leaving Rain's lips aching for more. He tried to press forward, but Colt wouldn't have any of it. He just repeated, "Yes, what, Rain?"

"Please," Rain whispered. He hoped it conveyed everything he felt right now: bound to Colt and his every whim, and ready to please him.

Colt set Rain on the ground and turned them around, but Rain still barely supported himself. Colt's grip on him was too strong—and he was easing him to the floor, one hand under each elbow.

Rain's jeans were so fucking tight that it almost hurt. Before long, it *would* hurt. But he knew better than to touch himself before Colt gave him permission.

When Rain was on his knees, Colt let go of his elbows and instead ran his hands up his arms all the way to his palms. He took Rain's hands in his own and leaned back against the door. Then, he spread his legs like he had all the time in the world.

Rain had to crane his neck to gaze up at Colt, barely restraining his whimper. The feeling of being helpless on his knees, ready to do Colt's bidding, was even better than he'd imagined.

Colt dropped one of Rain's hands but kept the other, pulling his hand toward his crotch. He pressed his palm over the back of Rain's hand, making Rain rub the length through his jeans.

Rain gulped, unable to look away from the bulge. His mouth watered with how much he wanted Colt, but he wasn't sure if he was allowed to dive in.

"You know what to do now." Colt's voice was low and demanding.

Rain lurched forward and fumbled with Colt's jeans, pulling them open as fast as he could. It took him a few seconds to get his fingers to work well enough to pull down his zipper and haul Colt's jeans down to his thighs.

Colt's quiet laugh made Rain's cheeks flush, but the

embarrassment felt good, too, in a way he couldn't put a finger on. It was nothing like the hot shame that had suffused him after those few hookups he'd so desperately sought out, or the boyfriend he'd foolishly placed his trust in before.

Yeah, Rain was unbearably eager to see and touch and taste Colt, and Colt was encouraging him onward. Seconds later, he pulled Colt free from his underwear and gasped.

Rain fucking loved that sight. Colt's erection bounced upright, nearly smacking him in the chin as he kneeled in front of him. It was flushed pink and gorgeous, and so big it made him squirm on his knees.

"Suck me." Colt didn't mince his words. One hand settled on the back of Rain's neck, the other tangling in his hair.

Rain smirked up at him. "Make m—hnnh!" He couldn't even finish the defiant words before Colt pushed Rain's mouth onto his cock, stifling him as his lips stretched around the shaft.

Fuck, Rain needed to touch himself so badly. He couldn't stop shifting now, his toes curling as he tried to put his pleasure out of mind. It was nearly impossible, though. He got so hot he could come on the spot whenever Colt was rough with him.

"That's it," Colt whispered. His hand slid from Rain's shoulder to cup his cheek tenderly, although every thrust of his hips was far from gentle.

Colt's dick filled his mouth and then some. It was a serious choking hazard, making Rain gasp for breath. Colt just hummed with pleasure and fucked his mouth without a care in the world for Rain's discomfort... and Rain only loved it more. He felt filthy, decadent, unleashed.

"You're so gorgeous," Colt murmured. "I love watching you choke on my dick. Don't you love it, too, my slutty little boyfriend? I can tell you do. You're so hard, aren't you?"

Rain managed a nod and tried to speak, to beg permission

to touch himself, but Colt wasn't hearing it. He held Rain's head down on his cock, all the while stroking Rain's hair and whispering sweet nothings.

"Not yet, my sweet. You're going to have to suck harder before I'm ready to let you go. Come on." He patted Rain's cheek forcefully, almost a smack but not quite. "Work for it."

Tears sprang to Rain's eyes, his cheek burning, but his cock only throbbed harder in his pants. He groaned around the length filling his mouth, swiping his tongue around it as best he could. Every time Colt pulled his hips back, Rain lapped at the swollen head that lay on his tongue while gasping for breath.

Rain couldn't help himself anymore. This was the hottest sex he'd had in his life, including his last hookup with Colt. He loved being used as Colt's plaything, but his arousal was building to a fever pitch. He might just come in his pants if he didn't get himself free now.

He slid a hand down his own pants and into his underwear, gasping and squeezing his eyes shut at the sparks that flew the moment his fingertips made contact with the aching length.

"Oh, don't think I don't see what you're up to." Colt's voice was a low growl. "But I'll let you put on a show for me, as long as you don't come."

Rain whimpered, trying to protest. Did Colt not see how turned on he was? He wanted—needed—to blow the lid off the tension that was building inside.

"You heard me." Colt patted his cheek again, a little harder, and then gripped the back of Rain's head, easing his hips forward until the head of his dick touched the back of Rain's throat. "That's it, baby. Now you get to take all of this in your hot little hole. You want that?"

Rain couldn't even nod. All he could do was squeeze

himself harder as he stroked awkwardly inside his jeans, staring up at Colt. *Yes*, he wanted to beg. *Please fuck me now.*

Colt's gaze softened like he was reading Rain's expression. He let go of Rain's hair and pulled back until his thick, glistening length popped free from Rain's lips.

"Hands out."

Rain whimpered, not sure for a few moments that he *could* obey that command. He had to fight every instinct to pull his hands out of his pants, leaving himself throbbing once again.

Colt gripped Rain's upper arms and pulled him to his feet with ease. "Take me to your bedroom."

As Rain walked through the small house to the bedroom, Colt's big hands settled on his hips. It felt like he was being steered, even if Rain was directing them.

He barely made it to the bed before Colt lifted him up onto it, tossing him down face-first.

"Fuck," Rain panted as the adrenaline shot through him, but Colt was already straddling the backs of his knees, reaching under him to unfasten his pants and yank them off.

Rain helped by arching his back, and the moment the jeans were off his ankles, he ground down against the silky surface of the duvet. It wasn't his hand, but anything at all would do.

Colt's hand tangled in the back of Rain's hair. "I hope you have lube. Spit won't go very far."

"Bedside table." Rain's whole body was tense with anticipation. "Condoms, too."

"Perfect." Colt ran a finger down Rain's spine, all the way from the back of his neck to the sensitive nerve endings around his hole.

As that fingertip slid between his cheeks, Rain couldn't hold back his whimper. He pushed up into the touch, but it was abruptly gone. "Stay," Colt whispered, and then his weight was gone.

Rain heard the rattling of his bedside drawer. He stayed put, as much as he wanted to reach under himself for a few sneaky jerks of his aching cock.

Then Colt was back over him, his lips against the back of Rain's neck. "Good boy," he praised. "You know what I do with a good boy?"

"Fuck him until he can't walk?" Rain helpfully suggested. "Ooh, I know. Or let him jerk himself off. Because he could really, *really* use the attention right now."

Rain was pretty sure his precum was soaking through the bed, and the slippery surface of the blanket wasn't enough for him. He needed a firm hand around his shaft.

"First suggestion, best suggestion. No touching, Rain."

Rain gasped, turning his head to stare over his shoulder. That was just cruel—even if the denial made him all the harder. "Please?"

Colt gave him another wide grin. "Nope." He slapped Rain's ass, sending heat jolting through his body. Pleasure prickled through the sting.

Rain cried out, his cheeks burning—both sets now. "No! Please, Colt. I'm so turned on it hurts. I need to, please."

But his begging was in vain. "I love hearing you so desperate. The more desperate you are, the more I'll make you wait."

Rain gasped, shifting onto hands and knees so he could reach himself, but Colt pressed one hand over each of Rain's to stop him from shifting his weight onto one hand and stroking himself.

"Not until I'm inside you," Colt whispered. "The longer I make you wait, the better it'll be. Trust me, darling."

The air rushed from Rain's lungs as Colt's fingers pressed

against him, then inside him. It wasn't quite what he sought, but it was close enough. As Colt found his prostate and crooked his fingers to rub it with every slide of his fingers, even deeper pleasure radiated through Rain's whole body.

"Yes," Rain whimpered when Colt pulled his hand away. Now came his cock, right? He needed to be filled to bursting, rode hard and wet. And he needed Colt's voice in his ear the whole time, soothing him and telling him how beautiful he was.

Colt seemed to intuitively grasp his needs. No wonder they were perfect together. "I'm all ready for you, Rain," he whispered. "Relax and work with me."

The heat of Colt pushing past Rain's tight ring of muscle quickly turned to pleasure. Rain gasped and pressed up against Colt. In answer, Colt stretched out over him, his chest settling against Rain's back as he tucked his nose into Rain's neck.

"Gorgeous," Colt whispered into his ear, sliding deeper inside Rain with each small thrust. He was stretching Rain open, filling him up completely. "You fit me so perfectly."

"So... So do you," Rain barely managed, his voice raw. He was steadier now, each spike of pleasure giving him the energy to work with Colt. They moved as one, Rain pushing back while Colt thrust into him.

Before long, the bed squeaked with the force of Colt's thrusts. Rain's arms buckled, and he folded them on the bed, letting his forehead rest against them. And God, what a view that was.

Between his legs and behind him, Rain saw Colt's balls smacking his skin, a sharp, rhythmic sound that overlaid both of their moans and gasps. Closer still was his own shaft, dripping wet, red, and harder than he'd ever seen it. It bounced through the air with each thrust, maddeningly unsatisfied.

But Colt was right—the longer he waited, the more tension built under his skin. Muscles that Rain hadn't even been aware of were taut.

At last, Colt's hand slid up the inside of his thigh, and then his strong fingers wrapped around Rain's aching cock. With Colt inside him and all around him, Rain's world narrowed to just their bodies.

All that mattered in the world was the two of them.

Every jerk of rough fingers across smooth skin made Rain quiver, and he pressed back into Colt even harder with each thrust. He was ready to explode, and he wasn't entirely sure he could hold back a second longer.

"You can come for me now, baby," Colt whispered. "My gorgeous new boyfriend."

All Rain had left in him was one word: "Colt!"

The waves of pleasure that crashed over him swept his mind away, making him lose track of everything else. Time itself collapsed, Rain's heart hammering in his ears too fast to believe.

The only thing he was vaguely conscious of was Colt's throaty groan and stuttering thrusts as his new boyfriend came, too, and joined him in the heights of this all-consuming ecstatic joy.

Colt's thrusts slowed and stopped as Rain's knees gave way, and they flopped together onto the bed with Colt spooning Rain.

"Good?" Colt whispered, his lips gently pressing the top of Rain's shoulder. "Or goody?"

"Oh, my God," Rain moaned, too out of breath to even laugh. How could he describe the pleasure to Colt? "I've never... been fucked like that."

And he'd sure as hell never been held like this afterward,

Colt's fingertips smoothing down his skin like he was tucking Rain's composure back into place.

Colt chuckled softly. "Me neither. I love that you can take everything I dish out." His voice was tinged with awe. "And then you push me for more."

Rain chuckled and closed his eyes. He just hummed in response, exhaustion setting in.

When Colt pulled away, he gave a low whine of protest before letting him clean up. Still, Rain counted down the seconds until Colt pulled the blankets over them both and wrapped around him again.

"I'm here," Colt whispered, flicking off the light.

Rain couldn't miss the sharp inhale when the darkness fell, nor the way Colt's grip on him tightened. "Leave on the lamp."

"You sure?" Colt rubbed his arm. "Is it going to keep you awake?"

Rain laughed breathlessly. "Baby, nothing in the world could keep me awake." The pet name just felt right coming from his lips right now. No overthinking it, no second-guessing himself.

The light clicked on again, but Rain tucked his arm over his eyes and it was perfectly dark. With Colt's arm around him, he couldn't fail to find sleep anyway. It was impossible to feel stressed when every part of him was satiated for the first time in ways he'd never even dreamed of.

If only they could stretch this perfect moment forever— never get up, never let morning come.

"I'll get a nightlight" was the last thing Rain remembered murmuring into the darkness. He just registered Colt squeezing him in silent thanks before sleep took him.

18

COLT

No sooner had Colt stepped into the stockroom to slip on his apron than Yolanda excused herself from the register and followed him. Late morning on Saturday, it was quiet enough that she could get away for a minute.

She grabbed his hand and shook it, beaming at him. "Dude. Word's leaked. Congrats!"

Colt grinned at her. He'd privately handed in his resignation to Lindon this week, since he wasn't the kind of person who would just stop showing up to work. He'd expected word would get out fast, though. It always did. "Yep, I'm taking the plunge."

"When's your last day?"

"Depends," Colt said, shrugging. "Lindon said he'll try to hire someone ASAP. I agreed to stay up to two weeks. If he finds my replacement sooner, I'll go with his blessing and it'll make my life easier. Otherwise, I get a little extra money."

"That's amazing." Yolanda high-fived him and then held open the stockroom door. "Here's to your future."

The smile on Colt's lips died as soon as he stepped behind the counter.

Right there, sitting at the corner table, was a certain unmistakable figure. He was built like Rain, but he had graying hair, and his thinner lips were hitched into an ugly smile. He wore a crisply tailored white shirt and smart slacks.

His gaze—exactly the shade of Rain's—was locked on Colt. That alone told him who it was: Floyd Hart. Colt would bet his life on it. And it looked like he was about to bet his future, like it or not.

The man got to his feet, acting leisurely, and then stretched and checked his watch. Like he'd just won the game.

And he might well have.

Colt's heart had dropped through the floorboards. Yolanda was talking to him, but he didn't hear a word. All he could think was *Where's he going?*

"I'd better head off," Floyd said as he approached, looking Colt up and down like he was sizing him up. He slid his empty mug across the counter. "Hart's Bay is a long drive, and Rain's expecting me."

Colt was still frozen on the spot. The blood had drained from his cheeks, leaving sparkles pricking at the edges of his vision.

He hadn't expected to be discovered *now*. Not when everything was going so well—when he was working toward fixing his mistakes. No more running away for "business meetings" or telling little white lies that would build up into storm clouds.

Without another word, Floyd turned and headed for the door.

It had no sooner shut than Colt yelped, "Fuck."

Lindon didn't care what they did out of earshot of customers, but there were a few tables of customers in the coffee shop today. Swearing in uniform was a big no-no.

Not that Colt gave a shit about that right now. He could see the snare that he'd stepped into it. He'd been hoisted by the ankle, and here he was—helplessly dangling miles away from where he needed to be.

"Colt." Yolanda snapped her fingers in front of his face, her voice sharp. She was pissed at him. "Dude. What the hell?"

He let her drag him back to the stockroom, muttering an apology to the customers. He wasn't even sure the words were put together in the right order.

"I... that guy." Colt gulped, pinching the bridge of his nose.

"Yeah, he was asking after you." Yolanda folded her arms. "I said you were coming in later, and he said he'd stick around to see you. But he just up and left. What was that all about?"

"I..." Colt tried to swallow his hysterical laugh. He didn't even know where to begin to explain his screwup.

"Okay, Colt, you look like you're about to faint. Sit." Yolanda pushed him to the chair in the corner and made him do it when he didn't move quick enough.

"He's my boyfriend's grandfather, and he hates both of us."

"Is he a homophobe? Ugh. I would've given him decaf," she muttered, folding her arms.

"Worse. I... I'm not supposed to be here. Rain doesn't know I work here. He thinks... I let him believe..." Colt's thoughts were coming in disjointed waves. "I mean, I made them all think I have experience developing properties."

Yolanda drew a sharp breath. "What the hell?"

"I know." Colt buried his face in his hands and then

tangled his fingers in his hair. He was about ready to tear it out. He could hardly breathe around the knot in his throat. "Rain's gonna be pissed that I lied to him, and I meant to tell him, but we had such a good date last night and I didn't want to ruin it, and..."

"Okay, okay." Yolanda paced back and forth in front of him. "I can't believe I'm about to say this, but... take off and sort that shit out."

"What?" Colt looked up so fast he nearly gave himself whiplash. "But I'll leave you short-handed. On a Saturday."

Yolanda eyed him and then huffed. "I know. Call me a romantic. You can send a thank-you card from your honeymoon."

Colt tried for a laugh, but it came out a strangled noise. Last night, he'd dared to let himself dream about that possibility. Now? He wasn't sure Rain wouldn't shut the door on his face. "But Lindon... if he comes in..."

"You've already quit." Yolanda shrugged. "What else can he do? It's just a job. It's not life or death." She pointed toward the door. "If what you have with this Rain guy and your new business *is* a new life, it's worth more than a job. Right?"

Colt nodded dumbly. He couldn't argue the point. "I... yes." He'd do anything to save this relationship with Rain, new and more precious than anything he'd had before.

"Then scram." Yolanda narrowed her gaze at Colt, then pinched his arm hard.

Colt yelped, pushing himself to his feet and shaking her hand off. "What was that for?"

"Snap out of this and drive safely. You can't send me a thank-you card from beyond the grave. Or flowers. I like daisies."

It went against all of Colt's instincts, but he unknotted the apron he'd put on scarcely three minutes ago. "Thank you," he breathed out. He was thinking a little clearer now. He had one job: get to Hart's Bay before it was too late.

"Don't mention it. But remember the daisies," Yolanda called after him as he sprinted for the door.

Colt managed a laugh this time and waved as he pushed open the door and burst out onto the busy street. Hell, if this worked, he'd plant a whole field of them in Yolanda's name.

His gut instinct didn't like his chances, but he had to try. Facing the odds had never daunted him before. What he'd found in Rain wasn't worth giving up on so easily.

Colt's gaze was nearly fixed on the horizon, just waiting for the coast to come within sight.

He'd been driving like this for the past ten minutes, scarcely able to pay attention to the road ahead. The moment he reached the coast, he'd dial his boyfriend from the car and tell him to wait for him because he was only ten minutes away.

Colt needed to get there first and explain.

There it was—an expanse of blue stretching on beyond the curve of the road. "Gotcha," Colt whispered and punched at the touchscreen in the dashboard.

He found Rain's number and hit the call button, but the ringing that emitted from his car speakers ended in a voicemail message.

"Hello. This is Rainier Hart." He sounded so formal that it would have made Colt smile if not for the situation.

Colt hung up, then cursed under his breath. What was he going to do now?

Maybe he was at work. No, it was Saturday, and Colt

knew that Rain was off. He'd only managed to arrange a meeting with Finn and Roy on Sunday as a family favor. They were going to go over the materials lists and plans in person to get on the same page.

Then, his phone chirped with an incoming text from Rain. Colt swallowed and pressed the button for the car to read out the text.

Through the car speakers, his phone read out Rain's words mechanically. "Hi. Can't talk, I'm at Floyd's. Coming out officially today!"

Colt gave a strangled groan. Fuck, this was bad.

Coming out was supposed to be Rain's big moment. He'd been waiting all his life for this day, and Colt was about to ruin it. He didn't want to rain on his parade, but it was unavoidable now. Floyd had set the perfect trap.

He dictated his response with shaking hands.

"Hi," Colt said, his mind racing. How much should he say? "Can you wait for me? I'm nearly in town." He glanced at the dashboard to make sure it had taken down the message properly, then hit the send button and prayed.

No response. Even as he approached the outskirts of Hart's Bay, his phone didn't go off with any response.

Fuck, he was screwed. Either Floyd had already gotten to Rain or he'd muted his phone before going to Floyd's place. Either way, those few minutes had made all the difference.

It wasn't hard to find Floyd's house. It looked more grand than any other place along the least familiar of the roads leading out from Hart Square. Just as Rain had once said, it looked like an old stagecoach inn.

Now, ivy grew up the sides of the building and a small garden grew on each side of the building, while a semicircular drive led up to the house. A gorgeous place, but tainted by the knowledge of who lived here. The name plaque above the mailbox by the road was a clue, too: *F. Hart, III*.

Colt had no choice. He had to walk in and pray that Rain was here. Instinct told him that he was—Floyd had met Rain on his home turf last time, so it seemed likely he'd pull the same move today.

He pulled up in the driveway in front of the house and got out, locking the doors before he headed up the stairs.

The moment he knocked, the door opened, and there he was—Floyd.

"Ah. I thought I'd see you soon." Floyd's smile was still thin and unpleasant, like he was taking great pleasure in this.

"I don't believe we've met. Floyd, isn't it?" Colt reached out to shake hands, not returning the smile. "I'm here to see Rain."

"Correct." Floyd looked down at the offered hand and sneered, then sidestepped to let him in. "We're having an informative conversation. I'm sure the subject of conversation would interest you."

That's the most polite way of saying "I know you two are gay" that I've ever heard, Colt thought. He forced a smile, even if he wanted to sucker punch Floyd for all the pain he'd caused them.

The moment Rain saw him, Colt's heart lifted for half a second. The way Rain rose to his feet, surprise and delight written over his face, told him that Floyd hadn't yet said a word about Colt's second life.

"Colt!" Rain greeted and patted the couch next to him. "Great timing."

But then he realized that he was going to have to watch Rain find out, and Colt's world crashed down.

"Yes," Floyd spoke up from behind him. "It is."

The triumph in his voice made Rain pause, his gaze wary as it flicked to Floyd. It followed Floyd as he walked to a high-backed chair on the other side of the room, his steps crisp and unhurried.

"What's going on?" Rain asked. He looked at Colt, his brows furrowed, like he needed comfort. And all Colt wanted to do was wrap his arms around him and steer him right out of that living room.

Colt took Rain's hand, casting him a quick look to see if that was okay. He was desperate to explain, even if he didn't know the right words to do so. *Don't listen to him*, he wanted to say. *I can explain later*. He squeezed hard, taking a tiny measure of comfort that Rain wasn't letting go. Yet.

"Yes," Floyd said, reaching his chair. He turned and sat in it, his hands folded in his lap. "Since you're not going to tell him what's going on, I will."

Colt's tongue felt thick in his mouth. He could hardly breathe. This was only the second time he'd met the man, and a chill of fear already crept down his spine at the cold way he watched them.

No wonder Rain had been so desperate for a way out that he was willing to go into business with a near stranger.

Colt closed his eyes for a few seconds and breathed out, trying to find the words. "Rain, I didn't tell you everything."

"It's all going to come out." Floyd's voice dripped with gloating glee. "Now, when your parents and I discussed your choice of business partner, I raised my concerns."

"Oh, for—" Rain started, exasperation in his tone.

"Allow me to finish." Floyd smirked. "Then you can use all the vulgar language you please."

"Yes, we're dating!" Rain burst out, cutting Floyd off. "So what? You've known I'm gay for years."

Colt sucked in a quick breath. It was all about to hit the fan.

"But do you know your boyfriend? Really?" Floyd pressed, leaning forward. He grinned. "Because I don't think you do."

"I don't need to. I already told you: Colt's the best man I've ever met," Rain said, his grip nearly crushing Colt's.

"And the best barista?" Floyd asked.

Rain blinked a few times and looked over at Colt. "Best... what?"

"Because you're not dating a property developer. Did he tell you that was what he was? His company was registered a month ago. His name doesn't appear on any property records in the whole state. And I happened to find myself in a grubby little independent coffee shop in downtown Portland this morning," Floyd pressed. "And who was behind the counter but Colt?"

Colt's eyes stung. He couldn't deny any of it.

Worse still, Rain went rigid, his grip on Colt's hand loosening a degree at a time. He looked over at Colt, as if seeking confirmation.

Colt nodded slightly, pressing his lips together. He'd give anything to be having this conversation anywhere else but in front of Rain's grandfather.

Sick bastard.

Rain pulled his hand free from Colt's and stood up. "Is this true? Why?"

"I'd guess he's a confidence man," Floyd pressed, his grin turning ugly again. "He saw a young, vulnerable target in you. He needed your confidence, and he probably spun stories to make you trust his track record. Who knows how many other people he's swindled? Or if this is his first attempt, somewhere he thought people would be gullible enough to fall for it?"

"Now, hold on," Colt burst out, his own temper flaring as he stood up. "I'm not scamming *anyone* here. I'm not even getting money from anyone. *I'm* the one funding the construction. And no, I don't know much, but I'm learning as I go. And... yes, I needed people's confidence, but only so we could get the ball rolling."

Rain drew away from him, and Colt couldn't look at his face. Couldn't see the hurt there. He was too focused on Floyd. He couldn't let the man get between them any more than he had. "You picked up your business experience a day at a time, too. Stop trying to punch holes in what we have."

Floyd raised an eyebrow. "I don't need to. Seems to me your ship is already sinking if you can't be honest to your own... *boyfriend*," he said with air quotes.

"What a dick," Colt scoffed. The man was never going to listen. All he cared about was hurting Rain, and to him, Colt was a tool to do the job. Instead, he gathered his courage to face his boyfriend. "Rain..."

But the hurt he saw in Rain's face made his throat close. And he knew he'd earned it, but *fuck*, it still hurt.

"So you'd better choose, Rain," Floyd said, his voice still smooth and unruffled. "Run away with another self-serving windbag—don't think I don't know about Desmond, boy—or stick with the people who want the best for you."

"Fuck you!" Rain snapped, lunging a step toward Floyd to snarl at his grandfather. Even under that fierce gaze, Floyd didn't flinch. Then, Rain turned to Colt and shook his head.

He didn't need to repeat the words: Colt could see them written over his face, and worse yet, disappointment.

"Fuck you all," Rain whispered, his voice cracking. He spun on his heel and rushed for the door.

Colt left Floyd behind to gloat over his victory and focused on the one thing that mattered right now. "Rain!"

"Don't," Rain snapped. "I don't want to hear anything." He didn't slow down, but Colt followed, hot on his heels, right out the front door. When they reached the front steps, Rain broke into a run.

"Rain!" he tried again, but his boyfriend didn't even acknowledge him, so Colt stumbled to a halt and watched his retreating back.

Shit. Colt had just fucked up the one good thing he had going in his life. And he had to get to Rain and explain. Or… apologize, at least.

But Rain didn't want to hear it, and it would only serve his own ego to try to force him to talk.

Colt's hands shook as he started up the stupid, expensive car he should never have wasted his money on. He'd drive it back to the dealer, trade in his fancy suit for jeans, and invite Rain to his coffee shop on the spot if he thought it would fix anything.

But it wouldn't, unless Rain was willing to give Colt a second chance that he didn't deserve.

There was no way Colt wanted to drive all the way back home when they had a construction meeting tomorrow. Or did they? God knew what would happen now.

All Colt could do was drive to the hotel a few miles outside town, on the edge of the highway, and numbly stumble into reception to ask for a room.

When he got in and shut the door, he didn't turn on the light. It felt like more than he deserved. Any light, at the end of the tunnel or on the horizon, was too much for him.

Colt just shrugged off his stupid coffee shop outfit—

comfortable shoes and white shirt and all—and crawled under the covers. He curled up, pulled them over his head, and cradled his phone by his cheek so he wouldn't miss a single alert.

All night long, it didn't make a sound.

19

RAIN

The phone rang before Rain was really awake. His eyes hurt, his throat hurt, and his pillow was still faintly damp.

He'd cried himself into numbness last night, until sleep had finally come for him. It couldn't have been more different from the night before, when he'd thought he'd found it all in Colt's arms.

Now he had no idea if it had all been a mirage or if Colt was as innocent as Rain wanted to believe. He hadn't wanted to hear more last night—hadn't wanted excuses and apologies and more bullshit lies.

But the call was from Finn.

"Hello?" Rain mumbled, rubbing his eyes. God only knew what time it was. It felt like noon, but it was probably still morning. He had no idea when he'd gotten to sleep.

"Hey, Rain." Finn's voice was soft, careful. Like he was worried. "How you holding up?"

"Um..." Rain searched his memory to see if anyone else had overheard last night's meeting. Surely not, though. "I'm pretty shitty, actually. Why?"

Finn hesitated. "Well, there's today's newsletter…"

It took a moment for Rain to realize what he meant. Scott, a retired journalist, ran the Hart's Bay town newsletter. He emailed it to everyone in town on Sunday mornings, and he often prided himself on scoops that wouldn't interest anyone outside the town.

Like finding out that Colt wasn't who he said he was.

"Maybe you should read it, then give me a call?" Finn encouraged.

"Fuck," Rain groaned. "Okay. Talk to you soon."

He switched from his phone to the email app when Finn hung up, then opened the beautifully formatted, three-page PDF.

There it was. The headline on the middle of the front page.

WHISTLE BLOWN ON HARBORFRONT DEVELOPMENT

Rain gave a strangled groan and rubbed his eyes, sitting up in bed to read the article underneath.

It was a short piece from an anonymous letter writer—obviously Floyd. In it, he said the same kind of shit as last night, except with less virulent homophobia.

The piece ended on another gut punch.

Colt Fuller, in other words, is a fraud. Why Hart's Bay city hall saw fit to approve this application I can't say, but my conscience compels me to speak out about this wolf among the sheep. Scammers are not welcome in this town, and never will be. Signed—anonymous.

Just like it was last night all over again, the same sensations rushed back to Rain. He felt sick, his heart pounded, his hands shook.

Had he been so badly deceived as Floyd was making out? Or was Floyd exaggerating to make Colt out to be the enemy?

There was only one way to find out, and Rain both needed and dreaded it.

Rain sent Finn a quick text: *The meeting's still on. We'll discuss it there.* He didn't know whether he'd be alone, or if he'd have his partner by his side.

Even thinking the word hurt—partner. Whether in the business or personal sense, that word implied that they were honest about everything with each other. Colt hadn't been, and Rain needed to know why.

His finger trembled as it hovered over the call button, Colt's name on his screen.

A small piece of Rain was afraid to make the call in case Colt never picked up. In case he just upped and left town, confirming all his worst fears.

But Rain didn't think Colt was capable of that. Things didn't add up, but Colt's sincerity had shone through in so many little moments—the kind Floyd would never see or appreciate.

He hit the button.

One ring later, sounding as bleary as Rain had felt until a few short minutes ago, Colt answered. "Hello?"

That much, at least, made Rain's nerves settle with relief, although a whole new kind of nervousness struck now. "Hi. It's... it's me."

"Rain," Colt breathed out, and the name had never sounded so sacred than when he uttered it. The single syllable instantly conjured up memories from Friday night—memories that hurt right now.

"I need to meet you," Rain said, trying to keep his voice businesslike. He didn't want to whine, or scream, or cry on the phone. He had plenty of chance to do that later. "Hart Square. How long will it take you to get there?"

"Fifteen minutes," Colt answered.

What? That meant he couldn't be in Portland. Rain paused for a moment, surprised. "Where are you?"

"The hotel by the highway." Colt groaned, sheets whispering and springs creaking in the background. "I think they cut costs by using plywood for mattresses."

The observation made Rain smile for a moment—just a brief moment of blissful ignorance, where he forgot the chasm looming between them. Then reality crashed in again, and he drew in a quick breath.

Even a day later, the sting hadn't faded. Rain could think straight and listen now, but he was still disoriented. His world had crashed out from under his feet.

Rain had to get answers—had to get this out of the way. And he wasn't sure if he looked forward to it or dreaded it more than anything in his life.

Fifteen minutes felt like a lifetime.

The moment the broad-shouldered man climbed out of his shiny car, Rain's heart twisted all over again. If he'd thought it was bad reading that news article, it was nothing compared to the sight of his face.

Colt walked differently—urgently, head bowed, like he was sheltering from some unseen gale. His clothes were the same rumpled ones he'd been in yesterday, and now Rain could see the distinctly service worker look to them.

That explained the smell of coffee that was always lingering around Colt, too. And his rush to get back to Portland sometimes. And his odd schedule of work in the city. They weren't meetings at all—they were shifts.

Everything had made sense the moment Floyd pointed it out, and Rain hated more than anything that Floyd had been the one to do so.

Colt slowed as he approached Rain, looking up at him. The trepidation on his face was easy to read.

"I don't know what the truth is right now," Rain greeted Colt, moving over to one side of the bench.

Colt sat on the other side, just about as far away from him as he could, but turned his body to face Rain. "I want to come out with all of it."

"I don't know if I want to hear it," Rain confessed. His throat hurt again, and his eyes stung like he was about to cry. *Fuck, no*, he told himself. *Enough crying for one lifetime.*

"Okay," Colt said, his voice a shadow of what it normally was. "What do you want?"

"Before you explain, I just... I want a promise that our contract is still solid." It took all Rain had not to lose his self-control. It hovered on a razor's edge right now, tears on one side and fury on the other.

"Our... contract," Colt repeated, sounding as numb as Rain wished he felt.

Rain chose the side of anger. "Yeah. The contract you signed, where you'll be funding the construction costs. Does that money exist?"

"Yes," Colt answered quickly, urgently. He twisted his hands together. "That's why I was working... yes."

Barista work would never pay for a commercial building. But Rain could see truth in Colt's eyes, and those two facts collided.

Now he needed the truth. He couldn't go a lifetime

without these questions being answered, and if he didn't ask now... he might never find out.

"So you're going to follow through?" Rain asked first, trying to forestall the inevitable.

"Yes," Colt said. His lips hardly moved until he licked them, then bit the lower one. "I know it's too late to say, but... I've quit the other job already. Walked out yesterday. I'm all in on this. It might be my first time, but I'm going to do it right, for both of us."

Us. Another word that hurt right now.

Rain flinched, taking a breath to let that sting pass before he answered. "Okay."

"And... I can't ask for forgiveness, but I need to apologize anyway." Colt's tone was deadly serious. "Floyd was right: I endangered us both by entering a contract in bad faith. It's illegal, and it's a shitty thing to do, and I never should have done it. I should have come clean from the start. I wish to God I had."

Colt's voice cracked on the last sentence, and he looked away quickly toward the art gallery, swiping at his eyes with the back of his hand.

Rain had never seen him like this. Fearful, boastful, joyful —but never devastated. Nobody could tell him that Colt wasn't being honest with him right now.

"Okay," Rain said. His voice barely carried far enough for Colt to hear. "What are you going to do about it?"

"The best thing I can do is stick around and fulfill my end of the deal. Show some integrity after all," Colt murmured. "I'm afraid—I'm really, really scared—that I've screwed up the best thing I ever found. It'll break my heart if I have to lose you. But I owe you the best I can do, and that's what I'm going to give you. If you want me to."

Tears trickled down Rain's nose now. He swiped them away, half-angry with himself for it. "I thought I knew you."

"And you do. I just... let you believe I'm more of a big deal than I am." Colt gave him a small, sad smile. "But I've never lied about who I am on the inside. I hoped that'd be enough. It was stupid of me to think so."

That much was true. Rain had already seen that he was a hard worker, curious, fiercely protective, and a dozen other traits. Hell, secretly working a second job proved how hard he worked.

"I know why you did it. You wanted me to be confident in you. It was still dumb... and unnecessary." That was what stung most of all—that none of it *had* to have happened. He could have been up-front, and Rain would have worked with him.

Colt nodded slightly, biting his lip again. "I guess that does make me a confidence man. But I didn't want to steal anything from you. I wanted to build us both up."

Rain shook his head. "But why didn't you tell me about the coffee shop thing?" It seemed like such a silly thing to lie about.

"I was afraid." Colt's voice was thick with emotion again. "At first, I was afraid that I'm never going to amount to anything. And then I got to know you, and I was even more afraid. That if you knew who I really was, you wouldn't love me."

He looked up at last, and those dark eyes caught Rain's gaze and held it. Just like they had the very first time they'd met. And every time since then. Even in Rain's dreams.

"Bullshit," Rain whispered. "I'd respect you even more. All this time I thought you were spoiled and flighty, taking off to Portland for meetings and driving out here on a whim. But retail and service work is fucking hard work, whatever my family says about it. If you'd just told me..." He trailed off.

"Are you afraid there's other stuff I haven't told you?" Colt folded his hands in his lap, fidgeting with his fingers.

Rain nodded. His tears had dried up now, at least.

"Well, I can't think of anything. That was it," Colt murmured. "The big, bad secret: I'm not that big a deal. I'm nobody, really."

Anger flared in Rain's chest. "Don't say that," he snapped. "Don't you dare."

Colt blinked at him, surprised but clueless. "What?"

Didn't he have any idea how he sounded? How much Rain wanted to knock it into his head? "This is the exact problem," Rain told him, the ferocity in his voice surprising even him. "You're acting like you're not good enough the way you are. And I didn't fall for that rich property developer who swaggers into town and puts it down. I fell for the man you showed me glimpses of underneath that mask."

Colt opened his mouth for a few moments, seemingly dumbfounded, and then closed it again. "Oh."

"And that man," Rain carried on, wiping his eyes, "isn't a nobody. I'm smarter than to fall for a nobody who's going nowhere in life. And you're not that, whatever you say. So don't insult us both."

Colt was just staring at him. "Sorry," he said after a few long moments had passed. "I didn't think you were falling for the real me."

"Why not?" Rain fought back his anger until he had a lid on it. He'd done enough boiling over lately. It was time to listen and try to understand. "Why didn't you think I saw you under all that crap?"

Colt's eyes widened for a few long moments. Then, he

cleared his throat and looked down. "It's gonna sound like a shitty excuse, but... I learned long ago to be the person I thought other people wanted me to be. I was always afraid that the minute I let someone in, I'd be shuffled along. Given up to a new family who would try to pry me open again, unpick me like I'm some mystery object. Go over my fucking *life story book.*"

Rain frowned and shook his head slightly, showing he didn't know what Colt meant.

"It's..." Colt breathed out a quick laugh. "It's a scrapbook you make in foster care, to show your new family who you are. You lug it around with you and hope you're writing the right things to make them take in an angry, stubborn teen instead of the cute little baby they wanted."

The air left Rain's lungs in a quick rush. Finally, he scooted closer and laid a hand over Colt's. "I'm sorry." He couldn't believe he hadn't made that connection before.

"No," Colt said quickly. "We're all responsible for dealing with our childhood shit. And I didn't, and then I went and hurt you by building our relationship on half-truths. That was shitty to you."

"It was," Rain agreed. "But I believe you. And I believe *in* you. You've shown me who you are, and every time you do it, I've fallen a little more for you. We have to stand together and make this work."

Colt blinked at him, his jaw dropping. "You mean... you're giving me another chance?" The fear and hope mingled in his voice unpicked the last of Rain's reservations.

This meant everything to Colt. It was plainly written across his face in the urgent way he stared at Rain, the way he slowly laid his other hand on the back of Rain's like he expected Rain to pull away from him again.

"Yes," Rain murmured. "You can show me you're going to stick around and fulfill your end of the deal, and then we'll see about dating. I'll give you a clean start as long as you face your fears and show me yourself, not who you think I want. Because it's that man I've fallen in love with."

The word hung between them, and Rain didn't move to take it back. If he knew nothing else, he knew it was true.

That was why the last day had hurt so much—he'd let Colt into his heart like no one before, and he'd been just as afraid of losing him as he was of finding out he was another people user like Desmond. Someone who trapped Rain into needing him and then exploited that fact.

And why the hell had he trusted Floyd's word on that, of all people? He had to make up his own damn mind from now on, or he'd never be free of people like that.

Colt, though? He trusted his word about the contract, and that he wasn't hiding any more secrets. Rain just didn't know where this left them as far as dating—and he wasn't sure if he could think through it just yet.

"I love you, too," Colt whispered, like he was afraid to hear the words out loud. "And I didn't think you'd give me this chance."

"Me, neither," Rain murmured with a frank little smile. "Good thing you're so damn cute."

A little laugh bubbled from Colt. He scooted closer to Rain, and when he put his arm around him, Rain leaned into him and closed his eyes.

He still smelled faintly like coffee.

"So you've been holding out on me with your coffee-making skills," Rain murmured. "You need to stay over and make more breakfasts."

Colt chuckled softly. "Sorry. I can't even claim that skill, if

I'm being honest. All I do is bus tables and man the register. They barely let me steam the milk. I'm a terrible barista. I don't have a future in coffee. Scrambled eggs, I can do."

"We'll stick with property development, then," Rain murmured. "And scrambled eggs."

Long minutes passed as Colt held Rain close, and Rain rested his head on his shoulder. Maybe they could make this work. Just maybe. They still had so much to talk about, but they'd filled the cracks in the foundation. Or at least, they were starting to.

Voices made them finally pull apart, and it took Rain a few moments to get his composure back.

Uncle Roy and Finn were walking up to greet them.

Right. The meeting.

They pulled apart and stood up, walking to the edge of the square to meet Rain's family members.

"Afternoon," Finn greeted, his tone distinctly chilly. His gaze flicked between Rain and Colt.

"Hello," Colt said. "Let's get this out of the way: I know you've heard rumors, and some of them are true. If you have questions, I'll answer them."

"Is the budget there?" Roy asked, tipping his chin back to look Colt up and down. "That's all I need to know. Budget and willpower."

"Yes," Colt promised. "I've made mistakes, but I genuinely want to make this project work for everyone. I don't want to hurt more people than I already have, and I was never in it to do a cheap, quick, bad job and run with the money." He spoke passionately, emotion creeping into his voice.

Before now, Colt's real feelings had been shielded, like a smooth-talking salesman who really wanted to close the deal. But now, Rain could hear the commitment in his voice.

Finn looked startled as he glanced between them. "And you're good with this?" he asked Rain. Roy held his breath as he waited for the response, too.

Rain couldn't help the smile that crept over his lips as he glanced sideways at his boyfriend. "More than good. Goody, even."

Finn gave him a puzzled look, but Colt cracked up. And that sound meant everything to Rain.

The air thawed as they walked to the warehouse. The connection between them was stronger again, even if it was fragile. At least it was something, and they could build on it.

Floyd had gotten to him last night by making him feel like this was Desmond all over again. He'd tried to find his freedom by running away with Desmond, and that hadn't worked. Then, he'd trusted Colt enough to go into business with him. He needed Colt to help find his freedom from his family. The idea that Colt might be exploiting that had ripped him apart.

But it was nothing like that, and Rain was pissed at himself for letting Floyd find that gap in his armor.

But Rain hadn't been chosen by Colt. They had chosen each other. And damn it, Rain was going to keep choosing Colt, over and over again.

Floyd's only weapon was fear. Maybe Colt had acted in fear, too, but Rain had a weapon stronger than any of Floyd's words: love. And Rain was going to act with love, the one thing Floyd had never succeeded in. That and sheer, stubborn force of will would win the day.

With Colt by his side again, their future in sight, Rain's spirits lifted. More than love, he'd found the one thing he'd never even thought to look for in this town: family. Finn and Roy's concern for him had been unmistakable.

Maybe he wasn't losing anything that wasn't worth losing.

And he was gaining a hell of a lot more in return—if he was willing to fight for it.

"Look! It's Lucy. We should say hi," Colt said to Finn while Rain walked behind them. "I'm gonna stop by the store and get fish. I think I'm supposed to bribe her."

"We can grab something on the way out," Finn agreed. He glanced back at Rain and smiled. "If Lucy likes him, we can keep him."

But his tone said more than that: it said that Finn considered Rain part of the *we*. A smile touched Rain's lips and then spread until his cheeks hurt.

Yeah, he had a family on his side after all. *Bring it, Grandpa.*

20

COLT

The light at the end of the tunnel was switched on at last. Problem was, it was a lot more expensive than Colt had expected.

He'd held it together while they talked about minutiae he didn't really understand—timelines, subcontractors, that kind of stuff—but the sticker shock was still sinking in.

Renovation was going to be expensive, and Roy had taken great care to warn him that building was almost always more expensive than planned. Plus, the units might not rent out immediately.

And Colt couldn't help but remember that he'd just quit his job. Lindon had texted him to tell him not to bother coming back in, that he'd found a replacement anyway. Which meant that continuing to pay Portland rent while working out here was just downright dumb.

And that left him with one solution.

"I'm gonna drop in and get some fish for Lucy," he told the others once they were finally done in the warehouse. Along the way, he planned to talk to the grocery store owner, Victor, about the apartment.

Colt walked into the little grocery store and immediately felt like someone was glaring at him. It didn't take long to find the source: Victor was behind one of the two checkouts, sitting on a stool with a newspaper open on his lap. The glare he aimed at Colt wasn't subtle.

In his buoyant mood of relief, Colt had forgotten that the rest of the town still didn't know the truth. Finn had brought up the town newsletter and shown him a copy of the "anonymous" letter.

It was nearly enough to make his confidence falter, but Colt took heart: if not physically by his side, Rain was with him.

He took a deep breath and walked up to the counter. "I'm looking for two things: a fish and an apartment."

The paper rustled as Victor closed it, his brow furrowed. "A fish... and an apartment?"

"Dead fish," Colt clarified. "For Lucy." He reached the counter and braced his hands on it. "And an apartment for me to live in."

There was no better way to prove that he was really invested in this town. If Floyd thought he'd come here, do a shitty job, and run away with the profits, he had another think coming.

"Hmm. The fish is easy." Victor pointed him toward the fridge along one wall. "The apartment, not so much."

"Let's start with the fish, then." Colt headed over to that wall, pulling open the fridge. He took the first plastic-wrapped bundle he could find, but when he turned around, Victor was there.

"No, not that kind. She likes ground fish more." Victor

pointed out another one, so Colt swapped his choice of fish. "Why do you want an apartment?"

"Because I'm working with Rain to renovate the warehouse by the harbor. It'll be a lot easier to supervise construction from here." That was the easy, pat, confident answer, so Colt reached a little deeper for the vulnerable one. "And I feel like people should know I'm invested in all of this."

"In the project, or in Rain?" The man's gaze was surprisingly perceptive.

Colt gulped, his hold on the plastic-wrapped bundle tightening. "Both. And in Hart's Bay itself."

"Good answer." Victor jerked his head toward the register and led him back, ringing him up. "Ask Cher. I left the applications with her in case she found someone. Drop it off here before closing time if you're really interested."

"Yes, sir." Colt smiled as he handed over a bill, then waited for his change. "Thanks very much."

"You're welcome. And... word of advice?"

Colt nearly held his breath as he turned on his heel to look at Victor again. "Yes?"

"When the mountain's out, don't take it for granted."

Colt blinked several times. He was pretty sure that kind of advice belonged on a scroll at the beginning of a computer game quest, but he also got the feeling he was supposed to understand it.

"Yes, sir. Thank you." Colt turned and left the store, still stunned as he made his way down to the dock.

As Colt approached, he slowed. Rain was talking seriously to the others, and he didn't feel like it was a conversation he should intrude upon.

"...didn't realize all this time?"

"We can't help who raised us," Roy said, his hand on Rain's shoulder.

Oh, shit. After all the chaos of the last day, Rain's coming-out had almost been a whisper in the wind when it should have been a big moment for him.

Colt wanted to slide his arm around Rain and ask how he could help, but the sideways glance the others gave him told him that this was a family conversation. And Colt wasn't quite confident that he was back in the family's good graces.

Not just yet.

"I'll leave this with you and go talk to Cher about an application for Victor's apartment," Colt said, his eyes lingering on Rain. His voice ticked up at the end of the sentence, silently questioning if Rain wanted him here. If he saw a hint that Rain wanted him to stay, he would.

But Rain just nodded once and looked back at Roy—a clear dismissal.

Colt couldn't pretend it didn't sting. But he also knew he damn well deserved much worse than that, so he swallowed it and headed for Cher's End Table once more.

He'd found the answers there before to questions he'd never known he had in his life. All he could hope was that this would hold true one more time.

Colt paused by the window of the art gallery for a look inside. He couldn't quite tell what compelled him to walk in, but he was following his instinct these days, so he did it.

"Hello—oh, hi." It was Ezra, the redheaded artist. He spun on the stool to face Colt, his long, straight hair flying out, and then came out from behind the counter. "How's it going?"

He was so warm and friendly that it made Colt stop in his tracks. Had he not read the newsletter? Or did he not care?

Ezra must have read the confusion on his face, because he

smiled softly. "There's an awful lot of half-truths out there. I choose not to believe them when there seems to be an agenda at work. And I could be wrong, but it seems like a very familiar agenda to me."

Colt let out a breath he hadn't even noticed himself holding, his shoulders sinking. "Yeah. It's still half-true, that's the problem." He wandered along the walls of the gallery, scanning the jewelry hanging on smaller racks, pottery on shelves, and art and photos on the walls.

"Are you looking for something to make things better?"

Colt nodded. He wasn't sure what, exactly, but he wanted to give Rain something to make him see that he was serious about fixing things between them.

"For a special someone?" Ezra came up behind him and gave him a knowing smile when he glanced around.

"Yeah."

"I think I have an idea." Ezra gently steered Colt by the elbow to the back wall, then gestured up.

Instantly, Colt saw what he meant, and a smile spread across his face. It was perfect. All he could do was hope Rain would take it the right way.

"Yeah. I'll buy it. But can I leave it here while I head to Cher's? I think I have to talk to him first."

"Sure thing." Ezra winked as they headed to the desk so he could pay. "I'll wrap it up for you and put it aside."

Colt smiled at Ezra and took his change. "Thanks."

"My pleasure. Good luck with everything." Ezra winked, humming to himself as Colt saw himself out of the gallery.

On the way out the door, Colt kept puzzling over Victor's words. It felt like he was just unpicking the meaning, but what he really needed was a friendly ear to help him out. Or, if not friendly, at least cheerful and bluntly honest.

And he knew just where to find that.

———

"So that's where we are now." Colt perched on a stool at the end of the bar, trying not to let the guilt and embarrassment overwhelm him once more. "What the hell do I do?"

Cher hummed under her breath as she wiped down glasses. "You know you've been an idiot."

"God, yeah," Colt said, sighing into his beer. He kept looking toward the door anytime it opened, part of him hoping it was Rain, but the other part afraid of the conversation they had yet to finish.

Cher nodded. "Good. You won't be an idiot again, then. You're not the type of guy to run into the same wall twice. You can keep tipping me outrageously if you want, though." She winked.

Colt managed a little smile. "I'll see what I can do. But what do I do about Rain? And what the hell did Victor mean?"

"Well, I'll tell you one thing for free: up in Seattle, they say *the mountain's out* when it's not too cloudy and you can see Mount Rainier."

Oh. Like that, it clicked into place, and Colt's cheeks flushed. "Of course."

Rain had come out for Colt. Or maybe Victor meant that Rain was letting Colt close and trusting him. Either way, he wouldn't take him for granted, if he was lucky enough to win his way back into Rain's good graces.

"And if you want to make it up to him, you don't let him push you away," Cher said with a shrug. "Easy as that. Own up to what you did. Go talk to him. Tell him what he means to you, and let him decide if he's ready to give you a chance."

Colt nodded. It sounded easier than it would be, he knew. "I started to, before. He said he'd give me another chance business-wise, but we never really agreed if we're dating again. It felt like we might be, but..." He trailed off. They hadn't really had a chance to hash it out yet.

He hadn't told her everything—like the fact they'd slept together a few nights ago, for instance—but he didn't have to. She'd seen enough of them in the bar together, and she knew Rain.

"What's the worst that can happen if you ask him to trust you again?"

"I let him down," Colt murmured, his heart twisting at the thought. "I do something dumb, or overspend on the budget, and somehow the project gets torpedoed..."

"No," Cher said, setting down the glass and tossing the towel across her shoulder. "The worst that happens is that you never get the courage to clear the air and you throw away something that could have been perfect. And then you have to watch him become someone else—hardened, hurt inside. And you know there's no going back to the man he used to be. All because someone messed with his heart and he never quite learned how to deal with it."

A shiver ran down Colt's spine at the serious note in her voice. He didn't know what to do or say.

Cher broke the stillness between them by nodding at the door. "The future's here."

Colt turned on his stool so fast he nearly slid right off it, and Cher snorted from nearby. Rain stood there in the doorway, by himself, his gaze searching the crowd.

He wants to see me.

And that fact alone made Colt's hopes rise. He stood more gracefully and waved Rain over.

Rain took the stool next to him and smiled. "Hey."

There was still a cautious note to his voice, but it wasn't the heartbroken, fearful tone he'd taken this morning. Colt would take the progress.

"Hi," he answered softly. "Did you get everything said to your family that you needed to?"

Rain looked startled for a long moment before a smile drew across his face. "My family," he repeated. His scoff wasn't meant in a bad way—more of an incredulous way, like he still had trouble believing it. "Yeah."

Colt's hopes lifted. "They're on your side, aren't they?"

"Yeah." Rain straightened up a little. "I guess I can start calling them that now. It's just strange."

"We choose our family," Cher said from behind the counter. Then, she pointedly looked at Colt before heading for the dishwasher.

Yeah. It's time for me to act on that choice, Colt thought.

He licked his lips and looked over at Rain, reaching out to take his hand. "Can I be honest with you?" As scary as it was, he didn't think he had much of a choice.

Rain's gaze flickered with surprise before he nodded. "Of course."

"Like I told you earlier, I'm in love with you," Colt said. He couldn't stop his voice wavering in those first few words. "I've never been in love before. I was stupid, and carrying old scars, and I let those affect how I treated you. It wasn't just that I needed you to trust me. I didn't think I deserved to be loved. And I would have stuck around by your side in whatever you were saying to your family, but... I felt like I didn't belong there."

Rain squeezed his hand tightly, but Colt wasn't done yet.

"I'm sorry. I'd do anything to save this between us. You're

the best man I've ever met, too. I wouldn't care if I lost every dollar I put into this project with you—though I'd try to make sure you came out ahead. Because you're worth more than all the money in the goddamn world."

That was it—the most words Colt could get out without choking up.

But it was all the words he needed, because Rain eased himself off his stool, took his other hand, and leaned in to kiss his forehead.

Then, as Colt looked up and met his gaze, Rain kissed him on the lips.

It was a gentle kiss, but not one of friendship. Not a chance. Not with the spark that still passed between them as Rain's warm breath ghosted across Colt's lips.

"If you'd rather wait and see, then that's okay," Colt murmured softly. "I plan to back up my words with actions. But I want you to know up front that I'm going to fight to keep you. I don't want this to just be business. I want to keep dating you."

Rain swayed slightly where he stood, and then he drew a deep breath. "I know. And I'm ready to forgive you. I want us to date, too. I know who the real enemy is, and it was never you. So let's call this our first fight and declare it over."

The relief that hit Colt felt like a wave had broken across his body. "Yes," he murmured and squeezed Rain's hands. "Let's do that."

Colt had never once expected vulnerability to be the answer, but it was right there all along.

And no matter who knew about that vulnerability—and wanted to exploit it for their own ends—embracing it still made Colt a stronger person than he'd ever been before.

21

RAIN

Rain had looked in the bottoms of plenty of glasses for courage in his life. Never before had he actually found it. He suspected that was down to the man at his side, not the drink in his hand.

Or maybe it was just being really, *really* done with this shit.

"I'll be right back," Rain said, a drink later. He slid his phone out of his pocket. "There's something I have to do."

Colt gave him a worried look. "Can I help?"

"No, thanks." Rain smiled and leaned in to kiss Colt's cheek. "Just hug me afterward."

"I can do that," Colt promised. He rubbed Rain's lower back before letting him go.

Rain strode for the door, drawing a breath when he was outside in the peace and quiet. He chose a plastic chair at one of the tables scattered outside the bar and dropped into it.

Then, he dialed his parents before he could second-guess himself. He breathed deeply, his gaze wandering toward the grocery store and art gallery. The latter was closing for the day, judging by the lights flickering off and the guys spilling from it.

One of them spotted him and waved, but he was too distracted to wave back.

"Rainier," his dad greeted, his tone solemn.

On instinct, his heart jolted before he caught himself. *No. He can't tell me off anymore. I'm a strong and independent adult*, he thought and braced himself.

"Dad, hello. Can you put the phone on speaker so Mom can hear?" No point in beating around the bush. He had no idea what Floyd had already told them, but they were probably expecting a coming-out phone call, complete with tearful confession and apology.

They were in for a surprise.

The line crackled. "Hello, Rainier." His mom sounded just as crisp, but this time, he was ready for it.

"Hi," Rain greeted them both. "So I'd talk to you in person, but I don't think you'd agree to meet me right now."

"After that stunt you pulled, I don't think so, either," his dad told him.

He ignored the jab. More importantly, if he did meet them, he'd be on the back foot. It would be in their living room, or on Floyd's footstool like he was a damn toddler.

Here, he was safe among his own family.

Ezra, Beau, Aaron, Ross, and Jesse were all heading toward him, the five of them chatting and laughing among themselves. They quieted down when they approached close enough to see he was on the phone.

"Sorry," Jesse whispered.

Rain waved them past while nodding in greeting. He'd have plenty of time to catch up later. "I have something to tell you guys," he said into the phone once the door had closed behind the group.

"Yes?" They didn't sound surprised. Wary, more like. And

he wasn't going to fall into whatever trap they'd devised for him—the lecture they'd no doubt prepared.

Instead, he cut to the heart of it.

"When Dad, Grandpa, Roy, and Joseph split the business and the family. It wasn't about the fishery collapsing, was it?"

There was silence on the other end of the line.

Fuck. Finn's version of history was right. He'd found out the truth about what happened all those years ago, and it hadn't come from his own so-called family.

"Damn it. You should have told me. But you didn't, because you were afraid I might take after Roy, weren't you?"

"Now, that's just not fair." His mom was speaking urgently. "Back then, nobody knew why some people turned out that way. We didn't want you to be led down the wrong path—"

"Oh, give it up. I'm gay. How long have you known? Years?" Rain asked. "Hell, you knew about Desmond, didn't you?"

Again, silence.

Rain's fury rose, white-hot. Far more than it had when talking to Floyd, that was for sure. His grandfather might be a prick, but his own parents? It was their job to protect him, or intervene, or help him in any way.

"We just hoped the experience would be... a positive one for you in the end."

Rain caught his breath, his nails digging into the table so hard a strip of plastic began lifting. It was so much worse than he'd feared. Now, a part of him wished that he *had* been as deep in the closet as he'd thought and his parents hadn't known until now. He'd prefer that to this knowledge.

"You hoped that dating an abuser would turn me off men?

That's despicable. When you're ready to love me for who I am, let me know. But the lies end here."

"You can't just walk away from family. Blood is thicker than water, you know," Dad burst out, finally snapping at him.

Rain smiled to himself and stood up from his chair, gazing out across the square. The moon was peeking over the harbor, just barely visible between the buildings now. "What about the blood, sweat, and tears I've shared with people who accept who I am? The family I make is stronger than the one that tried to make me something I'm not."

"Only for your own good."

Rain shook his head. "No, it was to soothe your own fears instead of dealing with them. Well, it's time to deal with them. Talk to you when you learn what family's really about."

He hung up and was surprised to find his hands perfectly steady. The nervousness that had flooded his system at the start of the phone call was gone.

Instead, he felt certain, grounded, and centered. Like he had a breakwater now and the once-choppy waters within him were as still as the mirror glass of the harbor nearby. Soon, the reflections in that water would be very different.

With a smile, Rain headed inside the bar.

He didn't expect to be ambushed. The table closest to the door was full now—the five guys who had just passed him by, plus Finn, Dash, and Colt were all there.

"Hi," Rain greeted, shy for just a moment when all their gazes turned to him. For half a second, he wondered if he'd made a mistake in putting his trust in these guys instead of his closest relatives.

But this wasn't a high school cafeteria anymore. They smiled, waving him over and offering greetings.

And Colt put his arms around Rain to squeeze him in a tight hug. "Everything go okay?"

"Really well," Rain answered honestly with a smile. "My parents fessed up a little bit to the lines they've fed me throughout my life and how they've been manipulating me. I told them I have a better family now." He bit his lip, looking around at the others.

Beau clapped, and Aaron reached in for a fist bump. That started a round of toasts and hugs, and Rain found himself swept into the middle of the group.

It was still a surprise, but he was happy about that. Better that than taking them for granted.

"Screw anyone who doesn't see you for who you are," Finn said with a small, rueful grin. "I'm only sorry that included me until not long ago."

Rain gave his cousin a smile. "I'm just glad it doesn't include you now."

"Aww," Ezra murmured, clasping his hands. Then, he elbowed Colt for no apparent reason.

"Oh!" Colt straightened up. "Come with me for a minute," he said to Rain, but for some reason, Ezra followed them outside. They didn't stop there, either.

"Where are we going?" Rain laughed, tagging along beside Ezra as Colt swept up his hand and clasped it tightly.

"Into the gallery. There's something I have to show you. Is it..." Colt trailed off.

"Yeah. Is that all right?" Ezra paused, the keys in the lock. "If you waited here for a minute, I could hang it...?"

They were talking so vaguely that Rain just blankly shook his head and stared.

"It's fine as is," Colt concluded. He only gave Rain a mysterious smile and led him into the dark space.

Ezra flicked on the light switch and then hurried behind the counter. He pulled out a flat package, maybe eighteen inches long, wrapped in silvery paper, with a single ribbon around it.

It looked like maybe a piece of art, but it didn't feel quite right for that when Ezra handed it to Rain.

"Um..." Rain looked at Colt.

"Go on, open it." Colt bit his lip and rested his hip against the counter, leaning there while Ezra stayed behind the counter and watched.

So Rain put the package down and unwrapped it, his hands slowing when he pulled apart the paper to take in what was underneath.

A silver photo frame with a series of three black-and-white photos. From left to right, Rain's gaze cast over them.

The harbor—gray, still, and quiet, with just a few boats moored on the slip.

The moon over the bay itself, trees jutting out across the clear, still waters.

The unmistakable hulking form of Lucy, surrounded by a vast expanse of empty dock.

It was the perfect juxtaposition, and it took Rain's breath away. The photos themselves were technically beautiful, but something about seeing them together...

The sight made him choke up, like it was tailor-made for him.

Better still, Colt had picked it out for him. And judging by the excited dance from foot to foot that Ezra was doing behind the counter, he'd had a helping hand, too.

Which meant they both knew him well enough to know which piece, of the many here in the gallery, would blow him away. At last, people around him actually knew the real him, and that meant everything.

Damn it, after all he'd been through today, *now* he was crying? Rain swiped at his nose.

"Thank you," Rain mumbled, turning to Colt. His arms were already open, so Rain just stepped in and let Colt rock him gently from side to side, his strong arms surrounding him.

A little sound escaped Ezra's throat, and then he pointedly made himself scarce, waiting outside the large plate glass front window and dabbing at his eyes.

"You're welcome. I hoped you'd like it," Colt murmured. "It seemed like some of your favorite parts of the town. Ross took the photos."

Of course he had. The guy dressed in all black himself—this was totally his style. A smile touched Rain's lips as he wiped his eyes and nodded. "Yeah? I'll compliment him on them later. And I know just where to hang this."

"Yeah?" Colt smiled. "Hopefully I'll get to see it more. Oh, shit." He suddenly let go of Rain and spun about, checking his phone for the time. "That reminds me—I have to pick up an application for the apartment and drop it off before closing time. When does Victor close up?"

He tried to make for the door, but Rain caught him by the hand. "No, you don't."

"I..." Colt trailed off, frowning in confusion as he looked back at Rain. "But I want to be near you." His voice wavered, like he wasn't sure he had the right to ask for that. "And I can't really afford Portland rent *and* all this construction, and be around to supervise enough from afar."

Rain just smiled. He'd already been thinking about it before the last few days had hit. The plan had vanished from mind given all that bullshit, but now that their secrets were out in the open, his determination had returned.

"I know. But if you move in with me, you'll save even more money and spend even more time with me. And you can supervise me whenever you like." He looked down so he could peek at Colt through his lashes. "That is, if supervising me is something you enjoy..."

Colt growled and moved closer, taking his hands. "You know it, you little minx." He swayed with Rain from side to side again, locking their fingers, palm to palm. "Are you sure, though? You wouldn't mind me living with you?"

"Wouldn't mind?" Rain nearly giggled. "I don't think it'll be any hardship. And besides... you never know 'til you try, right?"

Colt pulled him in for a long, long kiss, and Rain flung his arms around Colt's neck and lost himself in it.

At last, when they were gasping for breath, their smiles more radiant than the moonlight pouring in through the shop window, Rain pulled back. "You'll never be alone in the dark again," he promised.

And he meant it.

22

COLT, TWELVE DAYS LATER

"This one's your sandwich, that one's mine." Colt rolled down the top of the second brown paper bag and nodded. "I'll leave them both in the trunk."

Rain beamed up at him and rose onto tiptoe for a kiss. "Thank you," he chirped. "I love the perks of having a boyfriend on the job."

Colt beamed at Rain, setting down both lunch bags in the back of the car and grabbing his boyfriend around the waist. He hauled Rain in for a surprise kiss and then nodded at the travel mugs on top of the car. "Coffee there, too."

"My hero." With that, they were off for a day of work. And not just any day—their first day of working together quite like this.

The last project had wrapped up, so Hart & Hart was on-site at the warehouse now, setting up construction. Today was Friday, so it was mostly building scaffolding and setting up supplies and tools, but Colt had hardly slept last night with excitement.

It was like Christmas. A very expensive and terrifying

Christmas, but still... there was magic in the air as they drove down to the harbor together in Rain's car.

Colt had traded in his car and bought a cheap one during that long, crazy week he'd just survived. It hadn't taken much time to pack up his Portland apartment and move his stuff into Rain's house. Another big stressor lifted just like that.

With no more long, lonely Portland drives and no more secrets looming between them, life with Rain had settled into an easy rhythm. The kind he'd never even thought existed.

Two weeks ago, he never would have thought anything about his life could look like this.

"Morning," Colt greeted Ross as they parked in the lot next to the art gallery.

Ross was just unlocking the art gallery, getting ready to open it to the public. He pushed his mop of black hair out of his eyes and then smiled at them. "Morning, guys. I'll send Aaron over with coffee when he gets in."

They'd need more than one cup to get through the day. "You're a star," Rain called out, already heading for the warehouse. Justin was there, and he held up a hand for a high five of greeting.

Colt had spent more time around Justin now that he lived here. Rain had invited him over for a movie, and they'd had a great evening together.

Finn and Roy were there, and so was Mike, the middle manager in between the two of them. Rain was near the bottom of the totem pole, but he seemed to like having others to tell him what to do.

As Colt had extensively tested out over the last few weeks. He bit back his smirk and let a contented sigh escape instead, locking up the car and heading over to join him.

Insurance rules wouldn't let him join in the hard parts of

construction until the work was nearly done, but Colt intended to be on the site as much as possible. He was there to help make decisions, run errands, and do whatever else he could.

Colt hung back as work started, making sure he stayed out of the way of the guys who had already jumped in and started to work.

Some people were driving by for a look at the new project. That included Scott, the editor of the town newsletter. The same guy who had personally called him last week to apologize profusely for his slip in journalistic standards.

Scott had admitted that he had gotten the anonymous letter so late at night that he hadn't fact-checked or asked for a statement from Colt—or really thought properly—before releasing it. And from the sounds of it, he wasn't too happy with the source, either.

Colt smiled into his coffee. "Morning," he greeted him. "Here for some juicy news?"

"I sure am." Scott swung out of his car. "Just a couple photos of the first day so I can run a before-and-after piece."

"Sure." Colt watched him head down to the harbor to get a better angle on the action and snap a shot.

When Scott returned, he reached out for a handshake. "Again, I can't apologize as much as I should..."

"Ah, hell." Colt waved it off. "You've already done enough." The piece Scott had published last week had more than made up for it. In it, he'd examined the positive side of the development: the jobs being created and work given to residents of the town, and the possibilities for further expansion.

Since then, people around here had thawed. They'd even started siding with Colt, shaking their heads and telling him how sorry they were that *someone* in Hart's Bay was a vicious gossipmonger. And the word *someone* was always said with a knowing look.

"Well, the day it opens, I'll be here to write it up," Scott promised. "And if you want to run ads to rent the space out to locals, you can do that for free."

Colt smiled back at Scott and clapped his shoulder. "That's good of you."

A man in a high-vis vest was walking up to the site, though, attracting his attention. He had a collared shirt and pants on underneath, and Colt didn't recognize him as being one of the crew.

"Excuse me a minute. Who's in charge here?"

Finn reached the guy at about the same time Colt did, and Rain was hot on Finn's heels.

"That would be... all of us. Developers"—Finn jerked a thumb between Rain and Colt—"and supervisor. What's up?"

"Well, hi. I'm from town hall." The guy looked apologetic as he said it. "I have, uh, a noise complaint from neighbors. Say there's been lots of trucks around, delivering construction supplies here and stuff."

"Trucks? It's not like we've been revving them at midnight," Rain started, but Colt laid a hand on his shoulder.

"No, indeed." The man pushed up his glasses nervously. "There's no grounds for a warning or anything. I just came to remind you that under town bylaws, construction hours are limited. Eight to six every day. But of course, you know that." He nodded at Finn.

"We know," Finn echoed, his lips hitching into a knowing smile. "There won't be any trouble from us, sir."

Relief crossed the man's face, and he shook hands with them all. "Thank you very much. Thank you, indeed." Then, he scurried off again, already taking off the orange vest.

"The bastard," Colt whispered, finally letting his own anger heat up his cheeks. "That's gotta be Floyd. Man, we're on a tight enough timeline already."

In his head, he was already picturing a February opening date. Or worse, next summer. Maybe never. They'd really been counting on getting it done before Christmas—with enough time to find tenants, help them move in, and give them some of the Christmas sales season, too.

"We'll make it work," Finn promised. He smiled. "Nobody around here is gonna be slacking on the job."

"You should have seen how fast we fixed up that art gallery after the fire." Rain put his arm around Colt's shoulder for a moment and kissed his cheek.

When someone behind gave a good-natured wolf whistle, Rain flipped them off casually over his shoulder.

Colt burst out laughing and cupped Rain's cheeks, kissing him back once. He loved seeing that bold spirit and defiant attitude in every area of Rain's life. No more timid wallflower here.

"In fact, you know what? We should have a barbecue in the town square after work's done today." Rain gave Finn a wicked little smile. "Nobody's gonna object to that."

"A nice, noisy celebration barbecue?" Finn innocently responded. "I can't see who would have a problem."

"Especially if we decorate it with rainbows."

Finn snickered. "Who could hate rainbows?"

"Soulless people," Colt chimed in on the cousins' discussion, grinning at them. "I'll go talk to Ross and the guys and see if they're in. I bet Victor won't mind the flurry of extra business."

Rain nodded. "They're always up for a good Friday-night

barbecue. We could even talk Cher into opening, maybe. Move the festivities down to the beach when it gets dark."

"A beach bonfire night? Sounds like a plan," Colt agreed and headed off for a word with the guys at the gallery.

Floyd held no power here anymore. All he could do was play mean little practical jokes and try to sneakily harass them, and there were far more creative minds around to outwit him. If Floyd wanted to keep trying, they could keep playing his game. But Colt had the distinct feeling that wasn't going to last long.

Already, a few people had talked to him about Floyd. Apparently he wasn't staying around here this winter. Instead, he was going to spend his retirement in better climes: SoCal or Hawaii, maybe. He had friends with golf courses, he'd bragged.

A few people around town would miss him. Most, though, seemed to have had trouble with him at one point or another. And that was the part that made Colt shake his head: if Floyd just admitted he'd been wrong, well, a lot of things might have turned out different.

But Colt couldn't complain. He was here to stay, and not one other person seemed to have a problem with him for who he was. Nor with Rain, or Jesse and Finn, or any of the other gay guys who had made their presence known.

Most people just said hello, asked how Rain was doing, and welcomed him to town.

One of us, they said sometimes. *You're one of us now* or *Glad to have you as one of us*. And it brought a tear to his eye every time.

Colt was one of Hart's Bay's own now, and he couldn't be prouder.

The end of a long workday couldn't come soon enough.

Colt had spent the afternoon watching Rain scramble around the roof and scaffolding. Sure, he was harnessed in, and his light weight and slender frame made him agile, but it would take him time to get used to seeing Rain at work.

"How was today?" Rain asked as he joined Colt in the town square to set up snacks and drinks.

Colt had already been by to invite the neighbors over. It was good to make friends with the people who'd have to put up with inconvenience over the next few months.

"You're a star," Colt told Rain, locking his arms around him. It was better to have him safely on the ground and in his hold, where he felt like he could keep him forever.

"Yeah?" Rain laughed. "Feeling the itch to join me on the roofing crew?"

"No." Colt shuddered. "Actually, let me change my answer. Fuck, no."

Rain's laugh was a melody to his ears, and then Rain pressed his lips against Colt's cheek. "Message received. I'll rope you in for the finishing tasks, though."

"Rope me in, huh?" Colt growled into his ear and nipped his neck. "Now you're giving me more ideas."

Rain squirmed against him, and Colt didn't miss the hitch in his breathing. "Maybe I need to lasso this wild animal before I find him in my bed tonight," Rain giggled.

Colt pinched Rain's ass. "Empty words. I know you want to see me from below, after all day seeing me from above."

Rain shivered. "Careful," he murmured. "I might just steal you home before the barbecue even starts."

"Oh, no," Colt smirked. "No, I'll make you wait. You know that makes it better, baby."

He pulled away from Rain, ignoring his whimper of

protest, and headed over to the grill that the artists had brought from their yard.

"Sure," Rain grumbled good-naturedly. "You'll handle *that* meat, but not mine."

"Oh, I'll take you on later," Colt finished in a whisper. "My sexy little piece of meat."

Rain pressed himself into Colt's side with a grin of delight. "And I can't wait."

A clearing throat behind them caught Colt's attention, and he turned to find Aaron there with three cups of coffee. "Oh, hey," he greeted, looping an arm around Rain's neck while reaching to accept a cup. "Thanks."

"Hope I'm not interrupting something. Do carry on for my viewing pleasure."

"Nothing that can't wait, unfortunately for you," Colt responded without missing a beat. "That costs extra."

"Damn." Aaron pretended to pout and scuffed the ground. "So, I wanted a word with you two about the units in the new building."

"Yes?" Rain asked, perking up as Colt's mind switched back to business, too.

"I saw the unit on the end was being designed for something like a coffee shop. Well... I've been thinking that I might open a shop of my own. People seem to like my roasts. Would you consider renting to me?" Aaron looked nervous and strangely formal for a moment, like he wasn't quite sure how to ask.

Colt swapped glances with Rain. He didn't have to ask for time to think about it—he could see the answer on Rain's face. So he nodded his permission.

"We'd be delighted," Rain answered, grinning at him. "Consider yourself first in line on the waiting list."

"There's a waiting list?" Aaron's jaw dropped.

Colt snickered. "There is now."

Aaron joined in the laugh a moment later. "Oh, awesome. Glad I asked! Also... Ezra wants to ask, but he's busy being shy and nervous about it." Aaron rolled his eyes. "So on his behalf, if you're looking for someone to paint murals or do custom artwork..."

"We were counting on hiring him, actually," Colt said with a laugh. He sipped his coffee and sighed contentedly, then held the cup out for a toast with the other two. "To business and friendship."

"And love," Rain added, his voice soft.

"And love," Colt echoed.

"Thanks." Aaron beamed, gesturing Ezra and Beau over since they were hovering nearby, looking anxious. "They said yes to both of us!" They piled in to hug Aaron and high-five him.

"Thanks for giving us all a chance," Ezra said to Colt when he pulled away.

"You're welcome. It's the least you all deserve. Your art is great... Ross's photography is great... and this coffee is great, too." Colt held up his cup.

"The coffee? Yeah. It's goody, even," Rain chimed in.

Colt gave Rain a rueful grin. "And I should know."

23

COLT

The door banged open with the combined force of Colt's and Rain's body weight. They nearly fell into the front hall.

"Shit. Fucksticks," Colt mumbled as he tried to get his footing, one arm still looped around Rain's waist.

Rain giggled hysterically. "Fucksticks? Is that what I felt pressing into me?"

"You'll find out," Colt threatened, but he tripped over a pair of shoes. "Damn it, who left those there?" They were his own, and he turned red the moment he spotted them. "Uh, other than me."

Rain laughed so hard he leaned on the wall. "I'll find out about your fuckstick... the moment you stop stumbling about deck like a landlubber."

"Oh, you," Colt growled playfully and pinched Rain's nipples.

The move caught him by surprise. He squealed and batted Colt's hands away, then made a break for the hallway.

Colt followed, hot on his heels, sweeping his arms around

Rain to stop him in his tracks. "Gotcha," Colt whispered and kissed the back of his neck.

Rain gasped. "Oh, no," he teased. "Whatever will you do now, to celebrate our first day of construction? Share a shower with me?"

"I thought I'd treat you to something else before you get all clean," Colt murmured, nipping Rain's ear.

Rain pressed back into him, his breathing harsh and quick. "Like what?" He played innocent, but one squeeze of his crotch, apart from making him squeal, told the truth.

Colt had kept him waiting all evening at the barbecue, taking every opportunity to drop filthy hints about what he was going to do to Rain later into his ear. Along the way, it had gotten hard to control his own desires.

But he had one more thing he wanted to do first.

"Come here," Colt murmured, steering Rain bodily to the couch. When Rain dug his heels in, Colt pinched a nipple again and ground against that sexy little ass, making him feel the hard line of him.

That got Rain moving to the couch—eagerly, too.

"What are you doing to me, you insatiable man?" Rain draped the back of his hand along his forehead as he flopped along the couch. "I just don't know if I have the energy. I'm all hot and sweaty and tired after building," he kept playing, even rolling his head back against the armrest.

Colt grinned. "I'm happy to wait until tomorrow," he said. He sat at Rain's feet, easing them into his lap. "But you can't sneakily clean the pipes in the shower. I'll watch to make sure, if I have to."

Rain gasped genuinely this time, his eyes widening. "You wouldn't." But his toes curled, and the squirm of his ass into the gap between the cushions told Colt to put that on his mental to-do list for the future.

"No," Colt relented. "I'm not going to be *that* mean. We have to celebrate a good first day of construction, after all. Wait here," he instructed Rain.

"Oooh." Rain squirmed. "Lube run?"

"I'll do you one better," Colt promised, smirking at Rain. When he returned, he brought a steaming hot washcloth draped over one arm, a bottle of massage oil in the other.

Rain blinked. "Getting a cloth ready for cleaning me up? I'm so spoiled."

"Snarky thing, aren't you?" Colt pulled Rain's feet onto his lap again as he sat at the other end of the couch. "Good thing I love you that way." He pulled off one sock and then the other before rubbing the hot cloth along the bottoms of Rain's feet.

"Ohhh," Rain sighed in simultaneous understanding and bliss, and Colt smiled as he gazed up the length of his body to his face.

A few more presses and squeezes later, Rain's feet were clean, warm, and limber. He set aside the cloth and trickled oil over his fingers, then started working out the knots from heel to toe, one foot at a time.

By God, the noises Rain made were exquisite. Eventually, Rain managed to speak when Colt took a break to grab more oil. "I thought you were going to fuck my mouth. This is possibly even better. Or maybe on par. I'm still a cock-hungry slut, even if I love this. And my smart mouth will just keep going until you do something with it."

Colt grinned up at him. Rain was learning to talk dirty—and he learned fast. Already, he was able to catch Colt by surprise frequently. Now that they'd been tested together and found the results all negative, they didn't have to bother with condoms, and sex was even more frequent and spontaneous.

"Oh, I know," Colt said. He ran a fingertip gently along the top of Rain's foot and up his leg. "I plan to have my way with you soon."

"Please," Rain whispered. It was impossible not to notice the tent in his pants that hadn't gone away. If anything, it had grown from Colt's long, languorous strokes along Rain's skin.

Colt wiped his hands off and grinned, sidling his way between Rain's knees. He ran a hand up each thigh as he did so, slowly approaching that bulge. Rain tensed up, his eyes rounding and mouth falling open.

"Oh," Rain sighed when Colt finally let one palm brush him. "I *have* been good today, haven't I?"

"Don't get used to it," Colt said with a wink. He unbuttoned Rain's jeans and hooked his fingertips through both waistbands before dragging everything down to his knees.

"Being pleasured first, or being good?"

"Mostly the second. You so rarely are." Colt grinned at the look of playful indignation.

He loved when Rain went toe-to-toe with him. Without the stakes that had dogged the first steps of their relationship, it was playful between them now and usually ended up in sex. Colt sure as hell wasn't complaining.

Colt crouched over Rain's hard cock, admiring the straight length that fit perfectly on his palm. He licked from balls to head in one quick swipe of his tongue and then lapped at the shaft. Every time he pressed his lips against the thin, sensitive skin, Rain's thighs tensed and quivered.

Rain's ecstasy was honestly his favorite sight in the world. Not a day went by where Colt didn't want to please him—even if that meant teasing him first. As he always said, it was all the better after waiting.

"Colt," Rain whispered, drawing his gaze. His deep blue eyes were wide and desperate. "Please."

Under that entreating gaze, he couldn't make Rain wait another moment. Colt wrapped his lips around the swollen head and let the length slide down his tongue, sucking his cheeks in.

As he bobbed his head, his nose filled with Rain's scent and mouth full of Rain's taste, Rain's noises grew sharp. They were music to Colt's ears. The sofa scratched and creaked as Colt shifted on his knees so he could get the perfect angle to take him in one quick gulp.

Just when Rain's noises were becoming rhythmic and high-pitched, Colt pulled back.

Maybe he *could* make him wait a little longer.

The long, exasperated moan Rain gave made Colt burst out laughing. "I know, baby," he whispered and patted his thigh. "Just you wait."

Rain eyed him darkly but didn't reach for himself. He was getting well-trained already. He just laced his hands behind his head and dug his feet into the couch, drawing quick, shaky breaths.

"My turn first," Colt said. He couldn't possibly miss the way Rain's eyes lit up, and it made him grin as he shifted to straddle Rain's chest.

He let himself free with a pop of his button, a snick of his zipper, and a few yanks of fabric. As soon as his rock-hard erection bobbed in the air, Rain's eyes were drawn to it, and he licked his lips.

"You want to taste this?" Colt whispered, taking hold of himself. His own grip was pleasant, but not enough.

Rain nodded jerkily. "Yes," he whispered, fixated by the sight. Colt tapped himself gently against Rain's chin and then his lips. Rain strained up, trying to catch the length in his mouth, before he realized what Colt was waiting for. He gasped and lay back again, then murmured, "Yes, please."

"That's it." Colt grinned. He patted Rain's cheek firmly as he slid into Rain's hot, wet mouth.

God, it was like heaven. He closed his eyes for a few moments just to enjoy the first gulp of Rain's mouth around his sensitive, pulsating shaft. Then, he set to work, gripping Rain's hair in one hand as he patted his cheek with the other.

Rain squirmed under him and moaned every time he did so. The vibrations traveled up Colt's shaft, curling deep in his belly and stoking the fire.

After another minute of this, he pulled himself slowly free and stood up. "Bed," he whispered, picking up the massage oil in one hand and offering Rain the other.

Rain sidled out of his pants and took the hand. Colt pulled him to his feet, slipping an arm around his waist to steady him as they walked to the bedroom.

By now, Colt could find the bed in the darkness, on autopilot, or in the middle of a blowjob. He didn't even need to look as he pushed Rain onto it and then stripped him down. Rain giggled and squirmed, trying to resist, but Colt was a man on a mission.

Within moments, Rain was naked and gazing up at him with those gorgeous, wide eyes that had so captivated him at first sight. Even now, they transfixed him sometimes, making Colt remember that he was the luckiest damn guy alive.

It took Colt a few moments just to get his brain to make his body move. When he did, he cracked open the massage oil again. "Roll over," he ordered while he stripped himself naked, too.

Rain bit his lip playfully. "My favorite words. Well, and *bend over*. And *suck me*. And *my slut*." He rolled over, stretching his arms out to either side of him.

Hearing him freely chatter about his desires made Colt grin every time. "I've already made you suck me, my gorgeous, sexy, smart, kind, and yes, slutty boyfriend."

"Can't help it if your cock is addictive," Rain muttered into the duvet with a shrug. "It's your fault, really."

Colt laughed. "Compliment accepted." He ran his slick hands from Rain's shoulders down to the small of his back, spreading oil along his skin.

The blissful sigh Rain gave him was just as rewarding as it had been earlier. This time, though, Colt was naked on top of him, the oil smoothing the way between their skin.

Every stroke of his thumbs around Rain's shoulder blades, along his ribs, or down his arms just made the sparks between them fly. It was impossible to keep his hands off Rain when he was around.

Better still, his erection nestled between Rain's cheeks, and every shift of his body made them both remember it. As he worked on Rain's lower back, Colt slowly thrust between his thighs, making both of them moan.

Colt held out as long as he could before he couldn't resist taking what he wanted. He shifted off Rain and leaned over to grab the lube. "Spread your legs."

"Maybe I won't," Rain said, batting his lashes as he rolled onto his back and scrabbled away. "Maybe you'll have to lasso *this* wild animal."

Colt growled. When Rain played hard to get, something in his brain just needed him that much more—and Rain knew it.

The look in his eyes was teasing him, daring him to come get him.

Every time he played this game, Colt ended up balls-deep inside him within a minute.

"Rain," he ordered, his voice dropping. "Come here."

"Make me," Rain said, his teeth flashing in a grin as he folded his hands under his chin in the most adorably infuriating way.

Colt ditched the lube bottle and pursued him on hands and knees, but when he got a hold of Rain's shoulder, Rain slipped free.

"Damn it," Colt muttered and tried again, grabbing him around the waist—but Rain's oily skin was impossible to get a grip of, and Rain pushed himself backward out of the hold, scampering across the bed with a laugh.

The third time he tried and failed to get a hold of him, even Colt had to start laughing. "Maybe oiling you up wasn't such a good idea. It's given you leverage," Colt complained.

"I'll make leverage wherever I can."

"What about making love?" Colt knelt upright at the end of the bed now, while Rain lay on his side, head on the pillows.

Rain went still and then rolled onto his back, spreading his legs as he beamed up at Colt. "I could do that."

He offered Colt a hand to pull him up the bed, but when Colt grabbed it, he slipped free and almost collapsed onto Rain. This time, they both burst out laughing together.

"This is the opposite of leverage," Colt managed after he caught his breath. "What was I thinking?"

"You were treating me to something nice and gentle and sweet, so I had to make you regret it. Maybe you'll be all rough with me now," Rain mock-gasped, covering his mouth.

Colt finally reached Rain, kneeling between his legs. He

grabbed them, eased them over his shoulders, and held them in place while he bent Rain in two. The move made his cock line up alongside Rain's, the firm shaft bumping against his own making him gasp.

"If you insist," Colt whispered against his lips.

They made out for minutes like this while Colt fingered Rain, Rain's flexible body crunched in two so he couldn't squirm more than a little under him. When he was good and ready, Colt let Rain's feet touch the bed again, and then lined himself up. He slid inside in one quick thrust.

Rain cried out, biting his lip as his whole body squeezed around Colt's cock. It sent a jolt of pleasure through Colt, making him fight to keep from doing it again. But Colt had grown to recognize that expression of pleasure mingled with pain, and sure enough, it didn't take long.

"More," Rain gasped as soon as he caught his breath, so Colt indulged him. He thrust in quick, short movements at first before finding his rhythm. As Rain relaxed under him, he deepened each move until he was pushing fluidly inside.

Rain panted Colt's name, his expression the picture of ecstasy as the bed shook under them. For them, making love wasn't an easy, gentle rhythm. It was Colt drilling Rain's tight little ass the way Rain needed him to, until they both spilled their loads across the nearest surface.

"Yes," Rain growled, his nails digging into Colt's shoulders now. He ran them down Colt's back, and the sharp lines of fire as he scratched only made Colt redouble his pace.

There was no time for words now, only openmouthed kisses that left them gasping across each other's cheeks for breath.

"I'm so close." Rain's eyelids fluttered closed. "Don't stop."

And Colt never would. He was here, with Rain, to the very

end. Even with Rain squeezing tight around him with every thrust, and the pulsating tingling building deep in his belly, Colt held back.

It was Rain's turn first.

His boyfriend finally cried out, unspeakably beautiful as he arched off the bed, bared his throat, and squeezed his eyes shut. Colt could feel every uncontrollable wave of pleasure that jolted through Rain's body as he came all over himself, a sticky and gorgeous mess.

"I love you," Colt whispered, his hand cupped around Rain's cheek. Rain ignited tenderness in Colt at the same time as insatiable lust, protectiveness, and a hundred other emotions.

That was the last rational thought before Colt tipped over the edge, too.

Colt buried his face in Rain's neck and clutched him close as he came inside him. He wanted them to be this close forever, locked together, like they were a tailor-made two halves of a whole.

When the shock waves finally subsided and Colt's whirling mind kicked back to life, Rain was stroking his back and shoulder, whispering to him.

"I love you so much," Rain said, smiling as Colt pulled back and met his gaze. "I'm so lucky."

"You're lucky? What about me? I won the boyfriend lottery."

"Mmm." Rain pretended to toss his hair. "I'll invoke this next time you make me wait for my orgasm, you know."

Colt laughed breathlessly and pulled Rain into his arms, pressing his face into his hair before he kissed him. "I love you, baby. Body and soul."

Rain's eyes widened, and suddenly they shimmered. He

gulped once, hard, and then pressed his nose into Colt's neck. "You better. I'm *your* slut, you know."

Colt rubbed Rain's back with a gentle chuckle. "I know. And I'd better get an actual hot cloth for my one and only slut. Or he'll be a gross mess by morning."

"Such a romantic," Rain sighed, cupping his own cheeks with his hands as he rolled onto his back. As Colt ducked into the bathroom, he kept on talking. "What would I do without you?"

Colt grinned as he came back with a hot, wet cloth. "Keep wasting your jizz on old T-shirts?"

"One time!" Rain exclaimed, snatching the cloth and cleaning up. "I swear. One indiscretion and it haunts you for life."

"I'll make sure it does," Colt promised, laughing, while Rain dramatically groaned.

When Rain was under the covers, Colt turned out the light and joined him. The nightlight Rain had bought flicked on automatically, projecting soft stars along the ceiling and walls of the room.

Colt smiled at the sight before he pressed his nose into the back of Rain's neck and breathed deeply.

Perfect. Everything, at last, was just perfect.

The last flecks of white paint, scrapes and dents from hard-ware, and bruises from unit fittings were all hidden under-neath Rain's best suit.

Only Colt, just as dented and standing by Rain's side in his dark gray suit, knew them all.

For today, they weren't up to their elbows in last-minute jobs and stress. Now, they were Colt Fuller and Rain Hart—property developers, and, for the first time, landlords.

Fuller Hart Development's first tenants had just moved in, and finally, the two of them could relax.

These two months hadn't been easy by any means. Even with Rain's boss giving him time off to work on the building once the crew moved on to their next job, they'd had long hours being as quiet as possible together.

If choosing finishing colors and plant pots hadn't pulled them apart, Rain was confident that nothing would.

Then, they'd had this launch event to plan. Ezra's art and Ross's photography decorated the walls of several units. Some of the other guys had helped finish up, too, and Rain and Colt felt they had owed them all—plus their patient neighbors—a good party.

The whole damn town seemed to have a soft spot for him now, and Rain wasn't quite sure what he'd done to deserve it, but he was never going to take it for granted.

Justin was wandering around the new place, holding hands with a cute blond guy Rain vaguely recognized. Rain was glad that he wouldn't feel like so much of a third wheel anymore, even if it meant less time they could spend together watching movies and talking about random shit.

"Coffee?" Aaron was working double time to serve everyone samples at the launch event. He'd hired a great crew, including Yolanda as the head barista. Already, word was spreading through town of this new place to stop and fuel up on the way to work.

"No, thanks," Rain laughed, for once. "If I have any more, I'll never sleep."

Aaron smirked and nodded toward Colt with a wink. "He ought to never let you sleep anyway."

"Don't worry," Colt said with a laugh. "I know a good thing when it's in my bed."

Rain couldn't stop himself beaming. He elbowed Colt and gave him a wink. "And maybe we can stay awake for one kind of hard work now that the other kind's done."

Not that they hadn't made plenty of time for that somehow, even in their long days. They'd christened the new place more than once when it was too late for heavy machinery or others to join them at work.

"You survived! Now it's my turn to be a sexless, joyless business owner," Aaron lamented with a wink before moving on.

For one weird moment earlier that week, when talking with Aaron about the new business, Colt had thought about asking for a job. It had taken him a full two seconds to remember he didn't need to do that again. He put it down to the sleep deprivation, but it was another little sign of how much his life had changed.

Their income would slowly come in now, and with his expenses so much lower and Rain already owning several properties, Fuller Hart Development had its eye on creating a B&B in the new year.

"Okay, guys." Scott had reached them, camera in tow. "Time for your photo op." He crouched and aimed the camera up toward the building.

Colt beamed and slid his arm around Rain's shoulder. "Pucker up," he teased, while others nearby chuckled and applauded.

Rain's cheeks were hot, but he rested his hands on Colt's bulging biceps and stretched up onto tiptoe for a kiss.

The "awww" from around them was unmistakable.

"Perfect," Scott concluded as he rose to his feet again and checked the screen. "I'll send you your copy tomorrow."

"Thanks," Colt said and shook hands like they'd already discussed the matter.

Rain waited until Scott moved on for other photos and quotes before he looked at Colt. "What was that?"

Colt tapped his chin in thought. "Well... I was going to surprise you... but I could tell you, I suppose."

"You horrible tease," Rain sighed, looping his arms around Colt's shoulders.

"Come here. They can cope without us for a little while."

Colt took Rain by the hand away from the noise and the

music, and toward the long, still, silent wooden dock that stretched beyond the concrete pilings into the water.

It was their favorite spot to eat lunch—sharing it with Lucy sometimes—or just sit and watch the stars. Right now, the party had stretched on late enough that the first few were glimmering above the sea.

"I'm going to frame the front page of that town newsletter and put it on the wall right underneath the photos I bought you that day."

Rain was startled for a moment. It was ridiculously thoughtful and specific—and just like Colt, who seemed to know what Rain needed even before Rain himself did.

"Oh," he breathed out. "That's... that's wonderful."

His chest was tight with emotions as he imagined it: a colorful news page preserved for life underneath those three stark, melancholic photos that hung on their bedroom wall. Change was coming to Hart's Bay indeed.

And maybe that collection would grow big enough to move to the office one day.

Rain flung his arms around Colt's neck and hugged him tightly. "Thank you."

"For what?" Colt chuckled and rubbed Rain's back anyway, holding him.

Rain shook his head wordlessly. "I can't even say it all. Everything." When he finally let go, he turned away to walk to the end of the dock, wiping at his eyes. At least there was no sign of Lucy around or anyone watching besides Colt to see the tears of joy rolling down his face.

And it wasn't like he hadn't cried earlier, while they snipped the red ribbon together.

Colt had made him feel more than he ever had before, and it seemed like he wasn't done yet.

"There's one more thing." Colt's voice was close to him, but... lower than usual?

Rain turned about, and then his eyes widened. He couldn't quite process the sight, but Colt was on one knee in front of him, a thin strip of red ribbon in his hand—like he'd saved it from the ribbon-cutting ceremony.

"Rainier Jameson Hart."

Rain hadn't heard that full name since his fight with his parents. This time, it was said so differently. It was said with all the love and tenderness he now found in his family—the Harts, Colt, Jesse's crew of misfit artists, and more.

"Yes?" He barely dared to breathe.

"You've pushed me further than I ever thought I could go, and you've made me a better man than I ever hoped I could be. If I can give you the same happiness you've given me these last few months—for the rest of our lives, together—I'd be honored beyond words. And I'll get you a real ring as soon as we can afford it."

Rain laughed despite the tears rolling down his cheeks. He was adding buckets of salt water to the ocean underfoot. He wiped at his eyes, his vision blurry now, and then let Colt take his left hand.

"Will you marry me?"

Rain nodded hard, tears shimmering on the ends of his lashes as he wiped them away with his right hand again. "Yes," he gasped. "Yes, a million times yes!"

"Yes!" Colt gasped himself, pumping his fist once while Rain grinned.

Colt tied the red ribbon gently around Rain's finger before he rose to standing. Those strong arms swept him off his feet and cradled him as Colt spun around once.

Rain laughed giddily, clutching at Colt's shirt. The man was completely, utterly, ridiculous.

And completely, utterly his own, through the interminable Oregon rain and the mist, into the brighter days that lay ahead.

AFTERWORD

Dear reader,

Thank you for reading *Changed Hart*, the second book in the cozy, heartwarming world of Hart's Bay!

I loved spending more time immersed in the gorgeous scenery, and Rain and Colt just sizzled from start to finish! And this is just the beginning of the change in Hart's Bay's fortunes. Lots more guys around town are still looking for Mr. Right...

Thanks again to my superstar team: Amy, Sandra, Meg, and Kitti, you're all lifesavers! Any remaining errors are my own to recall with embarrassment in the wee hours of the morning. I want to give a big shoutout to my Facebook group Petals for embracing this little town and big-spirited family and asking for more. And, of course, all my love to the usual suspects.

Many more stories are waiting to be told... so I'm thrilled to announce that the next Hart's Bay novel is available now! *Wild Hart* is Ezra's story, and you can click here to buy it on Amazon.

In the meantime, make sure you grab the exclusive, free short story about Justin by signing up to my newsletter! You'll hear about freebies and deals; exclusive bonus stories; new releases and preorders; sneak peeks at upcoming books; event appearances; and other exciting news as it happens.

Changed Hart will be brought to life as an audiobook narrated by Greg Boudreaux in November 2019!

I also have a reader group on Facebook if you want to chat about your favorite parts of *Changed Hart*, see cute bee photos and good news stories, and keep on top of my upcoming releases with a whole bunch of lovely readers: https://www.facebook.com/groups/edavies

Last but not least: always be you!

~Ed

NEXT IN HART'S BAY...

WILD HART

"Everything I want is here, in front of me."

Rusty Campbell left Hart's Bay after high school to work in the wilderness. Now he's back home for one purpose: seaweed farming. To succeed, he'll need to fight the tide and win over his skeptical family, once-burned by the fishing industry collapse. But there are intriguing new faces bringing good fortune to Hart's Bay—like the captivating redhead who watches him from the art gallery.

Six months after moving to this small town, Ezra Carter's bed feels empty. Painting and running an art co-op with his friends doesn't fill the same need. The city boy is seriously considering lowering his standards… until the man of his dreams walks in and throws his no-good hookup out of the bar. Why does Rusty have to be straight?

Rusty is mystified at the surging chemistry between them as their friendship grows. Is Ezra the missing piece to the puzzle of Rusty's love life? As Rusty struggles to make sense of his feelings, he guides Ezra through his home territory to give the artist new inspiration—but he winds up becoming Ezra's muse himself.

Before long, they're fumbling their way through uncharted waters. Can their picture-perfect, no-labels relationship weather the storm brewing under their feet?

Click here to check it out on Amazon!

ABOUT THE AUTHOR

E. Davies grew up moving constantly, which taught him what people have in common, the ways relationships are formed, and the dangers of "miscellaneous" boxes. As a young gay author, Ed prefers to tell feel-good stories that are brimming with hope.

He writes full-time, goes on long nature walks, tries to fill his passport, drinks piña coladas on the beach, flees from cute guys, coos over fuzzy animals (especially bees), and is liable to tilt his head and click his tongue if you don't use your turn signal.

facebook.com/edaviesbooks

twitter.com/edaviesauthor

instagram.com/thisboyisstrange

bookbub.com/authors/e-davies

Hart's Bay:

Hard Hart

Changed Hart

Wild Hart

Stolen Hart

Significant Brothers:

Splinter

Grasp

Slick

Trace

Clutch

Tremble

Riley Brothers:

Buzz

Clang

Swish

Crunch

Slam

Grind

Brooklyn Boys:

Electric Sunshine

Live Wire

Boiling Point

F-Word:

Flaunt

Freak

Faux

Forever

After:

Afterburn

Afterglow

Aftermath

Men of Hidden Creek:

Shelter

Adore

Miracle

Redemption

Coauthored with Zach Jenkins:

Sugar Topped

Just a Summer Deal

Audiobooks:

The list is growing rapidly! You can see all my books available in audio here: www.edaviesbooks.com/audiobooks